HALF PORTIONS

HALF PORTIONS

EDNA FERBER

University of Illinois Press
Urbana and Chicago

Illinois paperback edition, 2003
Manufactured in the United States of America
P 5 4 3 2 1

♾ This book is printed on acid-free paper.

First published in 1920 by Doubleday, Page and Company.

Library of Congress Cataloging-in-Publication Data
Ferber, Edna, 1887–1968.
Half portions / Edna Ferber.
p. cm.
ISBN 0-252-02843-0 (cloth : alk. paper)
ISBN 0-252-07129-8 (pbk. : alk. paper)
1. United States—Social life and customs—
20th century—Fiction.
I. Title.
PS3511.E46H3 2003
813'.52—dc21   2002032230

CONTENTS

		PAGE
I.	THE MATERNAL FEMININE	3
II.	APRIL 25TH, AS USUAL	36
III.	OLD LADY MANDLE	76
IV.	YOU'VE GOT TO BE SELFISH	113
V.	LONG DISTANCE	148
VI.	UN MORSO DOO PANG	157
VII.	ONE HUNDRED PER CENT.	201
VIII.	FARMER IN THE DELL	239
IX.	THE DANCING GIRLS	280

Half Portions

THE MATERNAL FEMININE

CALLED upon to describe Aunt Sophy you would have to coin a term or fall back on the dictionary definition of a spinster. "An unmarried woman," states that worthy work, baldly, "especially when no longer young." That, to the world, was Sophy Decker. Unmarried, certainly. And most certainly no longer young. In figure she was, at fifty, what is known in the corset ads as a "stylish stout." Well dressed in blue serge, with broad-toed health shoes and a small, astute hat. The blue serge was practical common sense. The health shoes were comfort. The hat was strictly business. Sophy Decker made and sold hats, both astute and ingenuous, to the female population of Chippewa, Wisconsin. Chippewa's East-End set bought the knowing type of hat, and the mill hands and hired girls bought the naïve ones. But whether lumpy or possessed of that indefinable thing known as line, Sophy Decker's hats were honest hats.

The world is full of Aunt Sophys, unsung. Plump, ruddy, capable women of middle age. Unwed, and rather looked down upon by a family of married sisters and tolerant, good-humoured brothers-in-law, and careless nieces and nephews.

"Poor Aunt Soph," with a significant half smile. "She's such a good old thing. And she's had so little in life, really."

She was, undoubtedly, a good old thing—Aunt Soph. Forever sending a spray of sweeping black paradise, like a jet of liquid velvet, to this pert little niece in Seattle; or taking Adele, sister Flora's daughter, to Chicago or New York, as a treat, on one of her buying trips. Burdening herself, on her business visits to these cities, with a dozen foolish shopping commissions for the idle women folk of her family. Hearing without partisanship her sisters' complaints about their husbands, and her sisters' husbands' complaints about their wives. It was always the same.

"I'm telling you this, Sophy. I wouldn't breathe it to another living soul. But I honestly think, sometimes, that if it weren't for the children——"

There is no knowing why they confided these things to Sophy instead of to each other, these wedded sisters of hers. Perhaps they held for each other an unuttered distrust or jealousy. Perhaps, in making a confidante of Sophy, there was something of the satisfaction that comes of dropping a surreptitious stone down a deep well and hearing it plunk, safe in the knowledge that it has struck no one and that it cannot rebound, lying there in the soft darkness. Sometimes they would end by saying, "But you don't know what it is, Sophy. You can't. I'm sure I don't know why I'm telling you all this."

But when Sophy answered, sagely, "I know; I know"—they paid little heed, once having unburdened themselves. The curious part of it is that she did know. She knew as a woman of fifty must know who, all her life, has given and given and in return has received nothing. Sophy Decker had never used the word inhibition in her life. I doubt if she knew what it meant. When you are busy copying French models for the fall trade you have little time or taste for Freud. She only knew (without in the least knowing she knew) that in giving of her goods, of her affections, of her time, of her energy, she found a certain relief. Her own people would have been shocked if you had told them that there was about this old maid aunt something rather splendidly Rabelaisian. Without being at all what is known as a masculine woman she had, somehow, acquired the man's viewpoint, his shrewd value sense. She ate a good deal, and enjoyed her food. She did not care for those queer little stories that married women sometimes tell, with narrowed eyes, but she was strangely tolerant of what is known as sin. So simple and direct she was that you wondered how she prospered in a line so subtle as the millinery business.

You might have got a fairly true characterization of Sophy Decker from one of fifty people: from a dapper salesman in a New York or Chicago wholesale millinery house; from Otis Cowan, cashier of the First National Bank of Chippewa; from Julia Gold, her head milliner and trimmer; from almost any one, in fact, except a member of her own family. They knew her least of all, as is often true of one's own people. Her three married sisters—Grace in Seattle, Ella in Chicago, and Flora in Chippewa—regarded her with a rather affectionate disapproval from the snug safety of their own conjugal ingle-nooks.

"I don't know. There's something—well— common about Sophy," Flora confided to Ella. Flora, on shopping bent and Sophy, seeking hats, had made the five-hour run from Chippewa to Chicago together. "She talks to everybody. You should have heard her with the porter on our train. Chums! And when the conductor took our tickets it was a social occasion. You know how packed the seven fifty-two is. Every seat in the parlour car taken. And Sophy asking the coloured porter about how his wife was getting along—she called him William—and if they were going to send her west, and all about her. I *wish* she wouldn't."

Aunt Sophy undeniably had a habit of regarding people as human beings. You found her talking to chambermaids and delivery boys, and elevator starters, and gas collectors, and hotel clerks—all that aloof, unapproachable, superior crew. Under her benign volubility they bloomed and spread and took on colour as do those tight little Japanese paper water-flowers when you cast them into a bowl. It wasn't idle curiosity in her. She was interested. You found yourself confiding to her your innermost longings, your secret tribulations, under the encouragement of her sympathetic, "You don't say!" Perhaps it was as well that sister Flora was in ignorance of the fact that the men millinery salesmen at Danowitz & Danowitz, Importers, always called Miss Decker Aunt Soph, as, with one arm flung about her plump blue serge shoulder, they revealed to her the picture of their girl in the back flap of their bill-folder.

Flora, with a firm grip on Chippewa society, as represented by the East-End set, did not find her position enhanced by a sister in the millinery business in Elm Street.

"Of course it's wonderful that she's self-supporting and successful and all," she told her husband. "But it's not so pleasant for Adele, now that she's growing up, having all the girls she knows buying their hats of her aunt. Not that I—but you know how it is."

H. Charnsworth Baldwin said yes, he knew. But perhaps you, until you are made more intimately acquainted with Chippewa, Wisconsin; with the Decker girls of twenty years ago; with Flora's husband, H. Charnsworth Baldwin; and with their children Adele and Eugene, may feel a little natural bewilderment.

The Deckers had lived in a sagging old frame house (from which the original paint had long ago peeled in great scrofulous patches) on an unimportant street in Chippewa. There was a worm-eaten russet apple tree in the yard; an untidy tangle of wild-cucumber vine over the front porch; and an uncut brush of sunburnt grass and weeds all about. From May until September you never passed the Decker place without hearing the plunketty-plink of a mandolin from somewhere behind the vines, accompanied by a murmur of young voices, laughter, and the creak-creak of the hard-worked and protesting hammock hooks. Flora, Ella, and Grace Decker had more beaux and fewer clothes than any other girls in

Chippewa. In a town full of pretty young things they were, undoubtedly, the prettiest; and in a family of pretty sisters (Sophy always excepted) Flora was the acknowledged beauty. She was the kind of girl whose nose never turns red on a frosty morning. A little, white, exquisite nose, purest example of the degree of perfection which may be attained by that vulgarest of features. Under her great gray eyes were faint violet shadows which gave her a look of almost poignant wistfulness. If there is a less hackneyed way to describe her head on its slender throat than to say it was like a lovely flower on its stalk, you are free to use it. Her slow, sweet smile gave the beholder an actual physical pang. Only her family knew she was lazy as a behemoth, untidy about her person, and as sentimental as a hungry shark. The strange and cruel part of it was that, in some grotesque, exaggerated way, as a cartoon may be like a photograph, Sophy resembled Flora. It was as though Nature, in prankish mood, had given a cabbage the colour and texture of a rose, with none of its fragile reticence and grace.

It was a manless household. Mrs. Decker, vague, garrulous, and given to ice-wool shawls, referred to her dead husband, in frequent reminiscence, as poor Mr. Decker. Mrs. Decker dragged one leg as she walked—rheumatism, or a

spinal affection.   Small wonder, then, that Sophy,
the plain, with a gift for hat-making, a knack at egg-
less cake-baking, and a genius for turning a sleeve so
that last year's style met this year's without a
struggle, contributed nothing to the sag in the centre of the old twine hammock on the front porch.

That the three girls should marry well, and
Sophy not at all, was as inevitable as the sequence
of the seasons.   Ella and Grace did not manage
badly, considering that they had only their girlish
prettiness and the twine hammock to work with.
But Flora, with her beauty, captured H. Charnsworth Baldwin.   Chippewa gasped.   H. Charnsworth Baldwin drove a skittish mare to a
high-wheeled yellow runabout (this was twenty
years ago); had his clothes made at Proctor
Brothers in Milwaukee, and talked about a game
called golf.   It was he who advocated laying out a
section of land for what he called links, and erect-
ing a club house thereon.

"The section of the bluff overlooking the river,"
he explained, "is full of natural hazards, besides
having a really fine view."

Chippewa—or that comfortable, middle-class
section of it which got its exercise walking home to
dinner from the store at noon, and cutting the
grass evenings after supper—laughed as it read
this interview in the Chippewa *Eagle*.

"A golf course," they repeated to one another, grinning. "Conklin's cow pasture, up the river. It's full of natural—wait a minute—what was?—oh, yeh, here it is—hazards. Full of natural hazards. Say, couldn't you die!"

For H. Charnsworth Baldwin had been little Henry Baldwin before he went East to college. Ten years later H. Charnsworth, in knickerbockers and gay-topped stockings, was winning the cup in the men's tournament played on the Chippewa golf-club course, overlooking the river. And his name, in stout gold letters, blinked at you from the plate-glass windows of the office at the corner of Elm and Winnebago:

NORTHERN LUMBER AND LAND COMPANY.
H. CHARNSWORTH BALDWIN, PRES.

Two blocks farther down Elm Street was another sign, not so glittering, which read:

MISS SOPHY DECKER
Millinery

Sophy's hat-making, in the beginning, had been done at home. She had always made her sisters' hats, and her own, of course, and an occasional hat for a girl friend. After her sisters had married Sophy found herself in possession of a rather bewildering amount of spare time. The hat trade grew so that sometimes there were six rather botchy little bonnets all done up in yellow paper pyramids with a pin at the top, awaiting their future wearers.　After her mother's death Sophy still stayed on in the old house.　She took a course in millinery in Milwaukee, came home, stuck up a home-made sign in the parlour window (the untidy cucumber vines came down), and began her hat-making in earnest.　In five years she had opened a shop on a side street near Elm; had painted the old house, installed new plumbing, built a warty stucco porch, and transformed the weedy, grass-tangled yard into an orderly stretch of green lawn and bright flower-beds.　In ten years she was in Elm Street, and the Chippewa *Eagle* ran a half column twice a year describing her spring and fall openings.　On these occasions Aunt Sophy, in black satin, and marcel wave, and her most relentless corsets was, in all the superficial things, not a pleat, or fold, or line, or wave behind her city colleagues.　She had all the catch phrases:

"This is awfully good this year."

"Here's a sweet thing. A Mornet model. . . . Well, but my dear, it's the style—the line—you're paying for, not the material."

"I've got the very thing for you.　I had you in mind when I bought it.　Now don't say you can't wear henna.　Wait till you see it on."

When she stood behind you as you sat, un-crowned and expectant before the mirror, she would poise the hat four inches above your head, holding it in the tips of her fingers, a precious, fragile thing. Your fascinated eyes were held by it, and your breath as well. Then down it descended, slowly, slowly. A quick pressure. Her fingers firm against your temples. A little sigh of relieved suspense.

"That's wonderful on you! . . . You don't! Oh, my dear! But that's because you're not used to it. You know how you said, for years, you had to have a brim, and couldn't possibly wear a turban, with your nose, until I proved to you that if the head-size was only big . . . Well, perhaps this needs just a lit-tle lift here. Ju-u-ust a nip. There! That does it."

And that did it. Not that Sophy Decker ever tried to sell you a hat against your judgment, taste, or will. She was too wise a psychologist and too shrewd a business woman for that. She preferred that you go out of her shop hatless rather than with an unbecoming hat. But whether you bought or not you took with you out of Sophy Decker's shop something more precious than any hatbox ever contained. Just to hear her admonishing a customer, her good-natured face all aglow:

"My dear, always put on your hat before you get into your dress. I do. You can get your arms above your head, and set it right. I put on my hat and veil as soon's I get my hair combed."

In your mind's eye you saw her, a stout, well-stayed figure in tight brassière and scant petticoat, bare-armed and bare-bosomed, in smart hat and veil, attired as though for the street from the neck up and for the bedroom from the shoulders down.

The East-End set bought Sophy Decker's hats because they were modish and expensive hats. But she managed, miraculously, to gain a large and lucrative following among the paper-mill girls and factory hands as well. You would have thought that any attempt to hold both these opposites would cause her to lose one or the other. Aunt Sophy said, frankly, that of the two, she would have preferred to lose her smart trade.

"The mill girls come in with their money in their hands, you might say. They get good wages and they want to spend them. I wouldn't try to sell them one of those little plain model hats. They wouldn't understand 'em, or like them. And if I told them the price they'd think I was trying to cheat them. They want a velvet hat with something good and solid on it. Their fathers wouldn't prefer caviar to pork roast, would they? It's the same idea."

Her shop windows reflected her business acumen. One was chastely, severely elegant, holding a single hat poised on a slender stick. In the other were a dozen honest arrangements of velvet and satin and plumes.

At the spring opening she always displayed one of those little toques completely covered with violets. No one ever bought a hat like that. No one ever will. That violet-covered toque is a symbol.

"I don't expect 'em to buy it," Sophy Decker explained. "But everybody feels there should be a hat like that at a spring opening. It's like a fruit centre-piece at a family dinner. Nobody ever eats it but it has to be there."

The two Baldwin children—Adele and Eugene— found Aunt Sophy's shop a treasure trove. Adele, during her doll days, possessed such boxes of satin and velvet scraps, and bits of lace, and ribbon and jet as to make her the envy of all her playmates. She used to crawl about the floor of the shop workroom and under the table and chairs like a little scavenger.

"What in the world do you do with all that truck, child?" asked Aunt Sophy. "You must have barrels of it."

Adele stuffed another wisp of tulle into the pocket of her pinafore. "I keep it," she said.

When she was ten Adele had said to her mother, "Why do you always say 'Poor Sophy'?"

"Because Aunt Sophy's had so little in life. She never has married, and has always worked."

Adele considered that. "If you don't get married do they say you're poor?"

"Well—yes——"

"Then I'll get married," announced Adele. A small, dark, eerie child, skinny and rather foreign looking.

The boy, Eugene, had the beauty which should have been the girl's. Very tall, very blond, with the straight nose and wistful eyes of the Flora of twenty years ago. "If only Adele could have had his looks," his mother used to say. "They're wasted on a man. He doesn't need them but a girl does. Adele will have to be well-dressed and interesting. And that's such hard work."

Flora said she worshipped her children. And she actually sometimes still coquetted heavily with her husband. At twenty she had been addicted to baby talk when endeavouring to coax something out of someone. Her admirers had found it irresistible. At forty it was awful. Her selfishness was colossal. She affected a semi-invalidism and for fifteen years had spent one day a week in bed. She took no exercise and a great deal of baking soda and tried to fight her fat with

baths. Fifteen or twenty years had worked a
startling change in the two sisters, Flora the
beautiful, and Sophy the plain. It was more
than a mere physical change. It was a spiritual
thing, though neither knew nor marked it. Each
had taken on weight, the one, solidly, comfortably;
the other, flabbily, unhealthily. With the en-
croaching fat Flora's small, delicate features
seemed, somehow, to disappear in her face, so
that you saw it as a large white surface bearing in-
dentations, ridges, and hollows like one of those
enlarged photographs of the moon's surface as
seen through a telescope. A self-centred face, and
misleadingly placid. Aunt Sophy's large, plain
features, plumply padded now, impressed you as
indicating strength, courage, and a great human
understanding.

From her husband and her children Flora
exacted service that would have chafed a galley-
slave into rebellion. She loved to lie in bed, in a
lavender bed-jacket with ribbons, and be read to
by Adele or Eugene, or her husband. They all
hated it.

"She just wants to be waited on, and petted,
and admired," Adele had stormed one day, in open
rebellion, to her Aunt Sophy. "She uses it as an
excuse for everything and has, ever since 'Gene
and I were children. She's as strong as an ox."

Not a very ladylike or daughterly speech, but shockingly true.

Years before a generous but misguided woman friend, coming in to call, had been ushered in to where Mrs. Baldwin lay propped up in a nest of pillows.

"Well, I don't blame you," the caller had gushed. "If I looked the way you do in bed I'd stay there forever. Don't tell me you're sick, with all that lovely colour!"

Flora Baldwin had rolled her eyes ceilingward. "Nobody ever gives me credit for all my suffering and ill-health. And just because all my blood is in my cheeks."

Flora was ambitious, socially, but too lazy to make the effort necessary for success in that direction.

"I love my family," she would say. "They fill my life. After all, that's a profession in itself— being a wife and mother."

She showed her devotion by taking no interest whatever in her husband's land schemes; by forbidding Eugene to play football at school for fear he might be injured; by impressing Adele with the necessity for vivacity and modishness because of what she called her unfortunate lack of beauty.

"I don't understand it," she used to say in the child's very presence. "Her father's handsome enough, goodness knows; and I wasn't such a fright when I was a girl. And look at her! Little, dark, skinny thing."

The boy Eugene grew up a very silent, handsome, shy young fellow. The girl dark, voluble, and rather interesting. The husband, more and more immersed in his business, was absent from home for long periods; irritable after some of these home-comings; boisterously high-spirited following other trips. Now growling about household expenses and unpaid bills; now urging the purchase of some almost prohibitive luxury. Any one but a nagging, self-absorbed, and vain woman such as Flora would have marked these unmistakable signs. But Flora was a taker, not a giver. She thought herself affectionate because she craved affection unduly. She thought herself a fond mother because she insisted on having her children with her, under her thumb, marking their devotion as a prisoner marks time with his feet, stupidly, shufflingly, advancing not a step.

Sometimes Sophy the clear-eyed and level-headed, seeing this state of affairs, tried to stop it.

"You expect too much of your husband and children," she said one day, bluntly, to her sister.

"I!" Flora's dimpled hands had flown to her breast like a wounded thing. "I! You're crazy! There isn't a more devoted wife and mother in the world. That's the trouble. I love them too much."

"Well, then," grimly, "stop it for a change. That's half Eugene's nervousness—your fussing over him. He's eighteen. Give him a chance. You're weakening him. And stop dinning that society stuff into Adele's ears. She's got brains, that child. Why, just yesterday, in the workroom, she got hold of some satin and a shape and turned out a little turban that Angie Hatton———"

"Do you mean to tell me that Angie Hatton saw my Adele working in your shop! Now, look here, Sophy. You're earning your living, and it's to your credit. You're my sister. But I won't have Adele associated in the minds of my friends with your hat store, understand. I won't have it. That isn't what I sent her away to an expensive school for. To have her come back and sit around a millinery workshop with a lot of little, cheap, shoddy sewing girls! Now understand, I won't have it! You don't know what it is to be a mother. You don't know what it is to have suffered. If you had brought two children into the world———"

So then, it had come about, during the years between their childhood and their youth, that Aunt Sophy received the burden of their confidences, their griefs, their perplexities. She seemed, somehow, to understand in some miraculous way, and to make the burden a welcome one.

"Well, now, you tell Aunt Sophy all about it. Stop crying, Della. How can Aunt Sophy hear when you're crying! That's my baby. Now, then."

This when they were children. But with the years the habit clung and became fixed. There was something about Aunt Sophy's house—the old frame house with the warty stucco porch. For that matter, there was something about the very shop downtown, with its workroom in the rear, that had a cozy, homelike quality never possessed by the big Baldwin house. H. Charnsworth Baldwin had built a large brick mansion, in the Tudor style, on a bluff overlooking the Fox River, in the best residential section of Chippewa. It was expensively and correctly furnished. The hall consol alone was enough to strik a preliminary chill to your heart.

The millinery workroom, winter days, was always bright and warm and snug. The air was a little close, perhaps, and heavy, but with a not unpleasant smell of dyes, and stuffs, and velvet, and glue, and steam, and flatiron, and a certain heady scent that Julia Gold, the head trimmer, always used. There was a sociable cat, white with a dark gray patch on his throat and a swipe

of it across one flank that spoiled him for style and
beauty but made him a comfortable-looking cat
to have around.   Sometimes, on very cold days,
or in the rush reason, the girls would not go home
to dinner or supper, but would bring their lunches
and cook coffee over a little gas heater in the corner.   Julia Gold, especially, drank quantities of
coffee.   Aunt Sophy had hired her from Chicago.
She had been with her for five years.   She said
Julia was the best trimmer she had ever had.   Aunt
Sophy often took her to New York or Chicago on
her buying trips.   Julia had not much genius for
original design, or she would never have been
content to be head milliner in a small-town shop.
But she could copy a fifty-dollar model from
memory down to the last detail of crown and brim.
It was a gift that made her invaluable.

The boy, Eugene, used to like to look at Julia
Gold.   Her hair was very black and her face was
very white, and her eyebrows met in a thick, dark
line.   Her face, as she bent over her work, was
sullen and brooding, but when she lifted her head
suddenly, in conversation, you were startled by a
vivid flash of teeth, and eyes, and smile.   Her
voice was deep and low.   She made you a little
uncomfortable.   Her eyes seemed always to be
asking something.   Around the work table, mornings, she used to relate the dream she had had the

night before. In these dreams she was always being pursued by a lover. "And then I woke up, screaming." Neither she nor the sewing girls knew what she was revealing in these confidences of hers. But Aunt Sophy, the shrewd, somehow sensed it.

"You're alone too much, evenings. That's what comes of living in a boarding house. You come over to me for a week. The change will do you good, and it'll be nice for me, too, having somebody to keep me company."

Julia often came for a week or ten days at a time. Julia, about the house after supper, was given to those vivid splashy kimonos with big flowers embroidered on them. They made her hair look blacker and her skin whiter by contrast. Sometimes Eugene or Adele or both would drop in and the four would play bridge. Aunt Sophy played a shrewd and canny game, Adele a rather brilliant one, Julia a wild and disastrous hand, always, and Eugene so badly that only Julia would take him on as a partner. Mrs. Baldwin never knew about these evenings.

It was on one of these occasions that Aunt Sophy, coming unexpectedly into the living room from the kitchen where she and Adele were foraging for refreshments after the game, beheld Julia Gold and Eugene, arms clasped about each other, cheek

to cheek. They started up as she came in and
faced her, the woman defiantly, the boy bravely.
Julia Gold was thirty (with reservations) at that
time, and the boy not quite twenty-one.

"How long?" said Aunt Sophy, quietly. She
had a mayonnaise spoon and a leaf of lettuce in
her hand at the time, and still she did not look
comic.

"I'm crazy about her," said Eugene. "We're
crazy about each other. We're going to be married."

Aunt Sophy listened for the reassuring sound of
Adele's spoons and plates in the kitchen. She
came forward. "Now, listen——" she began.

"I love him," said Julia Gold, dramatically.
"I love him!"

Except that it was very white and, somehow,
old looking, Aunt Sophy's face was as benign as
always. "Now, look here, Julia, my girl. That
isn't love and you know it. I'm an old maid, but
I know what love is when I see it. I'm ashamed
of you, Julia. Sensible woman like you. Hug-
ging and kissing a boy like that, and old enough to
be his mother, pretty near."

"Now, look here, Aunt Soph! I'm fond of you
but if you're going to talk that way—— Why,
she's wonderful. She's taught me what it means
to really——"

"Oh, my land!" Aunt Sophy sat down, look-ing, suddenly, very sick and old.

And then, from the kitchen, Adele's clear young voice: "Heh! What's the idea! I'm not going to do all the work. Where's everybody?"

Aunt Sophy started up again. She came up to them and put a hand—a capable, firm, steadying hand on the arm of each. The woman drew back but the boy did not.

"Will you promise me not to do anything for a week? Just a week! Will you promise me? Will you?"

"Are you going to tell Father?"

"Not for a week if you'll promise not to see each other in that week. No, I don't want to send you away, Julia, I don't want to—— You're not a bad girl. It's just—he's never had—at home they never gave him a chance. Just a week, Julia. Just a week, Eugene. We can talk things over then."

Adele's footsteps coming from the kitchen.

"Quick!"

"I promise," said Eugene. Julia said nothing.

"Well, really," said Adele, from the doorway, "you're a nervy lot, sitting around while I slave in the kitchen. 'Gene, see if you can open the olives with this fool can opener. I tried."

There is no knowing what she expected to do

in that week, Aunt Sophy; what miracle she meant to perform. She had no plan in her mind. Just hope. She looked strangely shrunken and old, suddenly. But when, three days later, the news came that America was to go into the war she knew that her prayers were answered.

Flora was beside herself. "Eugene won't have to go. He isn't quite twenty-one, thank God! And by the time he is it will be over. Surely." She was almost hysterical.

Eugene was in the room. Aunt Sophy looked at him and he looked at Aunt Sophy. In her eyes was a question. In his was the answer. They said nothing. The next day Eugene enlisted. In three days he was gone. Flora took to her bed. Next day Adele, a faint, unwonted colour marking her cheeks, walked into her mother's bedroom and stood at the side of the recumbent figure. Her father, his hands clasped behind him, was pacing up and down, now and then kicking a cushion that had fallen to the floor. He was chewing a dead cigar, one side of his face twisted curiously over the cylinder in his mouth so that he had a sinister and crafty look.

"Charnsworth, won't you please stop ramping up and down like that! My nerves are killing me. I can't help it if the war has done something or other to your business. I'm sure no wife could have been more economical than I have. Nothing matters but Eugene, anyway. How could he do such a thing! I've given my whole life to my children——"

H. Charnsworth kicked the cushion again so that it struck the wall at the opposite side of the room. Flora drew her breath in between her teeth as though a knife had entered her heart.

Adele still stood at the side of the bed, looking at her mother. Her hands were clasped behind her, too. In that moment, as she stood there, she resembled her mother and her father so startlingly and simultaneously that the two, had they been less absorbed in their own affairs, must have marked it.

The girl's head came up, stiffly. "Listen. I'm going to marry Daniel Oakley."

Daniel Oakley was fifty, and a friend of her father's. For years he had been coming to the house and for years she had ridiculed him. She and Eugene had called him Sturdy Oak because he was always talking about his strength and endurance, his walks, his golf, his rugged health; pounding his chest meanwhile and planting his feet far apart. He and Baldwin had had business relations as well as friendly ones.

At this announcement Flora screamed and sat up in bed. H. Charnsworth stopped short in his

pacing and regarded his daughter with a queer
look; a concentrated look, as though what she had
said had set in motion a whole maze of mental
machinery within his brain.

"When did he ask you?"

"He's asked me a dozen times. But it's different now. All the men will be going to war.
There won't be any left. Look at England and
France. I'm not going to be left." She turned
squarely toward her father, her young face set and
hard. "You know what I mean. You know
what I mean."

Flora, sitting up in bed, was sobbing. "I think
you might have told your mother, Adele. What
are children coming to! You stand there and say,
'I'm going to marry Daniel Oakley.' Oh, I *am* so
faint . . . all of a sudden . . . get the
spirits of ammonia. . . ."

Adele turned and walked out of the room. She
was married six weeks later. They had a regular
pre-war wedding—veil, flowers, dinner, and all.
Aunt Sophy arranged the folds of her gown and
draped her veil. The girl stood looking at herself
in the mirror, a curious half-smile twisting her lips.
She seemed slighter and darker than ever.

"In all this white, and my veil, I look just like
a fly in a quart of milk," she said, with a laugh.
Then, suddenly, she turned to her aunt who stood

behind her and clung to her, holding her tight, tight. "I can't!" she gasped. "I can't! I can't!"

Aunt Sophy held her off and looked at her, her eyes searching the girl.

"What do you mean, Della? Are you just nervous or do you mean you don't want to marry him? Do you mean that? Then what are you marrying for? Tell me! Tell your Aunt Sophy."

But Adele was straightening herself and pulling out the crushed folds of her veil. "To pay the mortgage on the old homestead, of course. Just like the girl in the play." She laughed a little. But Aunt Sophy did not laugh.

"Now look here, Della. If you're——"

But there was a knock at the door. Adele caught up her flowers. "It's all right," she said.

Aunt Sophy stood with her back against the door. "If it's money," she said. "It is! It is, isn't it! Listen. I've got money saved. It was for you children. I've always been afraid. I knew he was sailing pretty close, with his speculations and all, since the war. He can have it all. It isn't too late yet. Adele! Della, my baby."

"Don't, Aunt Sophy. It wouldn't be enough, anyway. Daniel has been wonderful, really. Don't look like that. I'd have hated being poor, anyway. Never could have got used to it. It is ridiculous, though, isn't it? Like one of those

melodramas, or a cheap movie. I don't mind.
I'm lucky, really, when you come to think of it.
A plain little black thing like me."

"But your mother——"

"Mother doesn't know a thing."

Flora wept mistily all through the ceremony
but Adele was composed enough for two.

When, scarcely a month later, Baldwin came
to Sophy Decker, his face drawn and queer, Sophy
knew.

"How much?" she said.

"Thirty thousand will cover it. If you've got
more than that——"

"I thought Oakley—Adele said——"

"He did, but he won't any more, and this thing's
got to be met. It's this damned war that's done it.
I'd have been all right. People got scared. They
wanted their money. They wanted it in cash."

"Speculating with it, were you?"

"Oh, well, a woman doesn't understand these
business deals."

"No, naturally," said Aunt Sophy, "a butterfly
like me."

"Sophy, for God's sake don't joke now. I tell
you this will cover it, and everything will be all
right. If I had anybody else to go to for the
money I wouldn't ask you. But you'll get it back.
You know that."

Aunt Sophy got up, heavily, and went over to her desk. "It was for the children, anyway. They won't need it now."

He looked up at that. Something in her voice. "Who won't? Why won't they?"

"I don't know what made me say that. I had a dream."

"Eugene?"

"Yes."

"Oh, well, we're all nervous. Flora has dreams every night and presentiments every fifteen minutes. Now, look here, Sophy. About this money. You'll never know how grateful I am. Flora doesn't understand these things but I can talk to you. It's like this——"

"I might as well be honest about it," Sophy interrupted. "I'm doing it, not for you, but for Flora, and Della—and Eugene. Flora has lived such a sheltered life. I sometimes wonder if she ever really knew any of you. Her husband, or her children. I sometimes have the feeling that Della and Eugene are my children—were my children."

When he came home that night Baldwin told his wife that old Soph was getting queer. "She talks about the children being hers," he said.

"Oh, well, she's awfully fond of them," Flora explained. "And she's lived her little narrow life, with nothing to bother her but her hats and her

house.   She doesn't know what it means to suffer
as a mother suffers—poor Sophy."

"Um," Baldwin grunted.

When the official notification of Eugene's death
came from the War Department Aunt Sophy was
so calm that it might have appeared that Flora
had been right.   She took to her bed now in
earnest, did Flora, and they thought that her grief
would end in madness.   Sophy neglected everything to give comfort to the stricken two.

"How can you sit there like that!" Flora would
rail.   "How can you sit there like that!   Even if
you weren't his mother surely you must feel something."

"It's the way he died that comforts me," said
Aunt Sophy.

"What difference does that make!   What difference does that make!"

This is the letter that made a difference to Aunt
Sophy.   You will have to read it to understand,
though you are likely to skip letters on the printed
page.   You must not skip this.

AMERICAN RED CROSS
(CROIX ROUGE AMÉRICAINE)

My dear Mrs. Baldwin:

I am sure you must have been officially notified, by now, by
the U. S. War Dept. of the death of your son Lieut. Eugene
H. Baldwin.   But I want to write you what I can of his last

hours. I was with him much of that time as his nurse. I'm sure it must mean much to a mother to hear from a woman who was privileged to be with her boy at the last.

Your son was brought to our hospital one night badly gassed from the fighting in the Argonne Forest. Ordinarily we do not receive gassed patients, as they are sent to a special hospital near here. But two nights before the Germans wrecked this hospital, so many gassed patients have come to us.

Your son was put in the officers' ward where the doctors who examined him told me there was absolutely no hope for him, as he had inhaled the gas so much that it was only a matter of a few hours. I could scarcely believe that a man so big and strong as he was could not pull through.

The first bad attack he had, losing his breath and nearly choking, rather frightened him, although the doctor and I were both with him. He held my hand tightly in his, begging me not to leave him, and repeating, over and over, that it was good to have a woman near. He was propped high in bed and put his head on my shoulder while I fanned him until he breathed more easily. I stayed with him all that night, though I was not on duty. You see, his eyes also were badly burned. But before he died he was able to see very well. I stayed with him every minute of that night and have never seen a finer character than he showed during all that dreadful fight for life. He had several bad sinking attacks that night and came through each one simply because of his great will power and fighting spirit. After each attack he would grip my hand and say, "Well, we made it that time, didn't we, nurse? And if you'll only stay with me we'll win this fight." At intervals during the night I gave him sips of black coffee which was all he could swallow. Each time I gave it to him he would ask me if I had had some. That was only one instance of his thoughtfulness even in his suffering. Toward

morning he asked me if he was going to die. I could not tell
him the truth. He needed all his strength. I told him he
had one chance in a thousand. He seemed to become very
strong then, and sitting bolt upright in bed and shaking his
fist, he said: "Then by the Lord I'll fight for it!" We kept
him alive for three days, and actually thought we had won
when on the third day. . . .

But even in your sorrow you must be very proud to have
been the mother of such a son. . . .

I am a Wisconsin girl—Madison. When this is over and I
come home will you let me see you so that I may tell you more
than I can possibly write?

Marian King.

It was in March, six months later, that Marian
King came. They had hoped for it, but never
expected it. And she came. Four people were
waiting in the living room of the big Baldwin house
overlooking the river. Flora and her husband,
Adele and Aunt Sophy. They sat, waiting. Now
and then Adele would rise, nervously, and go to the
window that faced the street. Flora was weeping
with audible sniffs. Baldwin sat in his chair
frowning a little, a dead cigar in one corner of his
mouth. Only Aunt Sophy sat quietly, waiting.

There was little conversation. None in the last
five minutes. Flora broke the silence, dabbing
at her face with her handkerchief as she spoke.

"Sophy, how can you sit there like that? Not
that I don't envy you. I do. I remember I used

to feel sorry for you. I used to say, 'Poor Sophy.' But you unmarried ones are the happiest, after all. It's the married woman who drinks the cup to the last bitter drop. There you sit, Sophy, fifty years old, and life hasn't even touched you. You don't know how cruel life is."

Suddenly, "There!" said Adele. The other three in the room stood up and faced the door. The sound of a motor stopping outside. Daniel Oakley's hearty voice: "Well, it only took us five minutes from the station. Pretty good."

Footsteps down the hall. Marian King stood in the doorway. They faced her, the four—Baldwin and Adele and Flora and Sophy. Marian King stood a moment, uncertainly, her eyes upon them. She looked at the two older women with swift, appraising glance. Then she came into the room, quickly, and put her two hands on Aunt Sophy's shoulders and looked into her eyes straight and sure.

"You must be a very proud woman," she said. "You ought to be a very proud woman."

APRIL 25TH, AS USUAL

MRS. HOSEA C. BREWSTER always cleaned house in September and April. She started with the attic and worked her purifying path down to the cellar in strict accordance with Article I, Section 1, Unwritten Rules for House Cleaning. For twenty-five years she had done it. For twenty-five years she had hated it—being an intelligent woman. For twenty-five years, towel swathed about her head, skirt pinned back, sleeves rolled up—the costume dedicated to house cleaning since the days of What's-Her-Name mother of Lemuel (see Proverbs)—Mrs. Brewster had gone through the ceremony twice a year.

Furniture on the porch, woollens on the line, mattresses in the yard—everything that could be pounded, beaten, whisked, rubbed, flapped, shaken, or aired was dragged out and subjected to one or all of these indignities. After which, completely cowed, they were dragged in again and set in their places. Year after year, in attic and in cellar, things had piled up higher and higher—useless things, sentimental things; things in trunks;

36

things in chests; shelves full of things wrapped up in brown-paper parcels.

And boxes—oh, above all, boxes: pasteboard boxes, long and flat, square and oblong, each bearing weird and cryptic pencillings on one end; cryptic, that is, to any one except Mrs. Brewster and you who have owned an attic. Thus "H's Fshg Tckl" jabberwocked one long, slim box. Another stunned you with "Cur Ted Slpg Pch." A cabalistic third hid its contents under "Slp Cov Pinky Rm." To say nothing of such curt yet intriguing fragments as "Blk Nt Drs" and "Sun Par Val." Once you had the code key they translated themselves simply enough into such homely items as Hosey's fishing tackle, canvas curtains for Ted's sleeping porch, slip covers for Pinky's room, black net dress, sun-parlour valance.

The contents of those boxes formed a commentary on normal American household life as lived by Mr. and Mrs. Hosea C. Brewster, of Winnebago, Wisconsin. Hosey's rheumatism had prohibited trout fishing these ten years; Ted wrote from Arizona that "the li'l' ol' sky" was his sleeping-porch roof and you didn't have to worry out there about the neighbours seeing you in your pyjamas; Pinky's rose-cretonne room had lacked an occupant since Pinky left the Winnebago

High School for the Chicago Art Institute, thence
to New York and those amazingly successful
magazine covers that stare up at you from your
table—young lady, hollow chested (she'd need to
be with that décolletage), carrying feather fan.
You could tell a Brewster cover at sight, without
the fan.   That leaves the black net dress and the
sun-parlour valance.   The first had grown too
tight under the arms (Mrs. Brewster's arms); the
second had faded.

Now, don't gather from this that Mrs. Brewster
was an ample, pie-baking, ginghamed old soul
who wore black silk and a crushed-looking hat with
a palsied rose atop it.   Nor that Hosea C. Brewster was spectacled and slippered.   Not at all.
The Hosea C. Brewsters, of Winnebago, Wisconsin,
were the people you've met on the veranda of the
Moana Hotel at Honolulu, or at the top of Pike's
Peak, or peering into the restless heart of Vesuvius.
They were the prosperous Middle-Western type of
citizen who runs down to Chicago to see the new
plays and buy a hat, and to order a dozen Wedg-
wood salad plates at Field's.

Mrs. Brewster knew about Dunsany and
georgette and alligator pears; and Hosea Brewster
was in the habit of dropping around to the Elks'
Club, up above Schirmer's furniture store on Elm
Street, at about five in the afternoon on his way

home from the cold-storage plant. The Brewster place was honeycombed with sleeping porches and sun parlours and linen closets, and laundry chutes and vegetable bins and electric surprises, as your well-to-do Middle-Western house is likely to be.

That house had long ago grown too large for the two of them—physically, that is. But as the big frame house had expanded, so had they—in tolerance and understanding and humanness—until now, as you talked with them, you felt that here was room and to spare of sun-filled mental chambers, and shelves well stored with experience; and pantries and bins and closets for all your worries and confidences.

But the attic! And the cellar! The attic was the kind of attic every woman longs for who hasn't one and every woman loathes who has. "If I only had some place to put things in!" wails the first. And, "If it weren't for the attic I'd have thrown this stuff away long ago," complains the second. Mrs. Brewster herself had helped plan it. Hardwood floored, spacious, light, the Brewster attic revealed to you the social, æsthetic, educational, and spiritual progress of the entire family as clearly as if a sociologist had charted it.

Take, for example (before we run down to the cellar for a minute), the crayon portraits of Gran'-

ma and Gran'pa Brewster. When Ted had been a junior and Pinky a freshman at the Winnebago High School the crayon portraits had beamed down upon them from the living-room wall. To each of these worthy old people the artist had given a pair of hectic pink cheeks. Gran'ma Brewster especially, simpering down at you from the labyrinthian scrolls of her sextuple gold frame, was rouged like a soubrette and further embellished with a pair of gentian-blue eyes behind steel-bowed specs. Pinky—and in fact the entire Brewster household—had thought these massive atrocities the last word in artistic ornament. By the time she reached her sophomore year, Pinky had prevailed upon her mother to banish them to the dining room. Then, two years later, when the Chicago decorator did over the living room and the dining room, the crayons were relegated to the upstairs hall.

Ted and Pinky, away at school, began to bring their friends back with them for the vacations. Pinky's room had been done over in cream enamel and rose-flowered cretonne. She said the chromos in the hall spoiled the entire second floor. So the gold frames, glittering undimmed, the cheeks as rosily glowing as ever, found temporary resting place in a nondescript back chamber known as the sewing room. Then the new sleeping porch

was built for Ted, and the portraits ended their
journeying in the attic.

One paragraph will cover the cellar. Sta-
tionary tubs, laundry stove. Behind that, bin for
potatoes, bin for carrots, bins for onions, apples,
cabbages. Boxed shelves for preserves. And
behind that Hosea C. Brewster's *bête noir* and
plaything, tyrant and slave—the furnace. "She's
eating up coal this winter," Hosea Brewster would
complain. Or: "Give her a little more draft,
Fred." Fred, of the furnace and lawn mower,
would shake a doleful head. "She ain't drawin'
good. I do' know what's got into her."

By noon of this particular September day—a
blue-and-gold Wisconsin September day—Mrs.
Brewster had reached that stage in the cleaning of
the attic when it looked as if it would never be
clean and orderly again. Taking into consideration Miz' Merz (Miz' Merz by-the-day, you understand) and Gussie, the girl, and Fred, there was
very little necessity for Mrs. Brewster's official
house-cleaning uniform. She might have unpinned her skirt, unbound her head, rolled down
her sleeves, and left for the day, serene in the knowledge that no corner, no chandelier, no mirror, no
curlicue so hidden, so high, so glittering, so ornate
that it might hope to escape the rag or brush of one
or the other of this relentless and expert crew.

Every year, twice a year, as this box, that trunk or chest was opened and its contents revealed, Miz' Merz would say: "You keepin' this, Miz' Brewster?"

"That? Oh, dear, yes!" Or: "Well—I don't know. You can take that home with you if you want it. It might make over for Minnie."

Yet, why in the name of all that's ridiculous did she treasure the funeral wheat wreath in the walnut frame? Nothing is more *passé* than a last summer's hat, yet the leghorn and pink-cambric-rose thing in the tin trunk was the one Mrs. Brewster had worn when a bride. Then the plaid kilted dress with the black velvet monkey jacket that Pinky had worn when she spoke her first piece at the age of seven—well, these were things that even the rapacious eye of Miz' Merz (by-the-day) passed by unbrightened by covetousness.

The smell of soap and water, and cedar, and moth balls, and dust, and the ghost of a perfumery that Pinky used to use pervaded the hot attic. Mrs. Brewster, head and shoulders in a trunk, was trying not to listen and not to seem not to listen to Miz' Merz's recital of her husband's relations' latest flagrancy.

"'Families is nix,' I says. 'I got my own fam'ly to look out fur,' I says. Like that. 'Well,' s's he, 'w'en it comes to *that*,' s's he, 'I guess I got some——'" Punctuated by thumps, spatterings, swashings, and much heavy breathing, so that the sound of light footsteps along the second-floor hallway, a young, clear voice calling, then the same footsteps, fleeter now, on the attic stairway, were quite unheard.

Pinky's arms were around her mother's neck and for one awful moment it looked as if both were to be decapitated by the trunk lid, so violent had been Mrs. Brewster's start of surprise.

Incoherent little cries, and sentences unfinished:

"Pinky! Why—my baby! We didn't get your telegram. Did you——"

"No; I didn't. I just thought I—— Don't look so dazed, mummy—— You're all smudged, too—what in the world!" Pinky straightened her hat and looked about the attic. "Why, mother! You're—you're house cleaning!" There was a stunned sort of look on her face. Pinky's last visit home had been in June, all hammocks, and roses, and especially baked things, and motor trips into the country.

"Of course. This is September. But if I'd known you were coming—— Come here to the window. Let mother see you. Is that the kind of hat they're—why, it's a winter one, isn't it? Already! Dear me, I've just got used to the

angle of my summer one. You must telephone
father."

Miz' Merz, damply calicoed, rose from a corner
and came forward, wiping a moist and parboiled
hand on her skirt. "Ha' do, Pinky. Ain't forgot
your old friends, have you?"

"It's Mrs. Merz!" Pinky put her cool, sweet
fingers into the other woman's spongy clasp.
"Why, hello, Mrs. Merz! Of course when
there's house cleaning—I'd forgotten all about
house cleaning—that there was such a thing, I
mean."

"It's got to be done," replied Miz' Merz, severely.

Pinky, suddenly looking like one of her own
magazine covers (in tailor clothes), turned swiftly
to her mother. "Nothing of the kind," she said,
crisply. She looked about the hot, dusty, littered
room. She included and then banished it all with
one sweeping gesture. "Nothing of the kind.
This is—this is an anachronism."

"Mebbe so," retorted Miz' Merz with equal
crispness. "But it's got to be cleaned just the
same. Yessir; it's got to be cleaned."

They smiled at each other then, the mother and
daughter. They descended the winding attic
stairs happily, talking very fast and interrupting
each other.

Mrs. Brewster's skirt was still pinned up. Her

hair was bound in the protecting towel. "You must telephone father. No, let's surprise him. You'll hate the dinner—built around Miz Merz; you know—boiled. Well, you know what a despot she is."

It was hot for September, in Wisconsin. As they came out to the porch Pinky saw that there were tiny beads of moisture under her mother's eyes and about her chin. The sight infuriated her somehow. "Well, really, mother!"

Mrs. Brewster unpinned her skirt and smoothed it down; and smiled at Pinky, all unconscious that she looked like a plump, pink Sister of Mercy with that towel bound tightly about her hair. With a swift movement Pinky unpinned the towel, unwound it, dabbed with it tenderly at her mother's chin and brow, rolled it into a vicious wad, and hurled it through the open doorway.

"Now just what does that mean?" said Mrs. Brewster, equably. "Take off your hat and coat, Pinky, but don't treat them that way—unless that's the way they're doing in New York. Everything is so informal since the war." She had a pretty wit of her own, Mrs. Brewster.

Of course Pinky laughed then, and kissed her mother and hugged her hard. "It's just that it seems so idiotic—your digging around in an attic in this day and age! Why, it's—it's——" Pinky could express herself much more clearly in colours than in words. "There is no such thing as an attic. People don't clean them any more. I never realized before—this huge house. It has been wonderful to come back to, of course. But just you and dad." She stopped. She raised two young fists high in impotent anger. "Do you *like* cleaning the attic?"

"Why, no. I hate it."

"Then why in the world——"

"I've always done it, Pinky. And while they may not be wearing attics in New York, we haven't taken them off in Winnebago. Come on up to your room, dear. It looks bare. If I'd known you were coming—the slip covers——"

"Are they in the box in the attic labelled 'Slp Cov Pinky Rm'?" She succeeded in slurring it ludicrously.

It brought an appreciative giggle from Mrs. Brewster. A giggle need not be inconsistent with fifty years, especially if one's nose wrinkles up delightfully in the act. But no smile curved the daughter's stern young lips. Together they went up to Pinky's old room (the older woman stopped to pick up the crumpled towel on the hall floor). On the way they paused at the door of Mrs. Brewster's bedroom, so cool, so spacious, all soft grays and blues.

Suddenly Pinky's eyes widened with horror. She pointed an accusing forefinger at a large, dark object in a corner near a window. "That's the old walnut desk!" she exclaimed.

"I know it."

The girl turned, half amused, half annoyed. "Oh, mother dear! That's the situation in a nutshell. Without a shadow of doubt there's an eradicable streak of black walnut in your gray-enamel make-up."

"Eradicable! That's a grand word, Pinky. Stylish! I never expected to meet it out of a book. And, fu'thermore, as Miz' Merz would say, I didn't know there was any situation."

"I meant the attic. And it's more than a situation. It's a state of mind."

Mrs. Brewster had disappeared into the depths of her clothes closet. Her voice sounded muffled. "Pinky, you're talking the way they did at that tea you gave for father and me when we visited New York last winter." She emerged with a cool-looking blue kimono. "Here. Put this on. Father'll be home at twelve-thirty, for dinner, you know. You'll want a bath, won't you, dear?"

"Yes. Mummy, is it boiled—honestly?—on a day like this?"

"With onions," said Mrs. Brewster, firmly

Fifteen minutes later Pinky, splashing in a cool
tub, heard the voice of Miz' Merz high-pitched
with excitement and a certain awful joy: "Miz'
Brewster! Oh, Miz' Brewster! I found a moth
in Mr. Brewster's winter flannels!"

"Oh!" in choked accents of fury from Pinky;
and she brought a hard young fist down in the
water—spat!—so that it splashed ceiling, hair, and
floor impartially.

Still, it was a cool and serene young daughter
who greeted Hosea Brewster as he came limping up
the porch stairs. He placed the flat of the foot
down at each step instead of heel and ball. It
gave him a queer, hitching gait. The girl felt a
sharp little constriction of her throat as she marked
that rheumatic limp. "It's the beastly Wisconsin
winters," she told herself. Then, darting out at
him from the corner where she had been hiding:
"S'prise! S'prise!"

His plump blond face, flushed with the unwonted
heat, went darkly red. He dropped his hat. His
arms gathered her in. Her fresh young cheek
was pressed against his dear prickly one. So they
stood for a long minute—close.

"Need a shave, dad."

"Well, gosh, how did I know my best girl was
coming!" He held her off. "What's the matter,
Pink? Don't they like your covers any more?"

"Not a thing, Hosey. Don't get fresh. They're decorating my studio—you know—plasterers and stuff. I couldn't work. And I was lonesome for you."

Hosea Brewster went to the open doorway and gave a long whistle with a little quirk at the end. Then he came back to Pinky in the wide-seated porch swing. "You know," he said, his voice lowered confidentially, "I thought I'd take mother to New York for ten days or so. See the shows, and run around and eat at the dens of wickedness. She likes it for a change."

Pinky sat up, tense. "For a change? Dad, I want to talk to you about that. Mother needs——"

Mrs Brewster's light footstep sounded in the hall. She wore an all-enveloping gingham apron. "How did you like your surprise, father?" She came over to him and kissed the top of his head. "I'm getting dinner so that Gussie can go on with the attic. Everything's ready if you want to come in. I didn't want to dish up until you were at the table, so's everything would be hot." She threw a laughing glance at Pinky.

But when they were seated, there appeared a platter of cold, thinly sliced ham for Pinky, and a crisp salad, and a featherweight cheese soufflé, and iced tea, and a dessert coolly capped with whipped cream.

"But, mother, you shouldn't have——" feebly.

"There are always a lot of things in the house. You know that. I just wanted to tease you."

Father Brewster lingered for an unwonted hour after the midday meal. But two o'clock found him back at the cold-storage plant. Pinky watched him go, a speculative look in her eyes.

She visited the attic that afternoon at four, when it was again neat, clean, orderly, smelling of soap and sunshine. Standing there in the centre of the big room, freshly napped, smartly coifed, blue-serged, trim, the very concentrated essence of modernity, she eyed with stern deliberation the funeral wheat wreath in its walnut frame; the trunks; the chests; the boxes all shelved and neatly inscribed with their "H's Fshg Tckl" and "Blk Nt Drs."

"Barbaric!" she said aloud, though she stood there alone. "Medieval! Mad! It has got to be stopped. Slavery!" After which she went downstairs and picked golden glow for the living-room vases and scarlet salvia for the bowl in the dining room.

Still, as one saw Mrs. Brewster's tired droop at supper that night, there is no denying that there seemed some justification for Pinky's volcanic remarks.

Hosea Brewster announced, after supper, that

he and Fred were going to have a session with the furnace; she needed going over in September before they began firing up for the winter.

"I'll go down with you," said Pinky.

"No, you stay up here with mother. You'll get all ashes and coal dust."

But Pinky was firm. "Mother's half dead. She's going straight up to bed, after that darned old attic. I'll come up to tuck you in, mummy."

And though she did not descend to the cellar until the overhauling process was nearly completed she did come down in time for the last of the scene. She perched at the foot of the stairs and watched the two men, overalled, sooty, tobacco-wreathed, and happy. When, finally, Hosea Brewster knocked the ashes out of his stubby black pipe, dusted his sooty hands together briskly, and began to peel his overalls, Pinky came forward.

She put her hand on his arm. "Dad, I want to talk to you."

"Careful there. Better not touch me. I'm all dirt. G'night, Fred."

"Listen, dad. Mother isn't well."

He stopped then, with one overall leg off and the other on, and looked at her. "Huh? What d'you mean—isn't well? Mother." His mouth was open. His eyes looked suddenly strained.

"This house—it's killing her. She could hardly keep her eyes open at supper. It's too much for her. She ought to be enjoying herself—like other women. She's a slave to the attic and all those huge rooms. And you're another."

"Me?" feebly.

"Yes. A slave to this furnace. You said yourself to Fred, just now, that it was all worn out, and needed new pipes or something—I don't know what. And that coal was so high it would be cheaper using dollar bills for fuel. Oh, I know you were just being funny. But it was partly true. Wasn't it? Wasn't it?"

"Yeh, but listen here, Paula." He never called her Paula unless he was terribly disturbed. "About mother—you said——"

"You and she ought to go away this winter—not just for a trip, but to stay. You"—she drew a long breath and made the plunge—"you ought to give up the house."

"Give up——"

"Permanently. Mother and you are buried alive here. You ought to come to New York to live. Both of you will love it when you are there for a few days. I don't mean to come to a hotel. I mean to take a little apartment, a furnished apartment at first, to see how you like it—two rooms and kitchenette, like a playhouse."

Hosey Brewster looked down at his own big bulk, then around the great furnace room. "Oh, but listen——"

"No, I want you to listen first. Mother's worn out, I tell you. It isn't as if she were the old-fashioned kind; she isn't. She loves the theatres, and pretty hats, and shoes with buckles, and lobster, and concerts."

He broke in again: "Sure; she likes 'em for a change. But for a steady diet—— Besides, I've got a business to 'tend to. My gosh! I've got a business to——"

"You know perfectly well that Wetzler practically runs the whole thing—or could, if you'd let him." Youth is cruel like that, when it wants its way.

He did not even deny it. He seemed suddenly old. Pinky's heart smote her a little. "It's just that you've got so used to this great barracks you don't know how unhappy it's making you. Why, mother said to-day that she hated it. I asked about the attic—the cleaning and all—and she said she hated it."

"Did she say that, Paula?"

"Yes."

He dusted his hands together, slowly, spiritlessly.

His eyes looked pained and dull. "She did, h'm? You say she did?" He was talking to himself, and thinking, thinking.

Pinky, sensing victory, left him. She ran lighly up the cellar stairs, through the first-floor rooms, and up to the second floor. Her mother's bedroom door was open.

A little mauve lamp shed its glow upon the tired woman in one of the plump, gray-enamel beds. "No, I'm not sleeping. Come here, dear. What in the world have you been doing in the cellar all this time?"

"Talking to dad." She came over and perched herself on the side of the bed. She looked down at her mother. Then she bent and kissed her. Mrs. Brewster looked incredibly girlish with the lamp's rosy glow on her face and her hair, warmly brown and profuse, rippling out over the pillow. Scarcely a thread of gray in it. "You know, mother, I think dad isn't well. He ought to go away."

As if by magic the youth and glow faded out of the face on the pillow. As she sat up, clutching her nightgown to her breast, she looked suddenly pinched and old. "What do you mean, Pinky! Father—but he isn't sick. He——"

"Not sick. I don't mean sick exactly. But sort of worn out. That furnace. He's sick and

tired of the thing; that's what he said to Fred.   He
needs a change.   He ought to retire and enjoy life.
He could.   This house is killing both of you.
Why in the world don't you close it up, or sell it,
and come to New York?"

"But we do.   We did.   Last winter——"

"I don't mean just for a little trip.   I mean to
live.   Take a little two-room apartment in one of
the new buildings—near my studio—and relax.
Enjoy yourselves.   Meet new men and women.
Live!   You're in a rut—both of you.   Besides,
dad needs it.   That rheumatism of his, with these
Wisconsin winters——"

"But California—we could go to California
for——"

"That's only a stop-gap.   Get your little place
in New York all settled, and then run away whenever you like, without feeling that this great hulk of
a house is waiting for you.   Father hates it; I
know it."

"Did he ever say so?"

"Well, practically.   He thinks you're fond of it.
He——"

Slow steps ascending the stairs—heavy, painful
steps.   The two women listened in silence.
Every footfall seemed to emphasize Pinky's words.
The older woman turned her face toward the sound,
her lips parted, her eyes anxious, tender.

"How tired he sounds," said Pinky; "and old. And he's only—why, dad's only fifty-eight."

"Fifty-seven," snapped Mrs. Brewster, sharply, protectingly.

Pinky leaned forward and kissed her. "Good-night, mummy dear. You're so tired, aren't you?"

Her father stood in the doorway.

"Good-night, dear. I ought to be tucking you into bed. It's all turned around, isn't it? Biscuits and honey for breakfast, remember."

So Pinky went off to her own room (*sans* slp cov) and slept soundly, dreamlessly, as does one whose work is well done.

Three days later Pinky left. She waved a good-bye from the car platform, a radiant, electric, confident Pinky, her work well done.

"*Au 'voir!* The first of November! Everything begins then. You'll love it. You'll be real New Yorkers by Christmas. Now, no changing your minds, remember."

And by Christmas, somehow, miraculously, there were they, real New Yorkers; or as real and as New York as any one can be who is living in a studio apartment (duplex) that has been rented (furnished) from a lady who turned out to be from Des Moines.

When they arrived, Pinky had four apartments

waiting for their inspection. She told them this in triumph, and well she might, it being the winter after the war, when New York apartments were as scarce as black diamonds and twice as costly.

Father Brewster, on hearing the price, emitted a long, low whistle and said: "How many rooms did you say?"

"Two—and a kitchenette, of course."

"Well, then, all I can say is the furniture ought to be solid gold for that; inlaid with rubies and picked out with platinum."

But it wasn't. In fact, it wasn't solid anything, being mostly of a very impermanent structure and style. Pinky explained that she had kept the best for the last. The thing that worried Father Brewster was that, no matter at what hour of the day they might happen to call on the prospective lessor, that person was always feminine and hatted. Once it was eleven in the morning. Once five in the afternoon.

"Do these New York women wear hats in the house all the time?" demanded Hosea Brewster, worriedly. "I think they sleep in 'em. It's a wonder they ain't bald. Maybe they are. Maybe that's why. Anyway, it makes you feel like a book agent."

He sounded excited and tired. "Now, father!" said Mrs. Brewster, soothingly.

They were in the elevator that was taking
them up to the fourth and (according to Pinky)
choicest apartment. The building was what is
known as a studio apartment, in the West Sixties.
The corridors were done in red flagstones, with
gray-tone walls. The metal doors were painted
gray.

Pinky was snickering. "Now she'll say: 'Well,
we've been very comfortable here.' They always
do. Don't look too eager."

"No fear," put in Hosey Brewster.

"It's really lovely. And a real fireplace.
Everything new and good. She's asking two
hundred and twenty-five. Offer her one seventy-
five. She'll take two hundred."

"You bet she will," growled Hosea.

She answered the door—hatted; hatted in henna,
that being the season's chosen colour. A small,
dark foyer, overcrowded with furniture; a studio
living room, bright, high-ceilinged, smallish; one
entire side was window. There were Japanese
prints, and a baby grand piano, and a lot of
tables, and a davenport placed the way they
do it on the stage, with its back to the room
and its arms to the fireplace, and a long table
just behind it, with a lamp on it, and books, and
a dull jar thing, just as you've see it in the second-
act library.

Hosea Brewster twisted his head around and up to gaze at the lofty ceiling. "Feel's if I was standing at the bottom of a well," he remarked.

But the hatted one did not hear him. "No; no dining room," she was saying, briskly. "No, indeed. I always use this gate-legged table. You see? It pulls out like this. You can easily seat six—eight, in fact."

"Heaven forbid!" in fervent *sotto voce* from Father Brewster.

"It's an enormous saving in time and labour."

"The—kitchen!" inquired Mrs. Brewster.

The hat waxed playful. "You'll never guess where the kitchen is!" She skipped across the room. "You see this screen?" They saw it. A really handsome affair, and so placed at one end of the room that it looked a part of it. "Come here." They came. The reverse side of the screen was dotted with hooks, and on each hook hung a pot, a pan, a ladle, a spoon. And there was the tiny gas range, the infinitesimal ice chest, the miniature sink. The whole would have been lost in one corner of the Brewster's Winnebago china closet.

"Why, how—how wonderful!" breathed Mrs. Brewster.

"Isn't it? So complete—and so convenient. I've cooked roasts, steaks, chops, everything right here. It's just play."

A terrible fear seized upon Father Brewster. He eyed the sink and the tiny range with a suspicious eye. "The beds," he demanded, "where are the beds?"

She opened the little oven door and his heart sank. But, "They're upstairs," she said. "This is a duplex, you know."

A little flight of winding stairs ended in a balcony. The rail was hung with a gay mandarin robe. Two more steps and you were in the bedroom—a rather breathless little bedroom, profusely rose-coloured, and with whole battalions of photographs in flat silver frames standing about on dressing table, shelf, desk. The one window faced a gray brick wall.

They took the apartment. And thus began a life of ease and gayety for Mr. and Mrs. Hosea C. Brewster, of Winnebago, Wisconsin.

Pinky had dinner with them the first night, and they laughed a great deal, what with one thing and another. She sprang up to the balcony, and let down her bright hair, and leaned over the railing, *à la* Juliet, having first decked Hosey out in a sketchy but effective Romeo costume consisting of a hastily snatched up scarf over one shoulder, Pinky's little turban, and a frying pan for a lute. Mother Brewster did the Nurse, and by the time

Hosea began his limping climb up the balcony, the turban over one eye and the scarf winding itself about his stocky legs, they ended by tumbling in a heap of tearful laughter.

After Pinky left there came upon them, in that cozy little two-room apartment, a feeling of desolation and vastness, and a terrible loneliness such as they had never dreamed of in the great twelve-room house in Winnebago. They kept close to each other. They toiled up the winding stairs together and stood a moment on the balcony, feigning a light-heartedness that neither of them felt.

They lay very still in the little stuffy rose-coloured room, and the street noises of New York came up to them—a loose chain flapping against the mud guard of a taxi; the jolt of a flat-wheeled Eighth Avenue street car; the roar of an L train; laughter; the bleat of a motor horn; a piano in the apartment next door, or upstairs, or down.

She thought, as she lay there, choking, of the great, gracious gray-and-blue room at home, many-windowed, sweet-smelling, quiet. Quiet!

He thought, as he lay there, choking, of the gracious gray-blue room at home, many-windowed, sweet-smelling, quiet. Quiet!

Then, as he had said that night in September: "Sleeping, mother?"

"N-no. Not yet. Just dozing off."

"It's the strange beds, I guess. This is going to be great, though. Great!"

"My, yes!" agreed Mrs. Brewster, heartily.

They awoke next morning unrefreshed. Pa Brewster, back home in Winnebago, always whistled mournfully, off key, when he shaved. The more doleful his tune the happier his wife knew him to be. Also, she had learned to mark his progress by this or that passage in a refrain. Sometimes he sang, too (also off key), and you heard his genial roar all over the house. The louder he roared, and the more doleful the tune, the happier his frame of mind. Milly Brewster knew this. She had never known that she knew it. Neither had he. It was just one of those subconscious bits of marital knowledge that make for happiness and understanding.

When he sang "The Dying Cowboy's Lament" and came to the passage, "Oh, take me to the churchyard and lay the sod o-o-over me," Mrs. Brewster used to say: "Gussie, Mr. Brewster'll be down in ten minutes. You can start the eggs."

In the months of their gay life in Sixty-Seventh Street Hosey Brewster never once sang "The Dying Cowboy's Lament," nor whistled "In the Sweet By-and-By." No; he whistled not at all, or

when he did, gay bits of jazz heard at the theatre
or in a restaurant the night before.   He deceived
no one, least of all himself.   Sometimes his voice
would trail off into nothingness, but he would
catch the tune and toss it up again, heavily, as
though it were a physical weight.

Theatres!   Music!   Restaurants!   Teas!
Shopping!   The gay life!

"Enjoying yourself, Milly?" he would say.
"Time of my life, father."

She had her hair dressed in those geometrical
undulations without which no New York audience
feels itself clothed.   They saw Pinky less fre-
quently as time went on and her feeling of responsibility lessened.   Besides, the magazine covers
took most of her day.   She gave a tea for her father
and mother at her own studio, and Mrs. Brewster's hat, slippers, gown, and manner equalled in
line, style, cut, and texture those of any other
woman present, which rather surprised her until
she had talked to five or six of them.

She and Hosey drifted together and compared
notes.   "Say, Milly," he confided, "they're all
from Wisconsin—or approximately; Michigan, and
Minnesota, and Iowa, and around.   Far's I can
make out there's only one New Yorker, really, in
the whole caboodle of 'em."

"Which one?"

"That kind of plain little one over there—sensible looking, with the blue suit. I was talking to her. She was born right here in New York, but she doesn't live here—that is, not in the city. Lives in some place in the country, in a house."

A sort of look came into Mrs. Brewster's eyes. "Is that so? I'd like to talk to her, Hosey. Take me over."

She did talk to the quiet little woman in the plain blue suit. And the quiet little woman said: "Oh, dear, yes!" She ignored her r's fascinatingly, as New Yorkers do. "We live in Connecticut. You see, you Wisconsin people have crowded us out of New York; no breathing space. Besides, how can one live here? I mean to say—live. And then the children—it's no place for children, grown up or otherwise. I love it—oh, yes, indeed. I love it. But it's too difficult."

Mrs. Brewster defended it like a true Westerner. "But if you have just a tiny apartment, with a kitchenette——"

The New York woman laughed. There was nothing malicious about her. But she laughed. "I tried it. There's one corner of my soul that's still wrinkled from the crushing. Everything in a heap. Not to speak of the slavery of it. That—that deceitful, lying kitchenette."

This was the first woman who Mrs. Brewster

had talked to—really talked to—since leaving Winnebago. And she liked women. She missed them. At first she had eyed wonderingly, speculatively, the women she saw on Fifth Avenue. Swathed luxuriously in precious pelts, marvellously coifed and hatted, wearing the frailest of boots and hose, exhaling a mysterious, heady scent, they were more like strange, exotic birds than women.

The clerks in the shops, too—they were so remote, so contemptuous. When she went into Gerretson's, back home, Nellie Monahan was likely to say: "You've certainly had a lot of wear out of that blue, Mrs. Brewster. Let's see, you've had it two—three years this spring? My land! Let me show you our new taupes."

Pa Brewster had taken to conversing with the doorman. That adamantine individual, unaccustomed to being addressed as a human being, was startled at first, surly and distrustful. But he mellowed under Hosey's simple and friendly advances. They became quite pals, these two— perhaps two as lonely men as you could find in all lonely New York.

"I guess you ain't a New Yorker, huh?" Mike said.

"Me? No."

"Th' most of the folks in th' buildin' ain't."

"Ain't!" Hosea Brewster was startled into it. "They're artists, aren't they? Most of 'em?"

"No! Out-of-town folks, mostly, like you. West—Iowa an' Californy an' around there. Livin' here, though. Seem t' like it better'n where they come from. I dunno."

Hosey Brewster took to eying them as Mrs. Brewster had eyed the women. He wondered about them, these tight, trim men, rather short of breath, buttoned so snugly into their shining shoes and their tailored clothes, with their necks bulging in a fold of fat above the back of their white linen collars. He knew that he would never be like them. It wasn't his square-toed shoes that made the difference, or his gray hat, or his baggy trousers. It was something inside him—something he lacked, he thought. It never occurred to him that it was something he possessed that they did not.

"Enjoying yourself, Milly?"

"I should say I am, father."

"That's good. No housework and responsibility to this, is there?"

"It's play."

She hated the toy gas stove, and the tiny ice chest, and the screen pantry. All her married life she had kept house in a big, bounteous way: apples in barrels; butter in firkins; flour in sacks;

eggs in boxes; sugar in bins; cream in crocks. Sometimes she told herself, bitterly, that it was easier to keep twelve rooms tidy and habitable than one combination kitchen-dining-and-living room.

"Chops taste good, Hosey?"

"Grand. But you oughtn't to be cooking around like this. We'll eat out to-morrow night somewhere, and go to a show."

"You're enjoying it, aren't you, Hosey, h'm?"

"It's the life, mother! It's the life!"

His ruddy colour began to fade. He took to haunting department store kitchenware sections. He would come home with a new kind of cream whipper, or a patent device for the bathroom. He would tinker happily with this, driving a nail, adjusting a screw. At such times he was even known to begin to whistle some scrap of a doleful tune such as he used to hum. But he would change, quickly, into something lively. The price of butter, eggs, milk, cream, and the like horrified his Wisconsin cold-storage sensibilities. He used often to go down to Fulton Market before daylight and walk about among the stalls and shops, piled with tons of food of all kinds. He would talk to the marketmen, and the buyers and grocers, and come away feeling almost happy for a time.

Then, one day, with a sort of shock, he remem-

bered a farmer he had known back home in Winnebago. He knew the farmers for miles around,
naturally, in his business. This man had been a
steady butter-and-egg acquaintance, one of the
wealthy farmers in that prosperous Wisconsin
farming community. For his family's sake he had
moved into town, a ruddy, rufous-bearded, clumping fellow, intelligent, kindly. They had sold the
farm with a fine profit and had taken a box-like
house on Franklin Street. He had nothing to do
but enjoy himself. You saw him out on the porch
early, very early summer mornings.

You saw him ambling about the yard, poking at
a weed here, a plant there. A terrible loneliness
was upon him; a loneliness for the soil he had
deserted. And slowly, resistlessly, the soil pulled
at him with its black strength and its green tendrils
down, down, until he ceased to struggle and lay
there clasped gently to her breast, the mistress he
had thought to desert and who had him again at
last, and forever.

"I don't know what ailed him," his widow had
said, weeping. "He just seemed to kind of pine
away."

It was one morning in April—one soft, golden
April morning—when this memory had struck
Hosey Brewster. He had been down at Fulton

Market. Something about the place—the dewy fresh vegetables, the crates of eggs, the butter, the cheese—had brought such a surge of homesickness over him as to amount to an actual nausea. Riding uptown in the Subway he had caught a glimpse of himself in a slot-machine mirror. His face was pale and somehow shrunken. He looked at his hands. The skin hung loose where the little pads of fat had plumped them out.

"Gosh!" he said. "Gosh, I——"

He thought, then, of the red-faced farmer who used to come clumping into the cold-storage warehouse in his big boots and his buffalo coat. A great fear swept over him and left him weak and sick.

The chill grandeur of the studio-building foyer stabbed him. The glittering lift made him dizzy, somehow, this morning. He shouldn't have gone out without some breakfast perhaps. He walked down the flagged corridor softly; turned the key ever so cautiously. She might still be sleeping. He turned the knob gently, gently; tiptoed in and, turning, fell over a heavy wooden object that lay directly in his path in the dim little hall.

A barked shin. A good, round oath.

"Hosey! What's the matter? What——" She came running to him. She led him into the bright front room.

"What was that thing? A box or something, right there in front of the door. What the——"

"Oh, I'm so sorry, Hosey. You sometimes have breakfast downtown. I didn't know——"

Something in her voice—he stopped rubbing the injured shin to look up at her. Then he straightened slowly, his mouth ludicrously open. Her head was bound in a white towel. Her skirt was pinned back. Her sleeves were rolled up. Chairs, tables, rugs, ornaments, were huddled in a promiscuous heap. Mrs. Hosea C. Brewster was cleaning house.

"Milly!" he began, sternly. "And that's just the thing you came here to get away from. If Pinky——"

"I didn't mean to, father. But when I got up this morning there was a letter—a letter from the woman who owns this apartment, you know. She asked if I'd go to the hall closet—the one she reserved for her own things, you know—and unlock it, and get out a box she told me about, and have the hall boy express it to her. And I did, and—look!"

Limping a little he followed her. She turned on the light that hung in the closet. Boxes—pasteboard boxes—each one bearing a cryptic pencilling on the end that stared out at you. "Drp Stud

Win," said one; "Sum Slp Cov Bedrm," another;
"Toil. Set & Pic Frms."

Mrs. Brewster turned to her husband, almost
shamefacedly, and yet with a little air of defiance.
"It—I don't know—it made me—not homesick,
Hosey. Not homesick, exactly; but—well, I
guess I'm not the only woman with a walnut streak
in her modern make-up. Here's the woman—she
came to the door with her hat on, and yet——"

Truth—blinding, white-hot truth—burst in upon
him. "Mother," he said—and he stood up, suddenly robust, virile, alert—"mother, let's go home."

Mechanically she began to unpin the looped-
back skirt. "When?"

"Now."

"But, Hosey! Pinky—this flat—until
June——"

"Now! Unless you want to stay. Unless you
like it here in this—this make-believe, double-
barrelled, duplex do-funny of a studio thing.
Let's go home, mother. Let's go home—and
breathe."

In Wisconsin you are likely to find snow in
April—snow or slush. The Brewsters found both.
Yet on their way up from the station in 'Gene
Buck's flivver taxi they beamed out at it as if it
were a carpet of daisies.

At the corner of Elm and Jackson streets Hosey

Brewster stuck his head out of the window. "Stop here a minute, will you, 'Gene?"

They stopped in front of Hengel's meat market, and Hosey went in. Mrs. Brewster leaned back without comment.

Inside the shop. "Well, I see you're back from the East," said Aug Hengel.

"Yep."

"We thought you'd given us the go-by, you stayed away so long."

"No, sir-ree! Say, Aug, give me that piece of bacon—the big piece. And send me up some corned beef to-morrow for corned beef and cabbage. I'll take a steak along for to-night. Oh, about four pounds. That's right."

It seemed to him that nothing less than a side of beef could take out of his mouth the taste of those fiddling little lamb chops and the restaurant fare of the past six months.

All through the winter Fred had kept up a little heat in the house, with an eye to frozen water pipes. But there was a chill upon the place as they opened the door now. It was late afternoon. The house was very still, with the stillness of a dwelling that has long been uninhabited. The two stood there a moment, peering into the darkened rooms. Then Hosea Brewster strode forward, jerked up this curtain, that curtain with a sharp snap, flap! He stamped his feet to rid them of slush. He took off his hat and threw it high in the air and opened his arms wide and emitted a whoop of sheer joy and relief.

"Welcome home! Home!"

She clung to him. "Oh, Hosey, isn't it wonderful? How big it looks! Huge!"

"Land, yes." He strode from hall to dining room, from kitchen to library. "I know how a jack-in-the-box feels when the lid's opened. No wonder it grins and throws out its arms."

They did little talking after that. By five o'clock he was down in the cellar. She heard him making a great sound of rattling and bumping and shaking and pounding and shovelling. She smelled the acrid odour of his stubby black pipe.

"Hosey!"—from the top of the cellar stairs. "Hosey, bring up a can of preserves when you come."

"What?"

"Can of preserves."

"What kind?"

"Any kind you like."

"Can I have two kinds?"

He brought up quince marmalade and her choicest damson plums. He put them down on the kitchen table and looked around, spatting his hands together briskly to rid them of dust. "Sh's burning pretty good now. That Fred! Don't any more know how to handle a boiler than a baby does. Is the house getting warmer?"

He clumped into the dining room, through the butler's pantry, but he was back again in a wink, his eyes round. "Why, say, mother! You've got out the best dishes, and the silver, and the candles, and all. And the tablecloth with the do-dads on it. Why——"

"I know it." She opened the oven door, took out a pan of biscuits and slid it deftly to one side. "It seems as if I can't spread enough. I'm going to use the biggest platters, and I've put two extra boards in the table. It's big enough to seat ten. I want everything big, somehow. I've cooked enough potatoes for a regiment, and I know it's wasteful, and I don't care. I'll eat in my kitchen apron, if you'll keep on your overalls. Come on."

He cut into the steak—a great, thick slice. He knew she could never eat it, and she knew she could never eat it. But she did eat it all, ecstatically. And in a sort of ecstatic Nirvana the quiet and vastness and peace of the big old frame house settled down upon them.

The telephone in the hall rang startlingly, unexpectedly.

"Let me go, Milly."

"But who in the world! Nobody knows we're——"

He was at the telephone. "Who? Who? Oh." He turned: "It's Miz' Merz. She says her little Minnie went by at six and saw a light in the house. She—— Hello! What? . . . She says she wants to know if she's to save time for you at the end of the month for the April cleaning."

Mrs. Brewster took the receiver from him: "The twenty-fifth, as usual, Miz' Merz. The twenty-fifth, as usual. The attic must be a sight."

OLD LADY MANDLE

OLD lady Mandle was a queen. Her demesne, undisputed, was a six-room flat on South Park Avenue, Chicago. Her faithful servitress was Anna, an ancient person of Polish nativity, bad teeth, and a cunning hand at cookery. Not so cunning, however, but that old lady Mandle's was more artful still in such matters as meat-soups, broad noodles, fish with egg sauce, and the like. As ladies-in-waiting, flattering yet jealous, admiring though resentful, she had Mrs. Lamb, Mrs. Brunswick, and Mrs. Wormser, themselves old ladies and erstwhile queens, now deposed. And the crown jewel in old lady Mandle's diadem was my son Hugo.

Mrs. Mandle was not only a queen but a spoiled old lady. And not only a spoiled old lady but a confessedly spoiled old lady. Bridling and wagging her white head she admitted her pampered state. It was less an admission than a boast. Her son Hugo had spoiled her. This, too, she acknowledged. "My son Hugo spoils me," she would say, and there was no proper humbleness in her voice. Though he was her only son she never spoke of him merely as "Hugo," or "My son," but always as "My son Hugo." She rolled the three words on her tongue as though they were delicious morsels from which she would extract all possible savour and sweetness. And when she did this you could almost hear the click of the stiffening spines of Mrs. Lamb, Mrs. Brunswick, and Mrs. Wormser. For they envied her her son Hugo, and resented him as only three old ladies could who were living, tolerated and dependent, with their married sons and their sons' wives.

Any pleasant summer afternoon at four o'clock you might have seen Mrs. Mandle holding court. The four old women sat, a decent black silk row, on a shady bench in Washington Park (near the refectory and afternoon coffee). Three of them complained about their daughters-in-law. One of them bragged about her son. Adjective crowding adjective, pride in her voice, majesty in her mien, she bragged about my son Hugo.

My son Hugo had no wife. Not only that, Hugo Mandle, at forty, had no thought of marrying. Not that there was anything austere or saturnine about Hugo. He made you think, somehow, of a cherubic, jovial monk. It may have been his rosy rotundity, or, perhaps, the way in which his thinning hair vanished altogether at the top of his head, so as to form a tonsure. Hugo

Mandle, kindly, generous, shrewd, spoiled his old mother in the way in which women of seventy, whose middle life has been hard, like to be spoiled. First of all, of course, she reigned unchecked over the South Park Avenue flat. She quarrelled wholesomely and regularly with Polish Anna. Alternately she threatened Anna with dismissal and Anna threatened Ma Mandle with impending departure. This had been going on, comfortably, for fifteen years. Ma Mandle held the purse and her son filled it. Hugo paid everything from the rent to the iceman, and this without once making his mother feel a beneficiary. She possessed an infinitesimal income of her own, left her out of the ruins of her dead husband's money, but this Hugo always waved aside did she essay to pay for her own movie ticket or an ice cream soda. "Now, now! None of that, Ma. Your money's no good to-night."

When he returned from a New York business trip he usually brought her two gifts, one practical, the other absurd. She kissed him for the first and scolded him for the second, but it was the absurdity, fashioned of lace, or silk, or fragile stuff, that she pridefully displayed to her friends.

"Look what my son Hugo brought me. I should wear a thing like that in my old days. But it's beautiful anyway, h'm? He's got taste, my son Hugo."

In the cool of the evening you saw them taking a slow and solemn walk together, his hand on her arm. He surprised her with matinée tickets in pairs, telling her to treat one of her friends. On Anna's absent Thursdays he always offered to take dinner downtown. He brought her pound boxes of candy tied with sly loops and bands of gay satin ribbon which she carefully rolled and tucked away in a drawer. He praised her cooking, and teased her with elephantine playfulness, and told her that she looked like a chicken in that hat. Oh, yes, indeed! Mrs. Mandle was a spoiled old lady.

At half-past one she always prepared to take her nap in the quiet of her neat flat. She would select a plump, after-lunch chocolate from the box in her left-hand bureau drawer, take off her shoes, and settle her old frame in comfort. No noisy grandchildren to disturb her rest. No fault-finding daughter-in-law to bustle her out of the way. The sounds that Anna made, moving about in the kitchen at the far end of the long hall, were the subdued homely swishings and brushings that lulled and soothed rather than irritated. At half-past two she rose, refreshed, dressed herself in her dotted swiss with its rows of val, or in black silk, modish both. She was, in fact, a modish old lady as were her three friends. They were not

the ultra-modern type of old lady who at sixty
apes sixteen. They were neat and rather tart-
tongued septuagenarians, guiltless of artifice.
Their soft white hair was dressed neatly and craft-
ily so as to conceal the thinning spots that revealed
the pink scalp beneath. Their corsets and their
stomachs were too high, perhaps, for fashion,
and their heavy brooches and chains and rings
appeared clumsy when compared to the hoar-
frost tracery of the platinumsmith's exquisite
art. But their skirts had pleats when pleated
skirts were worn, and their sleeves were snug when
snug sleeves were decreed. They were inclined to
cling over-long to a favourite leather reticule,
scuffed and shapeless as an old shoe, but they
could hold their own at bridge on a rainy afternoon. In matters of material and cut Mrs.
Mandle triumphed. Her lace was likely to be
real where that of the other three was imitation.

So there they sat on a park bench in the pleasant
afternoon air, filling their lives with emptiness.
They had married, and brought children into the
world; sacrificed for them, managed a household,
been widowed. They represented magnificent
achievement, those four old women, though they
themselves did not know it. They had come up
the long hill, reached its apex, and come down.
Their journey was over and yet they sat by the

roadside. They knew that which could have helped younger travellers over the next hill, but those fleet-footed ones pressed on, wanting none of their wisdom. Ma Mandle alone still moved. She still queened it over her own household; she alone still had the delightful task of making a man comfortable. If the world passed them by as they sat there it did not pass unscathed. Their shrewd old eyes regarded the panorama, undeceived. They did not try to keep up with the procession, but they derived a sly amusement and entertainment from their observation of the modes and manners of this amazing day and age. Perhaps it was well that this plump matron in the overtight skirt or that miss mincing on four-inch heels could not hear the caustic comment of the white-haired four sitting so mildly on the bench at the side of the path.

Their talk, stray as it might, always came back to two subjects. They seemed never to tire of them. Three talked of their daughters-in-law, and bitterness rasped their throats. One talked of her son, and her voice was unctuous with pride.

"My son's wife——" one of the three would begin. There was something terribly significant in the mock respect with which she uttered the title.

"If I had ever thought," Mrs. Brunswick would say, shaking her head, "if I had ever thought that I would live to see the day when I had to depend on strangers for my comfort, I would have wished myself dead."

"You wouldn't call your son a stranger, Mrs. Brunswick!" in shocked tones from Mrs. Mandle.

"A stranger has got more consideration. I count for nothing. Less than nothing. I'm in the way. I don't interfere in that household. I see enough, and I hear enough, but I say nothing. My son's wife, she says it all."

A silence, thoughtful, brooding. Then, from Mrs. Wormser: "What good do you have of your children? They grow up, and what do you have of them?"

More shaking of heads, and a dark murmur about the advisability of an Old People's Home as a refuge. Then:

"My son Hugo said only yesterday, 'Ma,' he said, 'when it comes to housekeeping you could teach them all something, believe me. Why,' he says, 'if I was to try and get a cup of coffee like this in a restaurant—well, you couldn't get it in a restaurant, that's all. You couldn't get it in any hotel, Michigan Avenue or I don't care where."

Goaded, Mrs. Lamb would look up from her knitting. "Mark my words, he'll marry yet." She was a sallow, lively woman, her hair still markedly streaked with black. Her rheumatism-twisted fingers were always grotesquely busy with some handiwork, and the finished product was a marvel of perfection.

Mrs. Wormser, plump, placid, agreed. "That's the kind always marries late. And they get it the worst. Say, my son was no spring chicken, either, when he married. And you would think the sun rises and sets in his wife. Well, I suppose it's only natural. But you wait."

"Some girl is going to have a snap." Mrs. Brunswick, eager, peering, a trifle vindictive, offered final opinion. "The girls aren't going to let a boy like your Hugo get away. Not nowadays, the way they run after them like crazy. All they think about is dress and a good time."

The three smiled grimly. Ma Mandle smiled, too, a little nervously, her fingers creasing and uncreasing a fold of her black silk skirt as she made airy answer: "If I've said once I've said a million times to my son Hugo, 'Hugo, why don't you pick out some nice girl and settle down? I won't be here always.' And he says, 'Getting tired of me, are you, Ma? I guess maybe you're looking for a younger fellow.' Only last night I said, at the table, 'Hugo, when are you going to get married?' And he laughed. 'When I find somebody that can cook dumplings like these. Pass me another, Ma'."

"That's all very well," said Mrs. Wormser. "But when the right one comes along he won't know dumplings from mud."

"Oh, a man of forty isn't such a——"

"He's just like a man of twenty-five—only worse."

Mrs. Mandle would rise, abruptly. "Well, I guess you all know my son Hugo better than his own mother. How about a cup of coffee, ladies?"

They would proceed solemnly and eagerly to the columned coolness of the park refectory where they would drink their thick, creamy coffee. They never knew, perhaps, how keenly they counted on that cup of coffee, or how hungrily they drank it. Their minds, unconsciously, were definitely fixed on the four-o'clock drink that stimulated the old nerves.

Life had not always been so plumply upholstered for old lady Mandle. She had known its sharp corners and cruel edges. At twenty-three, a strong, healthy, fun-loving girl, she had married Herman Mandle, a dour man twenty-two years her senior. In their twenty-five years of married life together Hattie Mandle never had had a five-cent piece that she could call her own. Her husband was reputed to be wealthy, and probably was, according to the standards of that day. There were three children: Etta, the oldest; a second child, a girl, who died; and Hugo. Her husband's miserliness, and the grind of the planning, scheming, and contriving necessary to clothe and feed her two children would have crushed the spirit of many women. But hard and glum as her old husband was he never quite succeeded in subduing her courage or her love of fun. The habit of heart-breaking economy clung to her, however, even when days of plenty became hers. It showed in little hoarding ways: in the saving of burned matches, of bits of ribbon, of scraps of food, of the very furniture and linen, as though, when these were gone, no more would follow.

Ten years after her marriage her husband retired from active business. He busied himself now with his real estate, with mysterious papers, documents, agents. He was forever poking around the house at hours when a household should be manless, grumbling about the waste where there was none, peering into bread boxes, prying into corners never meant for masculine eyes. Etta, the girl, was like him, sharp-nosed, ferret-faced, stingy. The mother and the boy turned to each other. In a wordless way they grew very close, those two. It was as if they were silently matched against the father and daughter.

It was a queer household, brooding, sinister, like something created in a Brontë brain. The two children were twenty-four and twenty-two when the financial avalanche of '93 thundered across the continent sweeping Herman Mandle, a mere speck, into the débris. Stocks and bonds and real estate became paper, with paper value. He clawed about with frantic, clutching fingers but his voice was lost in the shrieks of thousands more hopelessly hurt. You saw him sitting for hours together with a black tin box in front of him, pawing over papers, scribbling down figures, muttering. The bleak future that confronted them had little of terror for Hattie Mandle. It presented no contrast with the bleakness of the past. On the day that she came upon him, his head fallen at a curious angle against the black tin box, his hands, asprawl, clutching the papers that strewed the table, she was appalled, not at what she found, but at the leap her heart gave at what she found. Herman Mandle's sudden death was one of the least of the tragedies that trailed in the wake of the devastating panic.

Thus it was that Hugo Mandle, at twenty-three, became the head of a household. He did not need to seek work. From the time he was seventeen he had been employed in a large china-importing house, starting as a stock boy. Brought up under the harsh circumstances of Hugo's youth, a boy becomes food for the reformatory or takes on the

seriousness and responsibility of middle age. In
Hugo's case the second was true. From his father
he had inherited a mathematical mind and a sense
of material values. From his mother, a certain
patience and courage, though he never attained
her iron indomitability.

It had been a terrific struggle. His salary at
twenty-three was most modest, but he was getting
on. He intended to be a buyer, some day, and
take trips abroad to the great Austrian and French
and English china houses.

The day after the funeral he said to his mother,
"Well, now we've got to get Etta married. But
married well. Somebody who'll take care of her."

"You're a good son, Hugo," Mrs. Mandle had
said.

Hugo shook his head. "It isn't that. If she's
comfortable and happy—or as happy as she knows
how to be—she'll never come back. That's what
I want. There's debts to pay, too. But I guess
we'll get along."

They did get along, but at snail's pace. There
followed five years of economy so rigid as to make
the past seem profligate. Etta, the acid-tongued,
the ferret-faced, was not the sort to go off without
the impetus of a dowry. The man for Etta, the
shrew, must be kindly, long-suffering, subdued—
and in need of a start. He was. They managed

a very decent trousseau and the miracle of five thousand dollars in cash. Every stitch in the trousseau and every penny in the dowry represented incredible sacrifice and self-denial on the part of mother and brother. Etta went off to her new home in Pittsburg with her husband. She had expressed thanks for nothing and had bickered with her mother to the last, but even Hugo knew that her suit and hat and gloves and shoes were right. She was almost handsome in them, the unwonted flush of excitement colouring her cheeks, brightening her eyes.

The next day Hugo came home with a new hat for his mother, a four-pound steak, and the announcement that he was going to take music lessons. A new era had begun in the life of Ma Mandle.

Two people, no matter how far apart in years or tastes, cannot struggle side by side, like that, in a common cause, without forging between them a bond indissoluble. Hugo, at twenty-eight, had the serious mien of a man of forty. At forty he was to revert to his slighted twenty-eight, but he did not know that then. His music lessons were his one protest against a beauty-starved youth. He played rather surprisingly well the cheap music of the day, waggling his head (already threatening baldness) in a professional vaudeville manner and

squinting up through his cigar smoke, happily.
His mother, seated in the room, sewing, would say,
"Play that again, Hugo. That's beautiful.
What's the name of that?" He would tell her,
for the dozenth time, and play it over, she humming, off-key, in his wake. The relation between
them was more than that of mother and son. It
was a complex thing that had in it something conjugal. When Hugo kissed his mother with a re-
sounding smack and assured her that she looked
like a kid she would push him away with little
futile shoves, pat her hair into place, and pretend
annoyance. "Go away, you big rough thing!"
she would cry. But all unconsciously she got from
it a thrill that her husband's withered kisses had
never given her.

Twelve years had passed since Etta's marriage.
Hugo's salary was a comfortable thing now, even
in these days of soaring prices. The habit of
economy, so long a necessity, had become almost
a vice in old lady Mandle. Hugo, with the
elasticity of younger years, learned to spend freely,
but his mother's thrift and shrewdness automatically swelled his savings. When he was on the
road, as he sometimes was for weeks at a time,
she spent only a tithe of the generous sum he left
with her. She and Anna ate those sketchy meals
that obtain in a manless household. When Hugo

was home the table was abundant and even choice,
though Ma Mandle often went blocks out of her
way to save three cents on a bunch of new beets.
So strong is usage. She would no more have
wasted his money than she would have knifed him
in the dark. She ran the household capably, but
her way was the old-fashioned way. Sometimes
Hugo used to protest, aghast at some petty act of
parsimony.

"But, Ma, what do you want to scrimp like that
for! You're the worst tightwad I ever saw.
Here, take this ten and blow it. You're worse
than the squirrels in the park, darned if you ain't!"

She couldn't resist the ten. Neither could she
resist showing it, next day, to Mrs. Brunswick,
Mrs. Lamb, and Mrs. Wormser. "How my son
Hugo spoils me! He takes out a ten-dollar bill,
and he stuffs it into my hand and says 'Ma,
you're the worst tightwad I ever saw.'" She
laughed contentedly. But she did not blow the
ten. As she grew older Hugo regularly lied to her
about the price of theatre tickets, dainties, articles
of dress, railway fares, luxuries. Her credulity
increased with age, shrewd though she naturally
was.

It was a second blooming for Ma Mandle.
When he surprised her with an evening at the
theatre she would fuss before her mirror for a full

hour. "Some gal!" Hugo would shout when finally she emerged. "Everybody'll be asking who the old man is you're out with. First thing I know I'll have a police-woman after me for going around with a chicken."

"Don't talk foolishness." But she would flush like a bride. She liked a musical comedy with a lot of girls in it and a good-looking tenor. Next day you would hear her humming the catch-tune in an airy falsetto. Sometimes she wondered about him. She was, after all, a rather wise old lady, and she knew something of men. She had a secret horror of his becoming what she called fast.

"Why don't you take out some nice young girl instead of an old woman like me, Hugo? Any girl would be only too glad." But in her heart was a dread. She thought of Mrs. Lamb, Mrs. Wormser, and Mrs. Brunswick.

So they had gone on, year after year, in the comfortable flat on South Park Avenue. A pleasant thing, life.

And then Hugo married, suddenly, breathlessly, as a man of forty does.

Afterward, Ma Mandle could recall almost nothing from which she might have taken warning. That was because he had said so little. She remembered that he had come home to dinner one evening and had spoken admiringly of a

woman buyer from Omaha. He did not often
speak of business.

"She buys like a man," he had said at dinner.
"I never saw anything like it. Knew what she
wanted and got it. She bought all my best
numbers at rock bottom. I sold her a four-figure
bill in half an hour. And no fuss. Everything
right to the point and when I asked her out to
dinner she turned me down. Good looking, too.
She's coming in again to-morrow for novelties."

Ma Mandle didn't even recall hearing her name
until the knife descended. Hugo played the piano
a great deal all that week, after dinner. Sentimental things, with a minor wail in the chorus.
Smoked a good deal, too. Twice he spent a full
hour in dressing, whistling absent-mindedly during
the process and leaving his necktie rack looking
like a nest of angry pythons when he went out,
without saying where he was going. The following week he didn't touch the piano and took long
walks in Washington Park, alone, after ten.
He seemed uninterested in his meals. Usually
he praised this dish, or that.

"How do you like the blueberry pie, Hugo?"

"'S all right." And declined a second piece.

The third week he went West on business.
When he came home he dropped his bag in the hall,
strode into his mother's bedroom, and stood before

her like a schoolboy. "Lil and I are going to be married," he said.

Ma Mandle had looked up at him, her face a blank. "Lil?"

"Sure. I told you all about her." He hadn't. He had merely thought about her, for three weeks, to the exclusion of everything else. "Ma, you'll love her. She knows all about you. She's the grandest girl in the world. Say, I don't know why she ever fell for a dub like me. Well, don't look so stunned. I guess you kind of suspicioned, huh?"

"But who——?"

"I never thought she'd look at me. Earned her own good salary, and strictly business, but she's a real woman. Says she wants her own home an——'n everything. Says every normal woman does. Says——"

Ad lib.

They were married the following month.

Hugo sub-leased the flat on South Park and took an eight-room apartment farther east. Ma Mandle's red and green plush parlour pieces, and her mahogany rockers, and her rubber plant, and the fern, and the can of grapefruit pits that she and Anna had planted and that had come up, miraculously, in the form of shiny, thick little green leaves, all were swept away in the upheaval that followed. Gone, too, was Polish Anna, with her

damp calico and her ubiquitous pail and dripping
rag and her gutturals. In her place was a trim
Swede who wore white kid shoes in the afternoon
and gray dresses and cob-web aprons. The sight
of the neat Swede sitting in her room at two-thirty
in the afternoon, tatting, never failed to fill Ma
Mandle with a dumb fury. Anna had been an all-
day scrubber.

But Lil. Hugo thought her very beautiful,
which she was not. A plump, voluble, full-bosomed
woman, exquisitely neat, with a clear, firm skin,
bright brown eyes, an unerring instinct for clothes,
and a shrewd business head. Hugo's devotion
amounted to worship.

He used to watch her at her toilette in their rose
and black mahogany front bedroom. Her plump
white shoulders gleamed from pink satin straps.
She smelled pleasantly of sachet and a certain
heady scent she affected. Seated before the mirror,
she stared steadily at herself with a concentration
such as an artist bestows upon a work that de-
pends, for its perfection, upon nuances of light and
shade. Everything about her shone and glittered.
Her pink nails were like polished coral. Her hair
gleamed in smooth undulations, not a strand out
of place. Her skin was clear and smooth as a
baby's. Her hands were plump and white. She
was always getting what she called a facial, from

which process she would emerge looking pinker
and creamier than ever. Lil knew when camisoles
were edged with filet, and when with Irish. Instinctively she sensed when taffeta was to be
superseded by foulard. The contents of her scented
bureau drawers needed only a dab of whipped
cream on top to look as if they might have been
eaten as something soufflé.

"How do I look in it, Hugo? Do you like
it?" was a question that rose daily to her lips. A
new hat, or frock, or collar, or negligée. Not that
she was unduly extravagant. She knew values,
and profited by her knowledge.

"Le's see. Turn around. It looks great on
you. Yep. That's all right."

He liked to fancy himself a connoisseur in
women's clothes and to prove it he sometimes
brought home an article of feminine apparel
glimpsed in a shop window or showcase, but Lil
soon put a stop to that. She had her own ideas
on clothes. He turned to jewellery. On Lil's
silken bosom reposed a diamond-and-platinum pin
the size and general contour of a fish-knife. She
had a dinner ring that crowded the second knuckle,
and on her plump wrist sparkled an oblong so en-
crusted with diamonds that its utilitarian dial
was almost lost.

It wasn't a one-sided devotion, however. Lil

knew much about men, and she had an instinct
for making them comfortable. It is a gift that
makes up for myriad minor shortcomings. She
had a way of laying his clean things out on the
bed—fresh linen, clean white socks (Hugo was
addicted to white socks and tan, low-cut shoes),
silk shirt, immaculate handkerchief. When he
came in at the end of a hard day downtown—hot,
fagged, sticky—she saw to it that the bathroom
was his own for an hour so that he could bathe,
shave, powder, dress, and emerge refreshed to eat
his good dinner in comfort. Lil was always waiting for him cool, interested, sweet-smelling.

When she said, "How's business, lover?" she
really wanted to know. More than that, when
he told her she understood, having herself been so
long in the game. She gave him shrewd advice,
too, so shrewdly administered that he never realized he had been advised, and so, man-like, could
never resent it.

Ma Mandle's reign was over.

To Mrs. Lamb, Mrs. Brunswick, and Mrs.
Wormser Ma Mandle lied magnificently. Their
eager, merciless questions pierced her like knives,
but she made placid answer: "Young folks are
young folks. They do things different. I got my
way. My son's wife has got hers." Their quick
ears caught the familiar phrase.

"It's hard, just the same," Mrs. Wormser insisted, "after you've been boss all these years to have somebody else step in and shove you out of the way. Don't I know!"

"I'm glad to have a little rest. Marketing and housekeeping nowadays is no snap, with the prices what they are. Anybody that wants the pleasure is welcome."

But they knew, the three. There was, in Ma Mandle's tone, a hollow pretence that deceived no one. They knew, and she knew that they knew. She was even as they were, a drinker of the hemlock cup, an eater of ashes.

Hugo Mandle was happier and more comfortable than he had ever been in his life. It wasn't merely his love for Lil, and her love for him that made him happy. Lil set a good table, though perhaps it was not as bounteous as his mother's had been. His food, somehow, seemed to agree with him better than it used to. It was because Lil selected her provisions with an eye to their building value, and to Hugo's figure. She told him he was getting too fat, and showed him where, and Hugo agreed with her and took off twenty-five burdensome pounds, but Ma Mandle fought every ounce of it.

"You'll weaken yourself, Hugo! Eat! How can a man work and not eat? I never heard of such a thing. Fads!"

But these were purely physical things. It was a certain mental relaxation that Hugo enjoyed, though he did not definitely know it. He only knew that Lil seemed, somehow, to understand. For years his mother had trailed after him, putting away things that he wanted left out, tidying that which he preferred left in seeming disorder. Lil seemed miraculously to understand about those things. He liked, for example, a certain grimy, gritty old rag with which he was wont to polish his golf clubs. It was caked with dirt, and most disreputable, but it was of just the right material, or weight, or size, or something, and he had for it the unreasoning affection that a child has for a tattered rag doll among a whole family of golden-haired, blue-eyed beauties. Ma Mandle, tidying up, used to throw away that rag in horror. Sometimes he would rescue it, crusted as it was with sand and mud and scouring dust. Sometimes he would have to train in a new rag, and it was never as good as the old. Lil understood about that rag, and approved of it. For that matter, she had a rag of her own which she used to remove cold cream from her face and throat. It was a clean enough bit of soft cloth to start with, but she clung to it as an actress often does, until it was smeared with the pink of makeup and the black of Chicago soot. She used to search remote corners of it

for an inch of unused, unsmeared space. Lil
knew about not talking when you wanted to read
the paper, too. Ma Mandle, at breakfast, had
always had a long and intricate story to tell
about the milkman, or the strawberries that she
had got the day before and that had spoiled overnight in the icebox. A shame! Sometimes he
had wanted to say, "Let me read my paper in
peace, won't you!" But he never had. Now it
was Lil who listened patiently to Ma Mandle's
small grievances, and Hugo was left free to peruse
the head-lines.

If you had told Ma Mandle that she was doing
her best to ruin the life of the one person she loved
best in all the world she would have told you that
you were insane. If you had told her that she was
jealous she would have denied it, furiously. But
both were true.

When Hugo brought his wife a gift he brought
one for his mother as well.

"You don't need to think you have to bring
your old mother anything," she would say, unrea-
sonably.

"Didn't I always bring you something, Ma?"

If seventy can be said to sulk, Ma Mandle
sulked.

Lil, on her way to market in the morning, was a
pleasant sight, trim, well-shod, immaculate. Ma,

whose marketing costume had always been neat but sketchy, would eye her disapprovingly. "Are you going out?"

"Just to market. I thought I'd start early, before everything was picked over."

"Oh—to market! I thought you were going to a party, you're so dressy."

In the beginning Lil had offered to allow Ma Mandle to continue with the marketing but Mrs. Mandle had declined, acidly. "Oh, no," she had said. "This is your household now."

But she never failed to inspect the groceries as they lay on the kitchen table after delivery. She would press a wise and disdainful thumb into a head of lettuce; poke a pot-roast with disapproving finger; turn a plump chicken over and thump it down with a look that was pregnant with meaning.

Ma Mandle disapproved of many things. Of Lil's silken, lacy lingerie; of her social activities; of what she termed her wastefulness. Lil wore the fewest possible undergarments, according to the fashion of the day, and she worried, good-naturedly, about additional plumpness that was the result of leisure and of rich food. She was addicted to afternoon parties at the homes of married women of her own age and station—pretty, well-dressed, over-indulged women who regularly ate too much. They served a mayonnaise chicken salad, and little hot buttery biscuits, and strong coffee with sugar and cream, and there were dishes of salted almonds, and great, shining, oily, black ripe olives, and a heavy, rich dessert. When she came home she ate nothing.

"I couldn't eat a bite of dinner," she would say. "Let me tell you what we had." She would come to the table in one of her silken, lace-bedecked teagowns and talk animatedly to Hugo while he ate his dinner and eyed her appreciatively as she sat there leaning one elbow on the cloth, the sleeve fallen back so that you saw her plump white forearm. She kept her clear, rosy skin in spite of the pastry and sweets and the indolent life, and even the layers of powder with which she was forever dabbing her face had not coarsened its texture.

Hugo, man-like, was unconscious of the undercurrent of animosity between the two women. He was very happy. He only knew that Lil understood about cigar ashes; that she didn't mind if a pillow wasn't plumped and patted after his Sunday nap on the davenport; that she never complained to him about the shortcomings of the little Swede, as Ma Mandle had about Polish Anna. Even at house-cleaning time, which Ma Mandle had always treated as a scourge, things were as smooth-running and peaceful as at ordinary times. Just a little bare, perhaps, as to floors, and smelling of cleanliness. Lil applied businesslike methods to the conduct of her house, and they were successful in spite of Ma Mandle's steady efforts to block them. Old lady Mandle did not mean to be cruel. She only thought that she was protecting her son's interests. She did not know that the wise men had a definite name for the mental processes which caused her, perversely, to do just the thing which she knew she should not do.

Hugo and Lil went out a great deal in the evening. They liked the theatre, restaurant life, gayety. Hugo learned to dance and became marvellously expert at it, as does your fat man.

"Come on and go out with us this evening, Mother," Lil would say.

"Sure!" Hugo would agree, heartily. "Come along, Ma. We'll show you some night life."

"I don't want to go," Ma Mandle would mutter. "I'm better off at home. You enjoy yourself better without an old woman dragging along."

That being true, they vowed it was not, and renewed their urging. In the end she went, grudgingly. But her old eyes would droop; the late supper would disagree with her; the noise, the music, the laughter, and shrill talk bewildered her. She did not understand the banter, and resented it.

Next day, in the park, she would boast of her life of gayety to the vaguely suspicious three.

Later she refused to go out with them. She stayed in her room a good deal, fussing about, arranging bureau drawers already geometrically precise, winding endless old ribbons, ripping the trimming off hats long passé and re-trimming them with odds and ends and scraps of feathers and flowers.

Hugo and Lil used to ask her to go with them to the movies, but they liked the second show at eight-thirty while she preferred the earlier one at seven. She grew sleepy early, though she often lay awake for hours after composing herself for sleep. She would watch the picture absorbedly, but when she stepped, blinking, into the bright glare of Fifty-third Street, she always had a sense of let-down, of depression.

A wise old lady of seventy, who could not apply her wisdom for her own good. A rather lonely old lady, with hardening arteries and a dilating heart. An increasingly fault-finding old lady. Even Hugo began to notice it. She would wait for him to come home and then, motioning him mysteriously into her own room, would pour a tale of fancied insult into his ear.

"I ran a household and brought up a family before she was born. I don't have to be told what's what. I may be an old woman but I'm not so old that I can sit and let my own son be made a fool of. One girl isn't enough, she's got to have a wash woman. And now a wash woman isn't enough she's got to have a woman to clean one day a week."

An hour later, from the front bedroom, where Hugo was dressing, would come the low murmur of conversation. Lil had reached the complaining point, goaded by much repetition.

The attitude of the two women distressed and bewildered Hugo. He was a simple soul, and this was a complex situation. His mind leaped from mother to wife, and back again, joltingly. After all, one woman at a time is all that any man can handle successfully.

"What's got into you women folks!" he would say. "Always quarrelling. Why can't you get along."

One night after dinner Lil said, quite innocently, "Mother, we haven't a decent picture of you. Why don't you have one taken? In your black lace."

Old lady Mandle broke into sudden fury. "I guess you think I'm going to die! A picture to put on the piano after I'm gone, huh? 'That's my dear mother that's gone.' Well, I don't have any picture taken. You can think of me the way I was when I was alive."

The thing grew and swelled and took on bitterness as it progressed. Lil's face grew strangely flushed and little veins stood out on her temples. All the pent-up bitterness that had been seething in Ma Mandle's mind broke bounds now, and welled to her lips. Accusation, denial; vituperation, retort.

"You'll be happy when I'm gone."

"If I am it's your fault."

"It's the ones that are used to nothing that always want the most. They don't know where to stop. When you were working in Omaha——"

"The salary I gave up to marry your son was more money than you ever saw."

And through it all, like a leit-motiv, ran Hugo's attempt at pacification: "Now, Ma! Don't, Lil. You'll only excite yourself. What's got into you two women?"

It was after dinner. In the end Ma Mandle slammed out of the house, hatless. Her old legs were trembling. Her hands shook. It was a hot June night. She felt as if she were burning up. In her frantic mind there was even thought of self-destruction. There were thousands of motor cars streaming by. The glare of their lamps and the smell of the gasoline blinded and stifled her. Once, at a crossing, she almost stumbled in front of an on-rushing car. The curses of the startled

driver sounded in her terrified ears after she had
made the opposite curb in a frantic bound. She
walked on and on for what seemed to her to be a
long time, with plodding, heavy step. She was
not conscious of being tired. She came to a park
bench and sat down, feeling very abused, and
lonely and agonized. This was what she had come
to in her old days. It was for this you bore
children, and brought them up and sacrificed for
them. How right they were—Mrs. Lamb, Mrs.
Brunswick, and Mrs. Wormser. Useless. Un-
considered. In the way.

By degrees she grew calmer. Her brain cooled
as her fevered old body lost the heat of anger.
Lil had looked kind of sick. Perhaps . . .
and how worried Hugo had looked. . . .

Feeling suddenly impelled she got up from the
bench and started toward home. Her walk,
which had seemed interminable, had really lasted
scarcely more than half an hour. She had sat in
the park scarcely fifteen minutes. Altogether
her flight had been, perhaps, an hour in duration.

She had her latchkey in her pocket. She
opened the door softly. The place was in darkness. Voices from the front bedroom, and the
sound of someone sobbing, as though spent. Old
lady Mandle's face hardened again. The door of
the front bedroom was closed. Plotting against

her! She crouched there in the hall, listening. Lil's voice, hoarse with sobs.

"I've tried and tried. But she hates me. Nothing I do suits her. If it wasn't for the baby coming sometimes I think I'd——"

"You're just nervous and excited, Lil. It'll come out all right. She's an old lady——"

"I know it. I know it. I've said that a million times in the last year and a half. But that doesn't excuse everything, does it? Is that any reason why she should spoil our lives? It isn't fair. It isn't fair!"

"Sh! Don't cry like that, dear. Don't! You'll only make yourself sick."

Her sobs again, racking, choking, and the gentle murmur of his soothing endearments. Then, unexpectedly, a little, high-pitched laugh through the tears.

"No, I'm not hysterical. I—it just struck me funny. I was just wondering if I might be like that. When I grow old, and my son marries, maybe I'll think everything his wife does is wrong. I suppose if we love them too much we really harm them. I suppose——"

"Oh, it's going to be a son, is it?"

"Yes."

Another silence. Then: "Come, dear. Bathe your poor eyes. You're all worn out from crying.

Why, sweetheart, I don't believe I ever saw you cry before."

"I know it. I feel better now. I wish crying could make it all right. I'm sorry. She's so old, dear. That's the trouble. They live in the past and they expect us to live in the past with them. You were a good son to her, Hughie. That's why you make such a wonderful husband. Too good, maybe. You've spoiled us both, and now we both want all of you."

Hugo was silent a moment. He was not a quick-thinking man. "A husband belongs to his wife," he said then, simply. "He's his mother's son by accident of birth. But he's his wife's husband by choice, and deliberately."

But she laughed again at that. "It isn't as easy as that, sweetheart. If it was there'd be no jokes in the funny papers. My poor boy! And just now, too, when you're so worried about business."

"Business'll be all right, Lil. Trade'll open up next winter. It's got to. We've kept going on the Japanese and English stuff. But if the French and Austrian factories start running we'll have a whirlwind year. If it hadn't been for you this last year I don't know how I'd have stood the strain. No importing, and the business just keeping its head above water. But you were right, honey. We've weathered the worst of it now."

"I'm glad you didn't tell Mother about it. She'd have worried herself sick. If she had known we both put every cent we had into the business——"

"We'll get it back ten times over. You'll see."

The sound of footsteps. "I wonder where she went. She oughtn't to be out alone. I'm kind of worried about her, Hugo. Don't you think you'd better——"

Ma Mandle opened the front door and then slammed it, ostentatiously, as though she had just come in.

"That you, Ma?" called Hugo.

He turned on the hall light. She stood there, blinking, a bent, pathetic little figure. Her eyes were averted. "Are you all right, Ma? We began to worry about you."

"I'm all right. I'm going to bed."

He made a clumsy, masculine pretence at heartiness. "Lil and I are going over to the drug store for a soda, it's so hot. Come on along, Ma."

Lil joined him in the doorway of the bedroom. Her eyes were red-rimmed behind the powder that she had hastily dabbed on, but she smiled bravely.

"Come on, Mother," she said. "It'll cool you off."

But Ma Mandle shook her head. "I'm better off at home. You run along, you two."

That was all. But the two standing there caught something in her tone. Something new, something gentle, something wise.

She went on down the hall to her room. She took off her clothes, and hung them away, neatly. But once in her nightgown she did not get into bed. She sat there, in the chair by the window. Old lady Mandle had lived to be seventy and had acquired much wisdom. One cannot live to be seventy without having experienced almost everything in life. But to crystallize that experience of a long lifetime into terms that would express the meaning of life—this she had never tried to do. She could not do it now, for that matter. But she groped around, painfully, in her mind. There had been herself and Hugo. And now Hugo's wife and the child to be. They were the ones that counted, now. That was the law of life. She did not put it into words. But something of this she thought as she sat there in her plain white nightgown, her scant white locks pinned in a neat knob at the top of her head. Selfishness. That was it. They called it love, but it was selfishness. She must tell them about it to-morrow—

Mrs. Lamb, Mrs. Brunswick, and Mrs. Wormser.
Only yesterday Mrs. Brunswick had waxed bitter
because her daughter-in-law had let a moth get
into her husband's winter suit.

"I never had a moth in my house!" Mrs.
Brunswick had declared. "Never. But nowadays housekeeping is nothing. A suit is ruined.
What does my son's wife care! I never had a moth
in my house."

Ma Mandle chuckled to herself there in the
darkness. "I bet she did. She forgets. We all
forget."

It was very hot to-night. Now and then there
was a wisp of breeze from the lake, but not often.
. . . How red Lil's eyes had been . . .
poor girl. Moved by a sudden impulse Ma
Mandle thudded down the hall in her bare
feet, found a scrap of paper in the writing-desk
drawer, scribbled a line on it, turned out the light,
and went into the empty front room. With a pin
from the tray on the dresser she fastened the note
to Lil's pillow, high up, where she must see it
the instant she turned on the light. Then she
scuttled down the hall to her room again.

She felt the heat terribly. She would sit by the
window again. All the blood in her body seemed
to be pounding in her head . . . pounding
in her head . . . pounding . . .

At ten Hugo and Lil came in, softly. Hugo tiptoed down the hall, as was his wont, and listened. The room was in darkness. "Sleeping, Ma?" he whispered. He could not see the white-gowned figure sitting peacefully by the window, and there was no answer. He tiptoed with painful awkwardness up the hall again.

"She's asleep, all right. I didn't think she'd get to sleep so early on a scorcher like this."

Lil turned on the light in her room. "It's too hot to sleep," she said. She began to disrobe languidly. Her eye fell on the scrap of paper pinned to her pillow. She went over to it, curiously, leaned over, read it.

"Oh, look, Hugo!" She gave a little tremulous laugh that was more than half sob. He came over to her and read it, his arm around her shoulder.

"My son Hugo and my daughter Lil they are the best son and daughter in the world."

A sudden hot haze before his eyes blotted out the words as he finished reading them.

YOU'VE GOT TO BE SELFISH

WHEN you try to do a story about three people like Sid Hahn and Mizzi Markis and Wallie Ascher you find yourself pawing around among the personalities helplessly. For the three of them are what is known in newspaper parlance as national figures. One n. f. is enough for any short story. Three would swamp a book. It's like one of those plays advertised as having an all-star cast. By the time each luminary has come on, and been greeted, and done his twinkling the play has faded into the background. You can't see the heavens for the stars.

Surely Sid Hahn, like the guest of honour at a dinner, needs no introduction. And just as surely will he be introduced. He has been described elsewhere and often; perhaps nowhere more concisely than on Page 16, paragraph two, of a volume that shall be nameless, though quoted, thus:

"Sid Hahn, erstwhile usher, call-boy, press agent, advance man, had a genius for things theatrical. It was inborn. Dramatic, sensitive, artistic, intuitive, he was often rendered inarticulate by the very force and variety of his feelings. A

little, rotund, ugly man, with the eyes of a dreamer,
the wide, mobile mouth of a humourist, the ears
of a comic ol' clo'es man. His generosity was
proverbial, and it amounted to a vice."

Not that that covers him. No one paragraph
could. You turn a fine diamond this way and
that, and as its facets catch the light you say,
"It's scarlet! No—it's blue! No—rose!—orange!
—lilac!—no——"

That was Sid Hahn.

I suppose he never really sat for a photograph
and yet you saw his likeness in all the magazines.
He was snapped on the street, and in the theatre,
and even up in his famous library-study-office on
the sixth and top floor of the Thalia Theatre Building. Usually with a fat black cigar—unlighted—
in one corner of his commodious mouth. Everyone interested in things theatrical (and whom does
that not include!) knew all about Sid Hahn—and
nothing. He had come, a boy, from one of those
middle-western towns with a high-falutin Greek
name. Parthenon, Ohio, or something incredible
like that. No one knows how he first approached
the profession which he was to dominate in America. There's no record of his having asked for a
job in a theatre, and received it. He oozed into it,
indefinably, and moved with it, and became a part
of it and finally controlled it. Satellites, fur-col-

lared and pseudo-successful, trailing in his wake,
used to talk loudly of I-knew-him-when. They
all lied. It had been Augustin Daly, dead these
many years, who had first recognized in this boy
the genius for discovering and directing genius.
Daly was, at that time, at the zenith of his career—
managing, writing, directing, producing. He fired
the imagination of this stocky, gargoyle-faced boy
with the luminous eyes and the humorous mouth.
I don't know that Sid Hahn, hanging about the
theatre in every kind of menial capacity, ever said
to himself in so many words:

"I'm going to be what he is. I'm going to concentrate on it. I won't let anything or anybody
interfere with it. Nobody knows what I'm going
to be. But I know. . . . And you've got to
be selfish. You've got to be selfish."

Of course no one ever really made a speech like
that to himself, even in the Horatio Alger books.
But if the great ambition and determination running through the whole fibre of his being could have
been crystallized into spoken words they would
have sounded like that.

By the time he was forty-five he had discovered more stars than Copernicus. They were
not all first-magnitude twinklers. Some of them
even glowed so feebly that you could see their
light only when he stood behind them, the steady

radiance of his genius shining through. But taken as a whole they made a brilliant constellation, furnishing much of the illumination for the brightest thoroughfare in the world.

He had never married. There are those who say that he had had an early love affair, but that he had sworn not to marry until he had achieved what he called success. And by that time it had been too late. It was as though the hot flame of ambition had burned out all his other passions. Later they say he was responsible for more happy marriages contracted by people who did not know that he was responsible for them than a popular east-side shadchen. He grew a little tired, perhaps, of playing with make-believe stage characters, and directing them, so he began to play with real ones, like God. But always kind.

No woman can resist making love to a man as indifferent as Sid Hahn appeared to be. They all tried their wiles on him: the red-haired ingénues, the blonde soubrettes, the stately leading ladies, the war horses, the old-timers, the ponies, the prima donnas. He used to sit there in his great, luxurious, book-lined inner office, smiling and inscrutable as a plump joss-house idol while the fair ones burnt incense and made offering of shewbread. Figuratively, he kicked over the basket of shew-bread, and of the incense said, "Take away that stuff! It smells!"

Not that he hated women. He was afraid of them, at first. Then, from years of experience with the femininity of the theatre, not nearly afraid enough. So, early, he had locked that corner of his mind, and had thrown away the key. When, years after, he broke in the door, lo! (as they say when an elaborate figure of speech is being used) lo! the treasures therein had turned to dust and ashes.

It was he who had brought over from Paris to the American stage the famous Renée Paterne of the incorrigible eyes. She made a fortune and swept the country with her song about those delinquent orbs. But when she turned them on Hahn, in their first interview in his office, he regarded her with what is known as a long, level look. She knew at that time not a word of English. Sid Hahn was ignorant of French. He said, very low, and with terrible calm to Wallie Ascher who was then acting as a sort of secretary, "Wallie, can't you do something to make her stop rolling her eyes around at me like that? It's awful! She makes me think of those heads you shy balls at, out at Coney. Take away my ink-well."

Renée had turned swiftly to Wallie and had said

something to him in French. Sid Hahn cocked a
quick ear. "What's that she said?"

"She says," translated the obliging and gifted
Wallie, "that monsieur is a woman-hater."

"My God! I thought she didn't understand
English!"

"She doesn't. But she's a woman. Not only
that, she's a French woman. They don't need to
know a language to understand it."

"Where did you get that, h'm? That wasn't
included in your Berlitz course, was it?"

Wallie Ascher had grinned—that winning flash
lighting up his dark, keen face. "No. I learned
that in another school."

Wallie Ascher's early career in the theatre, if
repeated here, might almost be a tiresome repetition of Hahn's beginning. And what Augustin
Daly had been to Sid Hahn's imagination and
ambition, Sid Hahn was to Wallie's. Wallie,
though, had been born to the theatre—if having a
tumbler for a father and a prestidigitator's foil
for a mother can be said to be a legitimate entrance
into the world of the theatre.

He had been employed about the old Thalia
for years before Hahn noticed him. In the beginning he was a spindle-legged office boy in the
upstairs suite of the firm of Hahn & Lohman,
theatrical producers; the kind of office-boy who is

addicted to shrill, clear whistling unless very firmly
dealt with. No one in the outer office realized how
faultless, how rhythmic were the arpeggios and
cadences that issued from those expertly puckered
lips. There was about his performance an unerring precision. As you listened you felt that
his ascent to the inevitable high note was a thing
impossible of achievement. Up—up—up he would
go, while you held your breath in suspense. And
then he took the high note—took it easily, in-
souciantly—held it, trilled it, tossed it.

"Now, look here," Miss Feldman would snap—
Miss Feldman of the outer office typewriter—
"look here, you kid. Any more of that bird
warbling and you go back to the woods where you
belong. This ain't a—a——"

"Aviary," suggested Wallie, almost shyly.

Miss Feldman glared. "How did you know
that word?"

"I don't know," helplessly. "But it's the word,
isn't it?"

Miss Feldman turned back to her typewriter.
"You're too smart for your age, you are."

"I know it," Wallie had agreed, humbly.

There's no telling where or how he learned to
play the piano. He probably never did learn.
He played it, though, as he whistled—brilliantly.
No doubt it was as imitative and as unconscious,

too, as his whistling had been. They say he didn't know one note from another, and doesn't to this day.

At twenty, when he should have been in love with at least three girls, he had fixed in his mind an image, a dream. And it bore no resemblance to twenty's accepted dreams. At that time he was living in one room (rear) of a shabby rooming house in Thirty-ninth Street. And this was the dream: By the time he was—well, long before he was thirty—he would have a bachelor apartment with a Jap, Saki. Saki was the perfect servant, noiseless, unobtrusive, expert. He saw little dinners just for four—or, at the most, six. And Saki, white-coated, deft, sliding hot plates when plates should be hot; cold plates when plates should be cold. Then, other evenings, alone, when he wanted to see no one—when, in a silken lounging robe (over faultless dinner clothes, of course, and wearing the kind of collar you see in the back of the magazines) he would say, "That will do, Saki." Then, all evening, he would play softly to himself those little, intimate, wistful Schumanny things in the firelight with just one lamp glowing softly—almost sombrely—at the side of the piano (grand).

His first real meeting with Sid Hahn had had much to do with the fixing of this image. Of course he had seen Hahn hundreds of times in the office and about the theatre. They had spoken, too, many times. Hahn called him vaguely, "Heh, boy!" but he grew to know him later as Wallie. From errand-boy, office-boy, call-boy he had become, by that time, a sort of unofficial assistant stage manager. No one acknowledged that he was invaluable about the place, but he was. When a new play was in rehearsal at the Thalia, Wallie knew more about props, business, cues, lights, and lines than the director himself. For a long time no one but Wallie and the director were aware of this. The director never did admit it. But that Hahn should find it out was inevitable.

He was nineteen or thereabouts when he was sent, one rainy November evening, to deliver a play manuscript to Hahn at his apartment. Wallie might have refused to perform an errand so menial, but his worship of Hahn made him glad of any service, however humble. He buttoned his coat over the manuscript, turned up his collar, and plunged into the cold drizzle of the November evening.

Hahn's apartment—he lived alone—was in the early fifties, off Fifth Avenue. For two days he had been ill with one of the heavy colds to which he was subject. He was unable to leave the house. Hence Wallie's errand.

It was Saki—or Saki's equivalent—who opened the door. A white-coated, soft-stepping Jap, world-old looking like the room glimpsed just beyond. Someone was playing the piano with one finger, horribly.

"You're to give this to Mr. Hahn. He's waiting for it."

"Genelmun come in," said the Jap, softly.

"No, he don't want to see me. Just give it to him, see?"

"Genelmun come in." Evidently orders.

"Oh, all right. But I know he doesn't want——"

Wallie turned down his collar with a quick flip, looked doubtfully at his shoes, and passed through the glowing little foyer into the room beyond. He stood in the doorway. He was scarcely twenty then, but something in him sort of rose, and gathered, and seethed, and swelled, and then hardened. He didn't know it then but it was his great resolve.

Sid Hahn was seated at the piano, a squat, gnomelike little figure, with those big ears, and that plump face, and those soft eyes—the kindest eyes in the world. He did not stop playing as Wallie appeared. He glanced up at him, ever so briefly, but kindly, too, and went on playing the thing with one short forefinger, excruciatingly. Wallie waited. He had heard somewhere that

Hahn would sit at the piano thus, for hours, the tears running down his cheeks because of the beauty of the music he could remember but not reproduce; and partly because of his own inability to reproduce it.

The stubby little forefinger faltered, stopped. He looked up at Wallie.

"God, I wish I could play!"

"Helps a lot."

"You play?"

"Yes."

"What?"

"Oh, most anything I've heard once. And some things I kind of make up."

"Compose, you mean?"

"Yes."

"Play one of those."

So Wallie Ascher played one of those. Of course you know "Good Night—Pleasant Dreams." He hadn't named it then. It wasn't even published until almost two years later, but that was what he played for Sid Hahn. Since "After The Ball" no popular song has achieved the success of that one. No doubt it was cheap, and no doubt it was sentimental, but so, too, are "The Suwannee River" and "My Old Kentucky Home," and they'll be singing those when more classical songs have long been forgotten. As Wallie played it his dark, thin face seemed to gleam and glow in the lamplight.

When he had finished Sid Hahn was silent for a moment. Then, "What're you going to do with it?"

"With what?"

"With what you've got. You know."

Wallie knew that he did not mean the song he had just played. "I'm going to—I'm going to do a lot with it."

"Yeh, but how?"

Wallie was looking down at his two lean brown hands on the keys. For a long minute he did not answer. Then: "By thinking about it all the time. And working like hell. . . . And you've got to be selfish . . . You've got to be selfish . . ."

As Sid Hahn stared at him, as though hypnotized, the Jap appeared in the doorway. So Hahn said, "Stay and have dinner with me," instead of what he had meant to say.

"Oh, I can't! Thanks. I——" He wanted to, terribly, but the thought was too much.

"Better."

They had dinner together. Even under the influence of Hahn's encouragement and two glasses of mellow wine whose name he did not know Wallie did not become fatuous. They talked about music—neither of them knew anything about it, really. Wallie confessed that he used it as an intoxicant and a stimulant.

"That's it!" cried Hahn, excitedly. "If I could play I'd have done more. More."

"Why don't you get one of those piano-players. What-you-call'ems?" Then, immediately, "No, of course not."

"Nah, that doesn't do it," said Hahn, quickly. "That's like adopting a baby when you can't have one of your own. It isn't the same. It isn't the same. It looks like a baby, and acts like a baby, and sounds like a baby—but it isn't yours. It isn't you. That's it! It isn't you!"

"Yeh," agreed Wallie, nodding. So perfectly did they understand each other, this ill-assorted pair.

It was midnight before Wallie left. They had both forgotten about the play manuscript whose delivery had been considered so important. The big room was gracious, quiet, soothing. A fire flickered in the grate. One lamp glowed softly— almost sombrely.

As Wallie rose at last to go he shook himself slightly like one coming out of a trance. He looked slowly about the golden, mellow room. "Gee!"

"Yes, but it isn't worth it," said Hahn, "after you've got it."

"That's what they all say"—grimly—"*after* they've got it."

The thing that had been born in Sid Hahn's mind thirty years before was now so plainly stamped on this boy's face that Hahn was startled into earnestness. "But I tell you, it's true! It's true!"

"Maybe. Some day, when I'm living in a place like this, I'll let you know if you're right."

In less than a year Wallie Ascher was working with Hahn. No one knew his official title or place. But "Ask Wallie. He'll know," had become a sort of slogan in the office. He did know. At twenty-one his knowledge of the theatre was infallible (this does not include plays unproduced; in this no one is infallible) and his feeling for it amounted to a sixth sense. There was something uncanny about the way he could talk about Lottie, for example, as if he had seen her; or Mrs. Siddons; or Mrs. Fiske when she was Minnie Maddern, the soubrette. It was as though he had the power to cast himself back into the past. No doubt it was that power which gave later to his group of historical plays (written by him between the ages of thirty and thirty-five) their convincingness and authority.

When Wallie was about twenty-three or -four Sid Hahn took him abroad on one of his annual scouting trips. Yearly, in the spring, Hahn swooped down upon London, Paris, Vienna, Berlin, seeking that of the foreign stage which might be translated, fumigated, desiccated, or otherwise rendered suitable for home use. He sent Wallie on to Vienna, alone, on the trail of a musical comedy rumoured to be a second Merry Widow in tunefulness, chic, and charm. Of course it wasn't. Merry Widows rarely repeat. Wallie wired Hahn, as arranged. The telegram is unimportant, perhaps, but characteristic.

Mr. Sid. Hahn,
Hotel Savoy,
London,
England.

It's a second all right but not a second Merry Widow. Heard of a winner in Budapest. Shall I go. Spent to-day from eleven to five running around the Ringstrasse looking for mythical creature known as the chic Viennese. After careful investigation wish to be quoted as saying the species if any is extinct.
Wallie.

This, remember, was in the year 1913, B.W. Wallie, obeying instructions, went to Budapest, witnessed the alleged winner, found it as advertised, wired Hahn to that effect, and was joined by that gentleman three days later.

Budapest, at that time, was still Little Paris, only wickeder. A city of magnificent buildings, and unsalted caviar, and beautiful, dangerous women, and frumpy men (civilian) and dashing officers in red pants, and Cigány music, and cafés and paprika and two-horse droshkies. Buda, low and flat, lay on one side; Pest, high and hilly, perched picturesquely on the other. Between the two rolled the Blue Danube (which is yellow).

It was here that Hahn and Wallie found Mizzi Markis. Mizzi Markis, then a girl of nineteen, was a hod carrier.

Wallie had three days in Budapest before Hahn met him there. As the manager stepped from the train, looking geometrically square in a long ulster that touched his ears and his heels, Wallie met him with a bound.

"Hello, S. H.! Great to see you! Say, listen, I've found something. I've found something big!"

Hahn had never seen the boy so excited. "Oh, shucks! No play's as good as that."

"Play! It isn't a play."

"Why, you young idiot, you said it was good! You said it was darned good! You don't mean to tell me——"

"Oh, that! That's all right. It's good—or will be when you get through with it."

"What you talking about then? Here, let's take one of these things with two horses. Gee, you ought to smoke a fat black seegar and wear a silk hat when you ride in one of these! I feel like a parade." He was like a boy on a holiday, as always when in Europe.

"But let me tell you about this girl, won't you!"

"Oh, it's a girl! What's her name? What's she do?"

"Her name's Mizzi."

"Mizzi what?"

"I don't know. She's a hod carrier. She——"

"That's all right, Wallie. I'm here now. An ice bag on your head and real quiet for two-three days. You'll come round fine."

But Wallie was almost sulking. "Wait till you see her, S. H. She sings."

"Beautiful, is she?"

"No, not particularly. No."

"Wonderful voice, h'm?"

"N-n-no. I wouldn't say it was what you'd call exactly wonderful."

Sid Hahn stood up in the droshky and waved his short arms in windmill circles. "Well, what the devil does she do then, that's so good? Carry bricks!"

"She is good at that. When she balances that

pail of mortar on her head and walks off with it,
her arms hanging straight at her sides———"

But Sid Hahn's patience was at an end. "You're
a humourist, you are. If I didn't know you I'd
say you were drunk. I'll bet you are, anyway.
You've been eating paprika, raw. You make me
sick."

Inelegant, but expressive of his feelings. But
Wallie only said, "You wait. You'll see."

Sid Hahn did see. He saw next day. Wallie
woke him out of a sound sleep so that he might
see. It was ten-thirty A. M. so that his peevishness
was unwarranted. They had seen the play the
night before and Hahn had decided that, translated and with interpolations (it was a comic
opera), it would captivate New York. Then and
there he completed the negotiations which Wallie
had begun. Hahn was all for taking the first
train out, but Wallie was firm. "You've got to
see her, I tell you. You've got to see her."

Their hotel faced the Corso. The Corso is a
wide promenade that runs along the Buda bank
of the Danube. Across the river, on the hill, the
royal palace looks down upon the little common
people. In that day the monde and the demi-
monde of Budapest walked on the Corso between
twelve and one. Up and down. Up and down.
The women, tall, dark, flashing-eyed, daringly

dressed. The men sallow, meagre, and wearing those trousers which, cut very wide and flappy at the ankles, make them the dowdiest men in the world. Hahn's room and Wallie's were on the second floor of the hotel, and at a corner. One set of windows faced the Corso, the river, and Pest on the hill. The other set looked down upon a new building being erected across the way. It was on this building that Mizzi Markis worked as hod carrier.

The war accustomed us to a million women in overalls doing the work of a million men. We saw them ploughing, juggling steel bars, making shells, running engines, stoking furnaces, handling freight. But to these two American men, at that time, the thing at which these labouring women were employed was dreadful and incredible.

Said Wallie: "By the time we've dressed, and had breakfast, and walked a little and everything, it'll be almost noon. And noon's the time. After they've eaten their lunch. But I want you to see her before."

By now his earnestness had impressed Hahn who still feigned an indifference he did not feel. It was about 11:30 when Wallie propelled him by the arm to the unfinished building across the way. And there he met Mizzi.

They were just completing the foundation. The

place was a busy hive.   Back and forth with pails.
Back and forth with loads of bricks.

"What's the matter with the men?" was Hahn's
first question.

Wallie explained.   "They do the dainty work.
They put one brick on top of the other, with a dab
of mortar between.   But none of the back-breaking stuff for them.   The women do that."

And it was so.   They were down in the pits
mixing the mortar, were the women.   They were
carrying great pails of it.   They were hauling
bricks up one ladder and down.   They wore short,
full skirts with a musical-comedy-chorus effect.
Some of them looked seventy and some seventeen.
It was fearful work for a woman.   A keen wind
was blowing across the river.   Their hands were
purple.

"Pick Mizzi," said Wallie.   "If you can pick
her I'll know I'm right.   But I know it, anyway."

Five minutes passed.   The two men stood
silent.   "The one with the walk and the face,"
said Hahn, then.   Which wasn't very bright of
him, because they all walked and they all had
faces.   "Going up the pit-ladder now.   With
the pail on her head."   Wallie gave a little laugh
of triumph.   But then, Hahn wouldn't have been
Hahn had he not been able to pick a personality
when he saw it.

Years afterward the reviewers always talked of Mizzi's walk. They called it her superb carriage. They didn't know that you have to walk very straight, on the balls of your feet, with your hips firm, your stomach held in flat, your shoulders back, your chest out, your chin out and a little down, if you are going to be at all successful in balancing a pail of mortar on your head. After a while that walk becomes a habit.

"Watch her with that pail," said Wallie.

Mizzi filled the pail almost to the top with the heavy white mixture. She filled it quickly, expertly. The pail, filled, weighed between seventeen and twenty kilos. One kilo is equal to about two and one fifth pounds. The girl threw down her scoop, stooped, grasped the pail by its two handles, and with one superb, unbroken motion raised the pail high in her two strong arms and placed it on her head. Then she breathed deeply, once, set her whole figure, turned stiffly, and was off with it. Sid Hahn took on a long breath as though he himself had just accomplished the gymnastic feat.

"Well, so far it's pretty good. But I don't know that the American stage is clamouring for any hod carriers and mortar mixers, exactly."

A whistle blew. Twelve o'clock. Bricks, mortar, scoops, shovels were abandoned. The women,

in their great clod-hopping shoes, flew chattering
to the tiny hut where their lunch boxes were stored.
The men followed more slowly, a mere handful of
them. Not one of them wore overalls or apron.
Out again with their bundles and boxes of food—
very small bundles. Very tiny boxes. They ate
ravenously the bread and sausage and drank their
beer in great gulps. Fifteen minutes after the
whistle had blown the last crumb had vanished.

"Now, then," said Wallie, and guided Hahn
nearer. He looked toward Mizzi. Everyone
looked toward her. Mizzi stood up, brushing
crumbs from her lap. She had a little four-cor-
nered black shawl, folded cross-wise, over her head
and tied under her chin. Her face was round and
her cheeks red. The shawl, framing this, made
her look very young and cherubic.

She did not put her hands on her hips, or do any
of those story-book things. She grinned, broadly,
showing strong white teeth made strong and white
through much munching of coarse black bread;
not yet showing the neglect common to her class.
She asked a question in a loud, clear voice.

"What's that?" asked Hahn.

"She's talking a kind of hunky Hungarian, I
guess. The people here won't speak German,
did you know that? They hate it."

The crowd shouted back with one voice. They

settled themselves comfortably, sitting or standing.   Their faces held the broad smile of anticipa-
tion.

"She asked them what they want her to sing.
They told her.   It's the same every day."

Mizzi Markis stood there before them in the
mud, and clay, and straw of the building débris.
And she sang for them a Hungarian popular song
of the day which, translated, sounds idiotic and
which runs something like this:

> A hundred geese in a row
> Going into the coop.
> At the head of the procession
> A stick over his shoulder——

No, you can't do it.   It means less than nothing that way, and certainly would not warrant the
shrieks of mirth that came from the audience
gathered round the girl.   Still, when you recall
the words of "A Hot Time":

When you hear dem bells go ding-ling-ling,
All join round and sweetly you must sing
And when the words am through in the chorus all join in
There 'll be a *hot time*
In the *old town*
To-night.
> My
> Ba-
>   By.

And yet it swept this continent, and Europe, and in Japan they still think it's our national anthem.

When she had finished, the crowd gave a roar of delight, and clapped their hands, and stamped their feet, and shouted. She had no unusual beauty. Her voice was untrained though possessed of strength and flexibility. It wasn't what she had sung, surely. You heard the song in a hundred cafés. Every street boy whistled it. It wasn't that expressive pair of shoulders, exactly. It wasn't a certain soothing tonal quality that made you forget all the things you'd been trying not to remember.

There is something so futile and unconvincing about an attempted description of an intangible thing. Some call it personality; some call it magnetism; some a rhythm sense; and some, genius. It's all these things, and none of them. Whatever it is, she had it. And whatever it is, Sid Hahn has never failed to recognize it.

So now he said, quietly, "She's got it."

"You bet she's got it!" from Wallie. "She's got more than Renée Paterne ever had. A year of training and some clothes——"

"You don't need to tell me. I'm in the theatrical business, myself."

"I'm sorry," stiffly.

But Hahn, too, was sorry immediately. "You

know how I am, Wallie. I like to run a thing off
by myself. What do you know about her? Find
out anything?"

"Well, a little. She doesn't seem to have any
people. And she's decent. Kind of a fierce kid,
I guess, and fights when offended. They say she's
Polish, not Hungarian. Her mother was a peasant.
Her father—nobody knows. I had a dickens of a
time finding out anything. The most terrible
language in the world—Hungarian. They'll stick
a *b* next to a *k* and follow it up with a *z* and put an
accent mark over the whole business and call it a
word. Last night I followed her home. And
guess what!"

"What?" said Hahn, obligingly.

"On her way she had to cross the big square—
the one they call Gisela Tér, with all the shops
around it. Well, when she came to Gerbeaud's——"

"What's Gerbeaud's?"

"That's the famous tea room and pastry shop
where all the swells go and guzzle tea with rum in it
and eat cakes—and say! It isn't like our pastry
that tastes like sawdust covered with shaving soap.
Marvellous stuff, this is!"

After all, he was barely twenty-four. So Hahn
said, good-naturedly, "All right, all right. We'll
go there this afternoon and eat an acre of it. Go
on. When she came to Gerbeaud's . . . ?"

"Well, when she came to Gerbeaud's she stopped and stood there, outside. There was a strip of red carpet from the door to the street. You know—the kind they have at home when there's a wedding on Fifth Avenue. There she stood at the edge of the carpet, waiting, her face, framed in that funny little black shawl, turned toward the window, and the tail of the little shawl kind of waggling in the wind. It was cold and nippy. I waited, too. Finally I sort of strolled over to her —I knew she couldn't any more than knock me down—and said, kind of casual, 'What's doing?' She looked up at me, like a kid, in that funny shawl. She knew I was an Englees, right away. I guess I must have a fine, open countenance. And I had motioned toward the red carpet, and the crowded windows. Anyway, she opens up with a regular burst of fireworks Hungarian, in that deep voice of hers. Not only that, she acted it out. In two seconds she had on an imaginary coronet and a court train. And haughty! Gosh! I was sort of stumped, but I said, 'You don't say!' and waited some more. And then they flung open the door of the tea shop thing. At the same moment up dashed an equipage—you couldn't possibly call it anything less—with flunkeys all over the outside, like trained monkeys. The people inside the shop stood up, with their mouths full of cake, and out came an old frump with a terrible hat and a fringe. And it was the Archduchess, and her name is Josefa."

"Your story interests me strangely, boy," Hahn said, grinning, "but I don't quite make you. Do archduchesses go to tea rooms for tea? And what's that got to do with our gifted little hod carrier?"

"This duchess does. Believe me, those tarts are good enough for the Queen of Hearts, let alone a duchess, no matter how arch. But the plot of the piece is this. The duchess person goes to Gerbeaud's about twice a week. And they always spread a red carpet for her. And Mizzi always manages to cut away in time to stand there in front of Gerbeaud's and see her come out. She's a gorgeous mimic, that little kid. And though I couldn't understand a word she said I managed to get out of it just this: That some day they're going to spread a red carpet for Mizzi and she's going to walk down it in glory. If you'd seen her face when she said it, S. H., you wouldn't laugh."

"I wouldn't laugh anyway," said Hahn, seriously.

And that's the true story of Mizzi Markis's beginning. Few people know it.

There they were, the three of them. And of the

three, Mizzi's ambition seemed to be the fiercest, the most implacable. She worked like a horse, cramming English, French, singing. In some things she was like a woman of thirty; in others a child of ten. Her gratitude to Hahn was pathetic. No one ever doubted that he was in love with her almost from the first—he who had resisted the professional beauties of three decades.

You know she wasn't—and isn't—a beauty, even in that portrait of her by Sargent, with her two black-haired, stunning-looking boys, one on either side. But she was one of those gorgeously healthy women whose very presence energizes those with whom she comes in contact. And then there was about her a certain bounteousness. There's no other word for it, really. She reminded you of those gracious figures you see posed for pictures entitled "Autumn Harvest."

While she was studying she had a little apartment with a middle-aged woman to look after her, and she must have been a handful. A born cook, she was, and Hahn and Wallie used to go there to dinner whenever she would let them. She cooked it herself. Hahn would give up any engagement for a dinner at Mizzi's. When he entered her little sitting room his cares seemed to drop from him. She never got over cutting bread as the peasant women do it—the loaf held firmly against her breast, the knife cutting toward her. Hahn used to watch her and laugh. Sometimes she would put on the little black head-shawl of her Budapest days and sing the street-song about the hundred geese in a row. A delightful, impudent figure.

With the very first English she learned she told Hahn and Wallie that some day they were going to spread a fine red carpet for her to tread upon and that all the world would gaze on her with envy. It was in her mind a symbol typifying all that there was of earthly glory.

"It'll be a long time before they do any red carpeting for you, my girl," Sid Hahn had said.

She turned on him fiercely. "I will not rest— I will not eat—I will not sleep—I will not love— until I have it."

Which was, of course, an exaggerated absurdity.

"Oh, what rot!" Wallie Ascher had said, angrily, and then he had thought of his own symbol of success, and his own resolve. And his face had hardened. Sid Hahn looked at the two of them; very young, both of them, very gifted, very electric. Very much in love with each other, though neither would admit it even in their own minds. Both their stern young faces set toward the goal which they thought meant happiness.

Now, Sid Hahn had never dabbled in this new stuff—you know—complexes and fixed ideas and images. But he was a very wise man, and he did know to what an extent these two were possessed by ambition for that which they considered desirable.

He must have thought it over for weeks. He was in love with Mizzi, remember. And his fondness for Wallie was a thing almost paternal. He watched these two for a long, long time, a queer, grim little smile on his gargoyle face. And then his mind was made up. He had always had his own way. He must have had a certain terrible enjoyment in depriving himself of the one thing he wanted most in the world—the one thing he wanted more than he had ever wanted anything.

He decided that Destiny—a ponderous, slow-moving creature at best—needed a little prodding from him. His plans were simple, as all effective plans are.

Mizzi had been in America just a year and a half. Her development was amazing, but she was far from being the finished product that she became in later years. Hahn decided to chance it. Mizzi had no fear of audiences. He had tried her out on that. An audience stimulated her. She took it to her breast. She romped with it.

He found a play at last. A comedy, with music. It was frankly built for Mizzi. He called Wallie Ascher into his office.

"I wouldn't try her out here for a million. New York's too fly. Some little thing might be wrong—you know how they are. And all the rest would go for nothing. The kindest audience in the world—when they like you. And the cruelest when they don't. We'll go on the road for two weeks. Then we'll open at the Blackstone in Chicago. I think this girl has got more real genius than any woman since—since Bernhardt in her prime. Five years from now she won't be singing. She'll be acting. And it'll *be* acting."

"Aren't you forcing things just a little?" asked Wallie, coolly.

"Oh, no. No. Anyway, it's just a try-out. By the way, Wallie, I'll probably be gone almost a month. If things go pretty well in Chicago I'll run over to French Lick for eight or ten days and see if I can't get a little of this stiffness out of my old bones. Will you do something for me?"

"Sure."

"Pack a few clothes and go up to my place and live there, will you? The Jap stays on, anyway. The last time I left it alone things went wrong. You'll be doing me a favour. Take it and play the piano, and have your friends in, and boss the Jap around. He's stuck on you, anyway. Says he likes to hear you play."

He stayed away six weeks. And any one who

knows him knows what hardship that was. He loved New York, and his own place, and his comfort, and his books; and hotel food gave him hideous indigestion.

Mizzi's first appearance was a moderate success. It was nothing like the sensation of her later efforts. She wasn't ready, and Hahn knew it. Mizzi and her middle-aged woman companion were installed at the Blackstone Hotel, which is just next door to the Blackstone Theatre, as any one is aware who knows Chicago. She was advertised as the Polish comedienne, Mizzi Markis, and the announcements hinted at her royal though remote ancestry. And on the night the play opened, as Mizzi stepped from the entrance of her hotel on her way to the stage door, just forty or fifty feet away, there she saw stretched on the pavement a scarlet path of soft-grained carpet for her feet to tread. From the steps of the hotel to the stage door of the theatre, there it lay, a rosy line of splendour.

The newspapers played it up as a publicity stunt. Every night, while the play lasted, the carpet was there. It was rolled up when the stage door closed upon her. It was unrolled and spread again when she came out after the performance. Hahn never forgot her face when she first saw it, and realized its significance. The look was there on the second night, and on the third, but after that it faded, vanished, and never came again. Mizzi had tasted of the golden fruit and found it dry and profitless, without nourishment or sweetness.

The show closed in the midst of a fairly good run. It closed abruptly, without warning. Together they came back to New York. Just outside New York Hahn knocked at the door of Mizzi's drawing room and stuck his round, ugly face in at the opening.

"Let's surprise Wallie," he said.

"Yes," said Mizzi, listlessly.

"He doesn't know the show's closed. We'll take a chance on his being home for dinner. Unless you're too tired."

"I'm not tired."

The Jap admitted them, and Hahn cut off his staccato exclamations with a quick and smothering hand. They tiptoed into the big, gracious, lamp-lighted room.

Wallie was seated at the piano. He had on a silk dressing gown with a purple cord. One of those dressing gowns you see in the haberdashers' windows, and wonder who buys them. He looked very tall in it, and rather distinguished, but not quite happy. He was playing as they came in. They said, "Boo!" or something idiotic like that. He stood up. And his face!

"Why, hello!" he said, and came forward, swiftly. "Hello! Hello!"

"Hello!" Hahn answered; "Not to say hello-hello."

Wallie looked at the girl. "Hello, Mizzi."

"Hello," said Mizzi.

"For God's sake stop saying 'hello!'" roared Hahn.

They both looked at him absently, and then at each other again.

Hahn flung his coat and hat at the Jap and rubbed his palms briskly together. "Well, how did you like it?" he said, and slapped Wallie on the back. "How'd you like it—the place I mean, and the Jap boy and all? H'm?"

"Very much," Wallie answered, formally. "Very nice."

"You'll be having one of your own some day, soon. That's sure."

"I suppose so," said Wallie, indifferently.

"I would like to go home," said Mizzi, suddenly, in her precise English.

At that Wallie leaped out of his lounging coat. "I'll take you! I'll—I'll be glad to take you."

Hahn smiled a little, ruefully. "We were going to have dinner here, the three of us. But if you're tired, Mizzi. I'm not so chipper myself when it comes to that." He looked about the room, gratefully. "It's good to be home."

Wallie, hat in hand, was waiting in the doorway. Mizzi, turning to go, suddenly felt two hands on her shoulders. She was whirled around. Hahn— he had to stand on tiptoe to do it—kissed her once on the mouth, hard. Then he gave her a little shove toward the door. "Tell Wallie about the red carpet," he said.

"I will not," Mizzi replied, very distinctly. "I hate red carpets."

Then they were gone. Hahn hardly seemed to notice that they had left. There were, I suppose, the proper number of Good-byes, and See-you-to-morrows, and Thank yous.

Sid Hahn stood there a moment in the middle of the room, very small, very squat, rather gnome-like, but not at all funny. He went over to the piano and seated himself, his shoulders hunched, his short legs clearing the floor. With the fore-finger of his right hand he began to pick out a little tune. Not a sad little tune. A Hungarian street song. He did it atrociously. The stubby fore-finger came down painstakingly on the white keys. Suddenly the little Jap servant stood in the door-way. Hahn looked up. His cheeks were wet with tears.

"God! I wish I could play!" he said.

LONG DISTANCE

CHET BALL was painting a wooden chicken yellow. The wooden chicken was mounted on a six-by-twelve board. The board was mounted on four tiny wheels. The whole would eventually be pulled on a string guided by the plump, moist hand of some blissful six-year-old.

You got the incongruity of it the instant your eye fell upon Chet Ball. Chet's shoulders alone would have loomed large in contrast with any wooden toy ever devised, including the Trojan horse. Everything about him, from the big, blunt-fingered hands that held the ridiculous chick to the great muscular pillar of his neck, was in direct opposition to his task, his surroundings, and his attitude.

Chet's proper milieu was Chicago, Illinois (the West Side); his job that of lineman for the Gas, Light and Power Company; his normal working position astride the top of a telegraph pole supported in his perilous perch by a lineman's leather belt and the kindly fates, both of which are likely to trick you in an emergency.

Yet now he lolled back among his pillows, dabbling complacently at the absurd yellow toy. A description of his surroundings would sound like Pages 3 to 17 of a novel by Mrs. Humphry Ward. The place was all greensward, and terraces, and sun dials, and beeches, and even those rhododendrons without which no English novel or country estate is complete. The presence of Chet Ball among his pillows and some hundreds similarly disposed revealed to you at once the fact that this particular English estate was now transformed into Reconstruction Hospital No. 9.

The painting of the chicken quite finished (including two beady black paint eyes) Chet was momentarily at a loss. Miss Kate had not told him to stop painting when the chicken was completed. Miss Kate was at the other end of the sunny garden walk, bending over a wheel-chair. So Chet went on painting, placidly. One by one, with meticulous nicety, he painted all his finger nails a bright and cheery yellow. Then he did the whole of his left thumb, and was starting on the second joint of the index finger when Miss Kate came up behind him and took the brush gently from his strong hands.

"You shouldn't have painted your fingers," she said.

Chet surveyed them with pride. "They look swell."

Miss Kate did not argue the point. She put the freshly painted wooden chicken on the table to dry in the sun. Her eyes fell upon a letter bearing an American postmark and addressed to Sergeant Chester Ball, with a lot of cryptic figures and letters strung out after it, such as A. E. F. and Co. 11.

"Here's a letter for you!" She infused a lot of Glad into her voice. But Chet only cast a languid eye upon it and said, "Yeh?"

"I'll read it to you, shall I? It's a nice fat one."

Chet sat back, indifferent, negatively acquiescent. And Miss Kate began to read in her clear young voice, there in the sunshine and scent of the centuries-old English garden.

It marked an epoch in Chet's life—that letter. But before we can appreciate it we'll have to know Chester Ball in his Chicago days.

Your true lineman has a daredevil way with the women, as have all men whose calling is a hazardous one. Chet was a crack workman. He could shinny up a pole, strap his emergency belt, open his tool kit, wield his pliers with expert deftness, and climb down again in record time. It was his pleasure—and seemingly the pleasure and privilege of all lineman's gangs the world over—to whistle blithely and to call impudently to any passing petticoat that caught his fancy.

Perched three feet from the top of the high pole he would cling, protected, seemingly, by some force working in direct defiance of the law of gravity. And now and then, by way of brightening the tedium of their job he and his gang would call to a girl passing in the street below, "Hoo-Hoo! Hello, sweetheart!"

There was nothing vicious in it. Chet would have come to the aid of beauty in distress as quickly as Don Quixote. Any man with a blue shirt as clean, and a shave as smooth, and a haircut as round as Chet Ball's has no meanness in him. A certain dare-deviltry went hand in hand with his work—a calling in which a careless load dispatcher, a cut wire, or a faulty strap may mean instant death. Usually the girls laughed and called back to them or went on more quickly, the colour in their cheeks a little higher.

But not Anastasia Rourke. Early the first morning of a two-weeks' job on the new plant of the Western Castings Company Chet Ball, glancing down from his dizzy perch atop an electric light pole, espied Miss Anastasia Rourke going to work. He didn't know her name nor anything about her, except that she was pretty. You could see that from a distance even more remote than

Chet's. But you couldn't know that Stasia was a lady not to be trifled with. We know her name was Rourke, but he didn't.

So then: "Hoo-Hoo!" he had called. "Hello, sweetheart! Wait for me and I'll be down."

Stasia Rourke had lifted her face to where he perched so high above the streets. Her cheeks were five shades pinker than was their wont, which would make them border on the red.

"You big coward, you!" she called, in her clear, crisp voice. "If you had your foot on the ground you wouldn't dast call to a decent girl like that. If you were down here I'd slap the face of you. You know you're safe up there."

The words were scarcely out of her mouth before Chet Ball's sturdy legs were twinkling down the pole. His spurred heels dug into the soft pine of the pole with little ripe, tearing sounds. He walked up to Stasia and stood squarely in front of her, six feet of brawn and brazen nerve. One ruddy cheek he presented to her astonished gaze. "Hello, sweetheart," he said. And waited. The Rourke girl hesitated just a second. All the Irish heart in her was melting at the boyish impudence of the man before her. Then she lifted one hand and slapped his smooth cheek. It was a ringing slap. You saw the four marks of her fingers upon his face. Chet straightened, his blue eyes bluer.

Stasia looked up at him, her eyes wide. Then down at her own hand, as if it belonged to somebody else. Her hand came up to her own face. She burst into tears, turned, and ran. And as she ran, and as she wept, she saw that Chet was still standing there, looking after her.

Next morning, when Stasia Rourke went by to work, Chet Ball was standing at the foot of the pole, waiting.

They were to have been married that next June. But that next June Chet Ball, perched perilously on the branch of a tree in a small woodsy spot somewhere in France, was one reason why the American artillery in that same woodsy spot was getting such a deadly range on the enemy. Chet's costume was so devised that even through field glasses (made in Germany) you couldn't tell where tree left off and Chet began.

Then, quite suddenly, the Germans got the range. The tree in which Chet was hidden came down with a crash, and Chet lay there, more than ever indiscernible among its tender foliage.

Which brings us back to the English garden, the yellow chicken, Miss Kate, and the letter.

His shattered leg was mended by one of those miracles of modern war surgery, though he never again would dig his spurred heels into the pine of a G. L. & P. Company pole. But the other thing—they put it down under the broad general head of shell shock. In the lovely English garden they set him to weaving and painting, as a means of soothing the shattered nerves. He had made everything from pottery jars to bead chains; from baskets to rugs. Slowly the tortured nerves healed. But the doctors, when they stopped at Chet's cot or chair, talked always of "the memory centre." Chet seemed satisfied to go on placidly painting toys or weaving chains with his great, square-tipped fingers—the fingers that had wielded the pliers so cleverly in his pole-climbing days.

"It's just something that only luck or an accident can mend," said the nerve specialist. "Time may do it—but I doubt it. Sometimes just a word—the right word—will set the thing in motion again. Does he get any letters?"

"His girl writes to him. Fine letters. But she doesn't know yet about—about this. I've written his letters for him. She knows now that his leg is healed and she wonders——"

That had been a month ago. To-day Miss Kate slit the envelope postmarked Chicago. Chet was fingering the yellow wooden chicken, pride in his eyes. In Miss Kate's eyes there was a troubled, baffled look as she began to read:

Chet, dear, it's raining in Chicago. And you know when it rains in Chicago, it's wetter, and muddier, and rainier than

any place in the world. Except maybe this Flanders we're
reading so much about. They say for rain and mud that
place takes the prize.

I don't know what I'm going on about rain and mud for,
Chet darling, when it's you I'm thinking of. Nothing else
and nobody else. Chet, I got a funny feeling there's something you're keeping back from me. You're hurt worse than
just the leg. Boy, dear, don't you know it won't make any
difference with me how you look, or feel, or anything? I don't
care how bad you're smashed up. I'd rather have you without any features at all than any other man with two sets.
Whatever's happened to the outside of you, they can't change
your insides. And you're the same man that called out to
me, that day, "Hoo-hoo! Hello, sweetheart!" and when I gave
you a piece of my mind climbed down off the pole, and put
your face up to be slapped, God bless the boy in you——

A sharp little sound from him. Miss Kate
looked up, quickly. Chet Ball was staring at
the beady-eyed yellow chicken in his hand.

"What's this thing?" he demanded in a strange
voice.

Miss Kate answered him very quietly, trying
to keep her own voice easy and natural. "That's
a toy chicken, cut out of wood."

"What'm I doin' with it?"

"You've just finished painting it."

Chet Ball held it in his great hand and stared
at it for a brief moment, struggling between anger
and amusement. And between anger and amuse-

ment he put it down on the table none too gently and stoop up, yawning a little.

"That's a hell of a job for a he-man!" Then in utter contrition: "Oh, beggin' your pardon! That was fierce! I didn't——"

But there was nothing shocked about the expression on Miss Kate's face. She was registering joy—pure joy.

UN MORSO DOO PANG

WHEN you are twenty you do not
patronize sunsets unless you are unhappy, in love, or both. Tessie Golden
was both. Six months ago a sunset that Belasco
himself could not have improved upon had wrung
from her only a casual tribute such as: "My!
Look how red the sky is!" delivered as unemotion-
ally as a weather bulletin.

Tessie Golden sat on the top step of the back
porch now, a slim, inert heap in a cotton kimono
whose colour and design were libels on the Nippon-
ese. Her head was propped wearily against the
porch post. Her hands were limp in her lap.
Her face was turned toward the west, where shone
that mingling of orange and rose known as salmon
pink. But no answering radiance in the girl's face
met the glow in the Wisconsin sky.

Saturday night, after supper in Chippewa, Wis.,
Tessie Golden of the pre-sunset era would have
been calling from her bedroom to the kitchen:
"Ma, what'd you do with my pink georgette
waist?"

And from the kitchen: "It's in your second bureau drawer. The collar was kind of mussed from Wednesday night, and I give it a little pressing while my iron was on."

At seven-thirty Tessie would have emerged from her bedroom in the pink georgette blouse that might have been considered alarmingly frank as to texture and precariously V-cut as to neck had Tessie herself not been so reassuringly unopulent; a black taffeta skirt, lavishly shirred and very brief; white kid shoes, high-laced, whose height still failed to achieve the two inches of white silk stocking that linked skirt hem to shoe top; finally, a hat with a good deal of French blue about it.

As she passed through the sitting room on her way out her mother would appear in the doorway, dish towel in hand. Her pride in this slim young thing and her love of her she concealed with a thin layer of carping criticism.

"Runnin' downtown again, I s'pose." A keen eye on the swishing skirt hem.

Tessie, the quick-tongued, would pat the arabesque of shining hair that lay coiled so submissively against either glowing cheek. "Oh, my, no! I just thought I'd dress up in case Angie Hatton drove past in her auto and picked me up for a little ride. So's not to keep her waiting."

Angie Hatton was Old Man Hatton's daughter.

Any one in the Fox River Valley could have told
you who Old Man Hatton was. You saw his
name at the top of every letterhead of any im-
portance in Chippewa, from the Pulp and Paper
Mill to the First National Bank, and including the
watch factory, the canning works, and the Mid-
Western Land Company. Knowing this, you
were able to appreciate Tessie's sarcasm. Angie
Hatton was as unaware of Tessie's existence as
only a young woman could be whose family resi-
dence was in Chippewa, Wis., but who wintered in
Italy, summered in the mountains, and bought
(so the town said) her very hairpins in New York.
When Angie Hatton came home from the East the
town used to stroll past on Mondays to view the
washing on the Hatton line. Angie's underwear,
flirting so audaciously with the sunshine and
zephyrs, was of voile and silk and crêpe de Chine
and satin—materials that we had always thought
of heretofore as intended exclusively for party
dresses and wedding gowns. Of course two years
later they were showing practically the same thing
at Megan's dry-goods store. But that was always
the way with Angie Hatton. Even those of us
who went to Chicago to shop never quite caught
up with her.

Delivered of this ironic thrust, Tessie would
walk toward the screen door with a little flaunting

sway of the hips.　Her mother's eyes, following the
slim figure, had a sort of grudging love in them.
A spare, caustic, wiry little woman, Tessie's
mother.　Tessie resembled her as a water colour
may resemble a blurred charcoal sketch.　Tessie's
wide mouth curved into humour lines.　She was
the cut-up of the escapement department at the
watch factory; the older woman's lips sagged at
the corners.　Tessie was buoyant and colourful
with youth.　The other was shrunken and faded
with years and labour.　As the girl minced across
the room in her absurdly high-heeled white kid
shoes the older woman thought: "My, but she's
pretty!"　But she said aloud: "Them shoes
could stand a cleaning.　I should think you'd stay
home once in a while and not be runnin' the streets
every night."

"Time enough to be sittin' home when I'm old
like you."

And yet between these two there was love, and
even understanding.　But in families such as
Tessie's demonstration is a thing to be ashamed of;
affection a thing to conceal.　Tessie's father was
janitor of the Chippewa High School.　A powerful
man, slightly crippled by rheumatism, loquacious,
lively, fond of his family, proud of his neat gray
frame house, and his new cement sidewalk, and his
carefully tended yard and garden patch.　In all

her life Tessie had never seen a caress exchanged between her parents.

Nowadays Ma Golden had little occasion for finding fault with Tessie's evening diversion. She no longer had cause to say: "Always gaddin' downtown, or over to Cora's or somewhere, like you didn't have a home to stay in. You ain't been in a evening this week, 'cept when you washed your hair."

Tessie had developed a fondness for sunsets viewed from the back porch—she who had thought nothing of dancing until three and rising at half-past six to go to work.

Stepping about in the kitchen after supper, her mother would eye the limp, relaxed figure on the back porch with a little pang at her heart. She would come to the screen door, or even out to the porch on some errand or other—to empty the coffee grounds; to turn the row of half-ripe tomatoes reddening on the porch railing; to flap and hang up a damp tea towel.

"Ain't you goin' out, Tess?"

"No."

"What you want to lop around here for? Such a grand evening. Why don't you put on your things and run downtown, or over to Cora's or somewhere, h'm?"

"What for?"—listlessly.

"What for! What does anybody go out for!"

"I don't know."

If they could have talked it over together, these two, the girl might have found relief. But the family shyness of their class was too strong upon them. Once Mrs. Golden had said, in an effort at sympathy: "Person'd think Chuck Mory was the only one who'd gone to war an' the last fella left in the world."

A grim flash of the old humour lifted the corners of the wide mouth. "He is. Who's there left? Stumpy Gans, up at the railroad crossing? Or maybe Fatty Weiman, driving the hack. Guess I'll doll up this evening and see if I can't make a hit with one of them."

She relapsed into bitter silence. The bottom had dropped out of Tessie Golden's world.

In order to understand the Tessie of to-day you will have to know the Tessie of six months ago; Tessie the impudent, the life-loving, the pleasure-ful. Tessie Golden could say things to the escapement-room foreman that any one else would have been fired for. Her wide mouth was capable of glorious insolences. Whenever you heard shrieks of laughter from the girls' wash room at noon you knew that Tessie was holding forth to an admiring group. She was a born mimic; audacious, agile, and with the gift of burlesque. The autumn that Angie Hatton came home from Europe wearing the first hobble skirt that Chippewa had ever seen Tessie gave an imitation of that advanced young woman's progress down Grand Avenue in this restricted garment. The thing was cruel in its fidelity, though containing just enough exaggeration to make it artistic. She followed it up by imitating the stricken look on the face of Mattie Haynes, cloak and suit buyer at Megan's, who, having just returned from the East with what she considered the most fashionable of the new fall styles, now beheld Angie Hatton in the garb that was the last echo of the last cry in Paris modes—and no model in Mattie's newly selected stock bore even the remotest resemblance to it.

You would know from this that Tessie was not a particularly deft worker. Her big-knuckled fingers were cleverer at turning out a shirt waist or retrimming a hat. Hers were what are known as handy hands, but not sensitive. It takes a light and facile set of fingers to fit pallet and arbour and fork together: close work and tedious. Seated on low benches along the tables, their chins almost level with the table top, the girls worked with pincers and gas flame, screwing together the three tiny parts of the watch's anatomy that was their particular specialty. Each wore a jeweller's glass in one eye. Tessie had worked at the watch factory for three years, and the pressure of the glass on the eye socket had given her the slightly hollow-eyed appearance peculiar to experienced watchmakers. It was not unbecoming, though, and lent her, somehow, a spiritual look which made her diablerie all the more piquant.

Tessie wasn't always witty, really. But she had achieved a reputation for wit which insured applause for even her feebler efforts. Nap Ballou, the foreman, never left the escapement room without a little shiver of nervous apprehension—a feeling justified by the ripple of suppressed laughter that went up and down the long tables. He knew that Tessie Golden, like a naughty schoolgirl when teacher's back is turned, had directed one of her sure shafts at him.

Ballou, his face darkling, could easily have punished her. Tessie knew it. But he never did, or would. She knew that, too. Her very insolence and audacity saved her.

"Some day," Ballou would warn her, "you'll get too gay, and then you'll find yourself looking for a job."

"Go on—fire me," retorted Tessie, "and I'll meet you in Lancaster"—a form of wit appreciated only by watchmakers. For there is a certain type of watch hand who is as peripatetic as the old-time printer. Restless, ne'er-do-well, spendthrift, he wanders from factory to factory through the chain of watchmaking towns: Springfield, Trenton, Waltham, Lancaster, Waterbury, Chippewa. Usually expert, always unreliable, certainly fond of drink, Nap Ballou was typical of his kind. The steady worker had a mingled admiration and contempt for him. He, in turn, regarded the other as a stick-in-the-mud. Nap wore his cap on one side of his curly head, and drank so evenly and steadily as never to be quite drunk and never strictly sober. He had slender, sensitive fingers like an artist's or a woman's, and he knew the parts of that intricate mechanism known as a watch from the jewel to the finishing room. It was said he had a wife or two. Forty-six, good-looking in a dissolute sort of way, possessing the charm of the wanderer, generous with his money, it was known that Tessie's barbs were permitted to prick him without retaliation because Tessie herself appealed to his errant fancy.

When the other girls teased her about this obvious state of affairs something fine and contemptuous welled up in her. "Him! Why, say, he ought to work in a pickle factory instead of a watch works. All he needs is a little dill and a handful of grape leaves to make him good eatin' as a relish."

And she thought of Chuck Mory, perched on the high seat of the American Express wagon, hatless, sunburnt, stockily muscular, shouting to his horse as he galloped clattering down Winnebago Street on his way to the depot and the 7.50 train.

I suppose there was something about the clear simplicity and uprightness of the firm little figure that appealed to Nap Ballou. He used to regard her curiously with a long, hard gaze before which she would grow uncomfortable. "Think you'll know me next time you see me?" But there was an uneasy feeling beneath her flip exterior. Not that there was anything of the beautiful, persecuted factory girl and villainous foreman about the situation. Tessie worked at watchmaking because it was light, pleasant, and well paid. She could have found another job for the asking. Her money went for white shoes and pink blouses and lacy boudoir caps which she affected Sunday mornings. She was forever buying a vivid necktie for her father and dressing up her protesting mother in gay colours that went ill with the drab, wrinkled face. "If it wasn't for me, you'd go round looking like one of those Polack women down by the tracks," Tessie would scold. "It's a wonder you don't wear a shawl!"

That was the Tessie of six months ago, gay, care-free, holding the reins of her life in her own

two capable hands. Three nights a week, and
Sunday, she saw Chuck Mory. When she went
downtown on Saturday night it was frankly to
meet Chuck, who was waiting for her on Schroeder's drug-store corner. He knew it, and she
knew it. Yet they always went through a little
ceremony. She and Cora, turning into Grand
from Winnebago Street, would make for the post
office. Then down the length of Grand with a
leaping glance at Schroeder's corner before they
reached it. Yes, there they were, very clean-
shaven, clean-shirted, slick looking. Tessie would
have known Chuck's blond head among a thousand. An air of studied hauteur and indifference
as they approached the corner. Heads turned the
other way. A low whistle from the boys.

"Oh, how do!"

"Good evening!"

Both greetings done with careful surprise.
Then on down the street. On the way back you
took the inside of the walk, and your hauteur was
now stony to the point of insult. Schroeder's
corner simply did not exist. On as far as Megan's
which you entered and inspected, up one brightly
lighted aisle and down the next. At the dress-
goods counter there was a neat little stack of
pamphlets entitled "In the World of Fashion."
You took one and sauntered out leisurely. Down

Winnebago Street now, homeward bound, talking animatedly and seemingly unconscious of quick footsteps sounding nearer and nearer. Just past the Burke House, where the residential district began, and where the trees cast their kindly shadows: "Can I see you home?" A hand slipped through her arm; a little tingling thrill.

"Oh, why, how do, Chuck! Hello, Scotty. Sure, if you're going our way."

At every turn Chuck left her side and dashed around behind her in order to place himself at her right again, according to the rigid rule of Chippewa etiquette. He took her arm only at street crossings until they reached the tracks, which perilous spot seemed to justify him in retaining his hold throughout the remainder of the stroll. Usually they lost Cora and Scotty without having been conscious of their loss.

Their talk? The girls and boys that each knew; the day's happenings at factory and express office; next Wednesday night's dance up in the Chute; and always the possibility of Chuck's leaving the wagon and assuming the managership of the office.

"Don't let this go any further, see? But I heard it straight that old Benke is goin' to be transferred to Fond du Lac. And if he is, why, I step in, see? Benke's got a girl in Fondy, and he's been pluggin' to get there. Gee, maybe I won't be glad when he does!" A little silence. "Will you be glad, Tess? H'm?"

Tess felt herself glowing and shivering as the big hand closed more tightly on her arm. "Me? Why, sure I'll be pleased to see you get a job that's coming to you by rights, and that'll get you better pay, and all."

But she knew what he meant, and he knew she knew. And the clasp tightened until it hurt her, and she was glad.

No more of that now. Chuck—gone. Scotty —gone. All the boys at the watch works, all the fellows in the neighbourhood—gone. At first she hadn't minded. It was exciting. You kidded them at first: "Well, believe me, Chuck, if you shoot the way you play ball, you're a gone goose already."

"All you got to do, Scotty, is to stick that face of yours up over the top of the trench and the Germans'll die of fright an' save you wastin' bullets."

There was a great knitting of socks and sweaters and caps. Tessie's big-knuckled, capable fingers made you dizzy, they flew so fast. Chuck was outfitted as for a polar expedition. Tess took half a day off to bid him good-bye. They marched down Grand Avenue, that first lot of them, in their every-

day suits and hats, with their shiny yellow suitcases and their paste-board boxes in their hands,
sheepish, red-faced, awkward. In their eyes,
though, a certain look. And so off for Camp
Sherman, their young heads sticking out of the car
windows in clusters—black, yellow, brown, red.
But for each woman on the depot platform there
was just one head. Tessie saw a blurred blond one
with a misty halo around it. A great shouting and
waving of handkerchiefs:

"Goo'-bye! Goo'-bye! Write, now! Be sure!
Mebbe you can get off in a week, for a visit.
Goo'-bye! Goo——"

They were gone. Their voices came back to
the crowd on the depot platform—high, clear
young voices; almost like the voices of children,
shouting.

Well, you wrote letters; fat, bulging letters, and
in turn you received equally plump envelopes with
a red triangle in one corner. You sent boxes of
homemade fudge (nut variety) and cookies and the
more durable forms of cake.

Then, unaccountably, Chuck was whisked all the
way to California. He was furious at parting with
his mates, and his indignation was expressed in his
letters to Tessie. She sympathized with him in
her replies. She tried to make light of it, but there
was a little clutch of terror in it, too. California!

My land! Might as well send a person to the end
of the world while they were about it. Two
months of that. Then, inexplicably again,
Chuck's letters bore the astounding postmark of
New York. She thought, in a panic, that he was
Franceward bound, but it turned out not to be so.
Not yet. Chuck's letters were taking on a cosmo-
politan tone. "Well," he wrote, "I guess the
little old town is as dead as ever. It seems funny
you being right there all this time and I've travelled
from the Atlantic to the Pacific. Everybody
treats me swell. You ought to seen some of those
California houses. They make Hatton's place
look sick."

The girls, Cora and Tess and the rest, laughed
and joked among themselves and assured one another, with a toss of the head, that they could have
a good time without the fellas. They didn't need
boys around. Well, I should say not!

They gave parties, and they were not a success.
There was one of the type known as a stag. They
dressed up in their brother's clothes, or their
father's or a neighbour boy's, and met at Cora's.
They looked as knock-kneed and slope-shouldered
and unmasculine as girls usually do in men's attire.
All except Tessie. There was something so as-
tonishingly boyish and straight about her; she
swaggered about with such a mannish swing of the

leg (that was the actress in her) that the girls flushed a little and said: "Honest, Tess, if I didn't know you was a girl, I'd be stuck on you. With that hat on a person wouldn't know you from a boy."

Tessie would cross one slim leg over the other and bestow a knowing wink upon the speaker. "Some hen party!" they all said. They danced to the music of the victrola and sang "Over There." They had ice cream and chocolate layer cake and went home in great hilarity, with their hands on each other's shoulders, still singing. When they met a passer-by they giggled and shrieked and ran.

But the thing was a failure, and they knew it. Next day, at the lunch hour and in the wash room, there was a little desultory talk about the stag. But the meat of such an aftergathering is contained in phrases such as "I says t' him" and "He says t' me." They wasted little conversation on the stag. It was much more exciting to exhibit letters on blue-lined paper with the red triangle at the top. Chuck's last letter had contained the news of his sergeancy.

Angie Hatton, home from the East, was writing letters, too. Everyone in Chippewa knew that. She wrote on that new art paper with the gnawed looking edges and stiff as a newly laundered cuff.

But the letters which she awaited so eagerly were written on the same sort of paper as were those Tessie had from Chuck: blue-lined, cheap in quality, a red triangle at one corner. A New York fellow, Chippewa learned; an aviator. They knew, too, that young Hatton was an infantry lieutenant somewhere in the East. These letters were not from him.

Ever since her home-coming Angie had been sewing at the Red Cross shop on Grand Avenue. Chippewa boasted two Red Cross shops. The Grand Avenue shop was the society shop. The East-End crowd sewed there, capped, veiled, aproned—and unapproachable. Were your fingers ever so deft, your knowledge of seams and basting mathematical, your skill with that complicated garment known as a pneumonia jacket uncanny; if you did not belong to the East-End set, you did not sew at the Grand Avenue shop. No matter how grossly red the blood which the Grand Avenue bandages and pads were ultimately to stanch, the liquid in the fingers that rolled and folded them was pure cerulean.

Tessie and her crowd had never thought of giving any such service to their country. They spoke of the Grand Avenue workers as "that stinkin' bunch," I regret to say. Yet each one of the girls was capable of starting a shirt waist in an emergency on Saturday night and finishing it in time for a Sunday picnic, buttonholes and all. Their help might have been invaluable. It never was asked.

Without warning Chuck came home on three days' leave. It meant that he was bound for France right enough this time. But Tessie didn't care.

"I don't care where you're goin'," she said, exultantly, her eyes lingering on the stocky, straight, powerful figure in its rather ill-fitting khaki. "You're here now. That's enough. Ain't you tickled to be home, Chuck? Gee!"

"I sh'd say," responded Chuck. But even he seemed to detect some lack in his tone and words. He elaborated somewhat shamefacedly: "Sure. It's swell to be home. But I don't know. After you've travelled around, and come back, things look so kind of little to you. I don't know—kind of——" he floundered about at a loss for expression. Then tried again: "Now, take Hatton's place, f'r example. I always used to think it was a regular palace, but, gosh, you ought to see places where I was asked in San Francisco and around there. Why, they was—were—enough to make the Hatton house look like a shack. Swimmin' pools of white marble, and acres of yard like a

park, and a Jap help always bringin' you something to eat or drink. And the folks themselves—
why, say! Here we are scrapin' and bowin' to
Hattons and that bunch. They're pikers to what
some people are that invited me to their houses in
New York and Berkeley, and treated me and the
other guys like kings or something. Take Megan's store, too"—he was warming to his subject,
so that he failed to notice the darkening of Tessie's
face—"it's a joke compared to New York and
San Francisco stores. Reg'lar rube joint."

Tessie stiffened. Her teeth were set, her eyes
sparkled. She tossed her head. "Well, I'm sure,
Mr. Mory, it's good enough for me. Too bad you
had to come home at all now you're so elegant and
swell, and everything. You better go call on
Angie Hatton instead of wastin' time on me.
She'd probably be tickled to see you."

He stumbled to his feet, then, awkwardly.
"Aw, say, Tessie, I didn't mean—why, say—you
don't suppose—why, believe me, I pretty near
busted out cryin' when I saw the Junction eatin'
house when my train came in. And I been
thinkin' of you every minute. There wasn't a
day——"

"Tell that to your swell New York friends. I
may be a rube, but I ain't a fool." She was
perilously near to tears.

"Why, say, Tess, listen! Listen! If you knew
—if you knew—a guy's got to—he's got no right
to——"

And presently Tessie was mollified, but only on
the surface. She smiled and glanced and teased
and sparkled. And beneath was terror. He
talked differently. He walked differently. It
wasn't his clothes or the army. It was something
else—an ease of manner, a new leisureliness of
glance, an air. Once Tessie had gone to Milwaukee over Labour Day. It was the extent of
her experience as a traveller. She remembered
how superior she had felt for at least two days
after. But Chuck! California! New York! It
wasn't the distance that terrified her. It was
his new knowledge, the broadening of his vision,
though she did not know it and certainly could not
have put it into words.

They went walking down by the river to Oneida
Springs, and drank some of the sulphur water that
tasted like rotten eggs. Tessie drank it with little
shrieks and shudders and puckered her face up into
an expression indicative of extreme disgust.

"It's good for you," Chuck said, and drank three
cups of it, manfully. "That taste is the mineral
qualities the water contains—sulphur and iron and
so forth."

"I don't care," snapped Tessie, irritably. "I

hate it!" They had often walked along the river and tasted of the spring water, but Chuck had never before waxed scientific. They took a boat at Baumann's boathouse and drifted down the lovely Fox River.

"Want to row?" Chuck asked. "I'll get an extra pair of oars if you do."

"I don't know how. Besides, it's too much work. I guess I'll let you do it."

Chuck was fitting his oars in the oarlocks. She stood on the landing looking down at him. His hat was off. His hair seemed blonder than ever against the rich tan of his face. His neck muscles swelled a little as he bent. Tessie felt a great longing to bury her face in the warm red skin. He straightened with a sigh and smiled at her. "I'll be ready in a minute." He took off his coat and turned his khaki shirt in at the throat, so that you saw the white, clean line of his untanned chest in strange contrast to his sunburnt throat. A feeling of giddy faintness surged over Tessie. She stepped blindly into the boat and would have fallen if Chuck's hard, firm grip had not steadied her. "Whoa, there! Don't you know how to step into a boat? There. Walk along the middle." She sat down and smiled up at him. "I don't know how I come to do that. I never did before."

Chuck braced his feet, rolled up his sleeves, and

took an oar in each brown hand, bending rhythmically to his task.   He looked about him, then at the
girl, and drew a deep breath, feathering his oars.
"I guess I must have dreamed about this more'n a
million times."

"Have you, Chuck?"

They drifted on in silence.   "Say, Tess, you
ought to learn to row.   It's good exercise.   Those
girls in California and New York, they play baseball and row and swim as good as the boys.
Honest, some of 'em are wonders!"

"Oh, I'm sick of your swell New York friends!
Can't you talk about something else?"

He saw that he had blundered without in the
least understanding how or why.   "All right.
What'll we talk about?"   In itself a fatal admission.

"About—you."   Tessie made it a caress.

"Me?   Nothin' to tell about me.   I just been
drillin' and studyin' and marchin' and readin'
some——   Oh, say, what d'you think?"

"What?"

"They been learnin' us—teachin' us, I mean—
French.   It's the darnedest language!   Bread is
pain.   Can you beat that?   If you want to ask
for a piece of bread, you say like this: *Donnay
ma un morso doo pang.*   See?"

"My!" breathed Tessie, all admiration.

And within her something was screaming: "Oh, my God! Oh, my God! He knows French. And those girls that can row and everything. And me, I don't know anything. Oh, God, what'll I do?"

It was as though she could see him slipping away from her, out of her grasp, out of her sight. She had no fear of what might come to him in France. Bullets and bayonets would never hurt Chuck. He'd make it, just as he always made the 7.50 when it seemed as if he was going to miss it sure. He'd make it there and back, all right. But he—he'd be a different Chuck, while she stayed the same Tessie. Books, travel, French, girls, swell folks——

And all the while she was smiling and dimpling and trailing her hand in the water. "Bet you can't guess what I got in that lunch box."

"Chocolate cake."

"Well, of course I've got chocolate cake. I baked it myself this morning."

"Yes, you did!"

"Why, Chuck Mory, I did so! I guess you think I can't do anything, the way you talk."

"Oh, don't I! I guess you know what I think."

"Well, it isn't the cake I mean. It's something else."

"Fried chicken!"

"Oh, now you've gone and guessed it." She pouted prettily.

"You asked me to, didn't you?"

Then they laughed together, as at something exquisitely witty.

Down the river, drifting, rowing. Tessie pointed to a house half hidden among the trees on the farther shore: "There's Hatton's camp. They say they have grand times there with their swell crowd some Saturdays and Sundays. If I had a house like that, I'd live in it all the time, not just a couple of days out of the whole year." She hesitated a moment. "I suppose it looks like a shanty to you now."

Chuck surveyed it, patronizingly. "No, it's a nice little place."

They beached their boat, and built a little fire, and had supper on the river bank, and Tessie picked out the choice bits for him—the breast of the chicken, beautifully golden brown; the ripest tomato; the firmest, juiciest pickle; the corner of the little cake which would give him a double share of icing. She may not have been versed in French, Tessie, but she was wise in feminine wiles.

From Chuck, between mouthfuls: "I guess you don't know how good this tastes. Camp grub's all right, but after you've had a few months of it you get so you don't believe there *is* such a thing as fried chicken and chocolate cake."

"I'm glad you like it, Chuck. Here, take this drumstick. You ain't eating a thing!" His fourth piece of chicken.

Down the river as far as the danger line just above the dam, with Tessie pretending fear just for the joy of having Chuck reassure her. Then back again in the dusk, Chuck bending to the task now against the current. And so up the hill homeward bound. They walked very slowly, Chuck's hand on her arm. They were dumb with the tragic, eloquent dumbness of their kind. If she could have spoken the words that were churning in her mind, they would have been something like this:

"Oh, Chuck, I wish I was married to you. I wouldn't care if only I had you. I wouldn't mind babies or anything. I'd be glad. I want our house, with a dining-room set, and a brass bed, and a mahogany table in the parlour, and all the housework to do. I'm scared. I'm scared I won't get it. What'll I do if I don't?"

And he, wordlessly: "Will you wait for me, Tessie, and keep on loving me and thinking of me? And will you keep yourself clean in mind and body so that if I come back———"

Aloud, she said: "I guess you'll get stuck on one of those French girls. I should worry! They say wages at the watch factory are going to be raised, workers are so scarce. I'll prob'ly be as rich as Angie Hatton time you get back."

And he, miserably: "Little old Chippewa girls are good enough for Chuck. I ain't counting on taking up with those Frenchies. I don't like their jabber, from what I know of it. I saw some pictures of 'em, last week, a fellow in camp had who'd been over there. Their hair is all funny, and fixed up with combs and stuff, and they look real dark like foreigners. Nix!"

It had been reassuring enough at the time. But that was six months ago. Which brings us to the Tessie who sat on the back porch, evenings, surveying the sunset. A listless, lackadaisical, brooding Tessie. Little point to going downtown Saturday nights now. There was no familiar, beloved figure to follow you swiftly as you turned off Elm Street, homeward bound. If she went downtown now, she saw only those Saturday-night family groups which are familiar to every small town. The husband, very wet as to hair and clean as to shirt, guarding the gocart outside while the woman accomplished her Saturday-night trading at Ding's or Halpin's. Sometimes there were as many as half a dozen gocarts outside Halpin's, each containing a sleeping burden, relaxed, chubby, fat-cheeked. The waiting men smoked their pipes and conversed largely. "Hello, Ed. Th' woman's inside, buyin' the store out, I guess."

"Tha' so? Mine, too. Well, how's everything?"

Tessie knew that presently the woman would come out, bundle laden, and that she would stow these lesser bundles in every corner left available by the more important sleeping bundle—two yards of goods; a spool of 100, white; a banana for the baby; a new stewpan at the Five-and-Ten.

There had been a time when Tessie, if she thought of these women at all, felt sorry for them; worn, drab, lacking in style and figure. Now she envied them. For the maternal may be strong at twenty.

There were weeks upon weeks when no letter came from Chuck. In his last letter there had been some talk of his being sent to Russia. Tessie's eyes, large enough now in her thin face, distended with a great fear. Russia! His letter spoke, too, of French villages and châteaux. He and a bunch of fellows had been introduced to a princess or a countess or something—it was all one to Tessie—and what do you think? She had kissed them all on both cheeks! Seems that's the way they did in France.

The morning after the receipt of this letter the girls at the watch factory might have remarked her pallor had they not been so occupied with a new and more absorbing topic.

"Tess, did you hear about Angie Hatton?"

"What about her?"

"She's going to France. It's in the Milwaukee paper, all about her being Chippewa's fairest daughter, and a picture of the house, and her being the belle of the Fox River Valley, and she's giving up her palatial home and all to go to work in a Y. M. C. A. canteen for her country and bleeding France."

"Ya-as she is!" sneered Tessie, and a dull red flush, so deep as to be painful, swept over her face from throat to brow. "Ya-as she is, the doll-faced simp! Why, say, she never wiped up a floor in her life, or baked a cake, or stood on them feet of hers. She couldn't cut up a loaf of bread decent. Bleedin' France! Ha! That's rich, that is." She thrust her chin out brutally, and her eyes narrowed to slits. "She's goin' over there after that fella of hers. She's chasin' him. It's now or never, and she knows it and she's scared, same's the rest of us. On'y we got to set home and make the best of it. Or take what's left."

She turned her head slowly to where Nap Ballou stood over a table at the far end of the room. She laughed a grim, unlovely little laugh. "I guess when you can't go after what you want, like Angie, why, you gotta take second choice."

All that day, at the bench, she was the reckless, insolent, audacious Tessie of six months ago. Nap Ballou was always standing over her, pretending to inspect some bit of work or other, his shoulder brushing hers. She laughed up at him so that her face was not more than two inches from his. He flushed, but she did not. She laughed a reckless little laugh.

"Thanks for helpin' teach me my trade, Mr. Ballou. 'Course I only been at it over three years now, so I ain't got the hang of it yet."

He straightened up slowly, and as he did so he rested a hand on her shoulder for a brief moment. She did not shrug it off.

That night, after supper, Tessie put on her hat and strolled down to Park Avenue. It wasn't for the walk. Tessie had never been told to exercise systematically for her body's good, or her mind's. She went in a spirit of unwholesome, brooding curiosity and a bitter resentment. Going to France, was she? Lots of good she'd do there. Better stay home and—and what? Tessie cast about in her mind for a fitting job for Angie. Guess she might's well go, after all. Nobody'd miss her, unless it was her father, and he didn't see her but about a third of the time. But in Tessie's heart was a great envy for this girl who could bridge the hideous waste of ocean that separated her from her man. Bleedin' France. Yeh! Joke!

The Hatton place, built and landscaped twenty years before, occupied a square block in solitary grandeur, the show place of Chippewa. In architectural style it was an impartial mixture of Norman castle, French château, and Rhenish Schloss, with a dash of Coney Island about its façade. It represented Old Man Hatton's realized dream of landed magnificence.

Tessie, walking slowly past it, and peering through the high iron fence, could not help noting an air of unwonted excitement about the place, usually so aloof, so coldly serene. Automobiles standing out in front. People going up and down. They didn't look very cheerful. Just as if it mattered whether anything happened to her or not!

Tessie walked around the block and stood a moment, uncertainly. Then she struck off down Grand Avenue and past Donovan's pool shack. A little group of after-supper idlers stood outside,

smoking and gossiping, as she knew there would be.
As she turned the corner she saw Nap Ballou
among them. She had known that, too. As she
passed she looked straight ahead, without bowing.
But just past the Burke House he caught up to
her. No half-shy "Can I walk home with you?"
from Nap Ballou. No. Instead: "Hello, sweetheart!"

"Hello, yourself."

"Somebody's looking mighty pretty this evening, all dolled up in pink."

"Think so?"

She tried to be pertly indifferent, but it was
good to have someone following, someone walking
home with you. What if he was old enough to be
her father, with graying hair? Lots of the movie
heroes had graying hair at the sides. Twenty
craves someone to tell it how wonderful it is.
And Nap Ballou told her.

They walked for an hour. Tessie left him at the
corner. She had once heard her father designate
Ballou as "that drunken skunk." When she
entered the sitting room her cheeks held an unwonted pink. Her eyes were brighter than they
had been in months. Her mother looked up
quickly, peering at her over a pair of steel-rimmed
spectacles, very much askew.

"Where you been, Tessie?"

"Oh, walkin'."

"Who with?"

"Cora."

"Why, she was here, callin' for you, not more'n an hour ago."

Tessie, taking the hatpins out of her hat on her way upstairs, met this coolly. "Yeh, I ran into her comin' back."

Upstairs, lying fully dressed on her hard little bed, she stared up into the darkness, thinking, her hands limp at her sides. Oh, well, what's the diff? You had to make the best of it. Everybody makin' a fuss about the soldiers: feedin' 'em, and askin' 'em to their houses, and sendin' 'em things, and givin' dances and picnics and parties so they wouldn't be lonesome. Chuck had told her all about it. The other boys told the same. They could just pick and choose their good times. Tessie's mind groped about, sensing a certain injustice. How about the girls? She didn't put it thus squarely. Hers was not a logical mind, trained to think. Easy enough to paw over the menfolks and get silly over brass buttons and a uniform. She put it that way. She thought of the refrain of a popular song: "What Are You Going to Do to Help the Boys?" Tessie, smiling a crooked little smile up there in the darkness, parodied the words deftly: "What're you going to do to help the girls?" she demanded. "What're you going to do——" She rolled over on one side and buried her head in her arms.

There was news again next morning at the watch factory. Tessie of the old days had never needed to depend on the other girls for the latest bit of gossip. Her alert eye and quick ear had always caught it first. But of late she had led a cloistered existence, indifferent to the world about her. The Chippewa *Courier* went into the newspaper pile behind the kitchen door without a glance from Tessie's incurious eye.

She was late this morning. As she sat down at the bench and fitted her glass in her eye the chatter of the others, pitched in the high key of unusual excitement, penetrated even her listlessness.

"An' they say she never screeched or fainted or anything. She stood there, kind of quiet, lookin' straight ahead, and then all of a sudden she ran to her pa——"

"Both comin' at once, like that——"

"I feel sorry for her. She never did anything to me. She——"

Tessie spoke, her voice penetrating the staccato fragments all about her and gathering them into a whole. "Say, who's the heroine of this picture? Somebody flash me a cut-in so I can kinda follow the story.   I come in in the middle of the reel, I guess."

They turned on her with the unlovely eagerness of those who have ugly news to tell.   They all spoke at once, in short sentences, their voices high with the note of hysteria.

"Angie Hatton's beau was killed——"

"They say his aireoplane fell ten thousan' feet——"

"The news come only last evenin' about eight——"

"She won't see nobody but her pa——"

Eight!   At eight Tessie had been standing outside Hatton's house envying Angie and hating her. So that explained the people, and the automobiles, and the excitement.   Tessie was not receiving the news with the dramatic reaction which its purveyors felt it deserved.   Tessie, turning from one to the other quietly, had said nothing.   She was pitying Angie.   Oh, the luxury of it!   Nap Ballou, coming in swiftly to still the unwonted commotion in work hours, found Tessie the only one quietly occupied in that chatter-filled room.   She was smiling as she worked.   Nap Ballou, bending over her on some pretence that deceived no one, spoke low-voiced in her ear.   But she veiled her eyes insolently and did not glance up.   She hummed contentedly all the morning at her tedious work.

She had promised Nap Ballou to go picnicking with him Sunday. Down the river, boating, with supper on shore. The small, still voice within her had said: "Don't go! Don't go!" But the harsh, high-pitched, reckless overtone said: "Go on! Have a good time. Take all you can get."

She would have to lie at home and she did it. Some fabrication about the girls at the watch works did the trick. Fried chicken, chocolate cake. She packed them deftly and daintily. High-heeled white kid shoes, flimsy blouse, rustling skirt. Nap Ballou was waiting for her over in the city park. She saw him before he espied her. He was leaning against a tree idly, staring straight ahead with queer, lack-lustre eyes. Silhouetted there against the tender green of the pretty square he looked very old, somehow, and different—much older than he looked in his shop clothes, issuing orders. Tessie noticed that he sagged where he should have stuck out, and protruded where he should have been flat. There flashed across her mind a vividly clear picture of Chuck as she had last seen him: brown, fit, high of chest, flat of stomach, slim of flank.

Ballou saw her. He straightened and came toward her swiftly: "Somebody looks mighty sweet this afternoon."

Tessie plumped the heavy lunch box into his

arms. "When you get a line you like you stick to it, don't you?"

Down at the boathouse even Tessie, who had confessed ignorance of boats and oars, knew that Ballou was fumbling clumsily. He stooped to adjust the oars to the oarlocks. His hat was off. His hair looked very gray in the cruel spring sunshine. He straightened and smiled up at her.

"Ready in a minute, sweetheart," he said. He took off his collar and turned in the neckband of his shirt. His skin was very white. Tessie felt a little shudder of disgust sweep over her, so that she stumbled a little as she stepped into the boat.

The river was very lovely. Tessie trailed her fingers in the water and told herself that she was having a grand time. She told Nap the same when he asked her.

"Having a good time, little beauty?" he said. He was puffing a little with the unwonted exercise. Alcohol-atrophied muscles do not take kindly to rowing.

Tessie tried some of her old-time pertness of speech. "Oh, good enough, considerin' the company."

He laughed, admiringly, at that and said she was a card.

When the early evening came on they made a clumsy landing and had supper. This time Nap fed her the titbits, though she protested. "White meat for you," he said, "with your skin like milk."

"You must of read that in a book," scoffed Tessie. She glanced around her at the deepening shadows. "We haven't got much time. It gets dark so early."

"No hurry," Nap assured her. He went on eating in a leisurely, finicking sort of way, though he consumed very little food actually.

"You're not eating much," Tessie said once, half-heartedly. She decided that she wasn't having such a very grand time, after all, and that she hated his teeth, which were very bad. Now, Chuck's strong, white double row——

"Well," she said, "let's be going."

"No hurry," again.

Tessie looked up at that with the instinctive fear of her kind. "What d'you mean, no hurry! 'Spect to stay here till dark?" She laughed at her own joke.

"Yes."

She got up then, the blood in her face. "Well, *I* don't."

He rose, too. "Why not?"

"Because I don't, that's why." She stooped and began picking up the remnants of the lunch, placing spoons and glass bottles swiftly and thriftily in the lunch box. Nap stepped around behind her.

"Let me help," he said. And then his arm was about her and his face was close to hers, and Tessie did not like it. He kissed her after a little wordless struggle. And then she knew. Tessie's lips were not virgin. She had been kissed before. But not like this. Not like this! She struck at him furiously. Across her mind flashed the memory of a girl who had worked in the finishing room. A nice girl, too. But that hadn't helped her. Nap Ballou was laughing a little as he clasped her.

At that she heard herself saying: "I'll get Chuck Mory after you—you drunken bum, you! He'll lick you black and blue. He'll——"

The face, with the ugly, broken brown teeth, was coming close again. With all the young strength that was in her she freed one hand and clawed at that face from eyes to chin. A howl of pain rewarded her. His hold loosened. Like a flash she was off. She ran. It seemed to her that her feet did not touch the earth. Over brush, through bushes, crashing against trees, on and on. She heard him following her, but the broken-down engine that was his heart refused to do the work. She ran on, though her fear was as

great as before. Fear of what might have happened . . . to her, Tessie Golden . . .
that nobody could even talk fresh to. She gave a
little sob of fury and fatigue. She was stumbling
now. It was growing dark. She ran on again, in
fear of the overtaking darkness. It was easier
now. Not so many trees and bushes. She came
to a fence, climbed over it, lurched as she landed,
leaned against it weakly for support, one hand on
her aching heart. Before her was the Hatton
summer cottage, dimly outlined in the twilight
among the trees. A warm, flickering light danced
in the window.

Tessie stood a moment, breathing painfully,
sobbingly. Then, with a little instinctive gesture,
she patted her hair, tidied her blouse, and walked
uncertainly toward the house, up the steps to the
door. She stood there a moment, swaying slightly.
Somebody'd be there. The light. The woman
who cooked for them or the man who took care of
the place. Somebody'd——

She knocked at the door feebly. She'd tell 'em
she had lost her way and got scared when it began
to get dark. She knocked again, louder now.
Footsteps. She braced herself and even arranged
a crooked smile. The door opened wide. Old
Man Hatton!

She looked up at him, terror and relief in her

face. He peered over his glasses at her. "Who is it?" Tessie had not known, somehow, that his face was so kindly.

Tessie's carefully planned story crumbled into nothingness. "It's me!" she whimpered. "It's me!"

He reached out and put a hand on her arm and drew her inside.

"Angie! Angie! Here's a poor little kid——"

Tessie clutched frantically at the last crumbs of her pride. She tried to straighten, to smile with her old bravado. What was that story she had planned to tell?

"Who is it, dad? Who——?" Angie Hatton came into the hallway. She stared at Angie. Then: "Why, my dear!" she said. "My dear! Come in here."

Angie Hatton! Tessie began to cry weakly, her face buried in Angie Hatton's expensive blouse. Tessie remembered later that she had felt no surprise at the act.

"There, there!" Angie Hatton was saying. "Just poke up the fire, dad. And get something from the dining room. Oh, I don't know. To drink, you know. Something——"

Then Old Man Hatton stood over her, holding a small glass to her lips. Tessie drank it obediently, made a wry little face, coughed, wiped her eyes, and sat up. She looked from one to the other, like a trapped little animal. She put a hand to her tousled head.

"That's all right," Angie Hatton assured her. "You can fix it after a while."

There they were, the three of them: Old Man Hatton with his back to the fire, looking benignly down upon her; Angie seated, with some knitting in her hands, as if entertaining bedraggled, tearstained young ladies at dusk were an everyday occurrence; Tessie, twisting her handkerchief in a torment of embarrassment. But they asked no questions, these two. They evinced no curiosity about this dishevelled creature who had flung herself in upon their decent solitude.

Tessie stared at the fire. She looked up at Old Man Hatton's face and opened her lips. She looked down and shut them again. Then she flashed a quick look at Angie, to see if she could detect there some suspicion, some disdain. None. Angie Hatton looked—well, Tessie put it to herself, thus: "She looks like she'd cried till she couldn't cry no more—only inside."

And then, surprisingly, Tessie began to talk. "I wouldn't never have gone with this fella, only Chuck, he was gone. All the boys're gone. It's fierce. You get scared, sittin' home, waitin', and

they're in France and everywheres, learnin' French
and everything, and meetin' grand people and
havin' a fuss made over 'em. So I got mad and
said I didn't care, I wasn't goin' to squat home all
my life, waitin'——"

Angie Hatton had stopped knitting now. Old
Man Hatton was looking down at her very kindly.
And so Tessie went on. The pent-up emotions
and thoughts of these past months were finding an
outlet at last. These things which she had never
been able to discuss with her mother she now was
laying bare to Angie Hatton and Old Man Hatton!
They asked no questions. They seemed to understand. Once Old Man Hatton interrupted with:
"So that's the kind of fellow they've got as escapement-room foreman, eh?"

Tessie, whose mind was working very clearly
now, put out a quick hand. "Say, it wasn't his
fault. He's a bum, all right, but I knew it, didn't
I? It was me. I didn't care. Seemed to me it
didn't make no difference who I went with, but it
does." She looked down at her hands clasped so
tightly in her lap.

"Yes, it makes a whole lot of difference," Angie
agreed, and looked up at her father.

At that Tessie blurted her last desperate problem: "He's learnin' all kind of new things. Me,
I ain't learnin' anything. When Chuck comes

home he'll just think I'm dumb, that's all.
He——"

"What kind of thing would you like to learn,
Tessie, so that when Chuck comes home——"

Tessie looked up then, her wide mouth quivering
with eagerness. "I'd like to learn to swim—and
row a boat—and play ball—like the rich girls—
like the girls that's makin' such a fuss over the
soldiers."

Angie Hatton was not laughing. So, after a
moment's hesitation, Tessie brought out the worst
of it. "And French. I'd like to learn to talk
French."

Old Man Hatton had been surveying his shoes,
his mouth grim. He looked at Angie now and
smiled a little. "Well, Angie, it looks as if you'd
found your job right here at home, doesn't it?
This young lady's just one of hundreds, I suppose.
Hundreds. You can have the whole house for
them, if you want it, Angie, and the grounds, and
all the money you need. I guess we've kind of
overlooked the girls. H'm, Angie. What d'you
say?"

But Tessie was not listening. She had scarcely
heard. Her face was white with earnestness.

"C'n you speak French?"

"Yes," Angie answered.

"Well," said Tessie, and gulped once, "well,

how do you say in French: 'Give me a piece of bread'? That's what I want to learn first."

Angie Hatton said it correctly.

"That's it! Wait a minute! Say it again, will you?"

Angie said it again.

Tessie wet her lips. Her cheeks were smeared with tears and dirt. Her hair was wild and her blouse awry. "Donnay-ma-un-morso-doo-pang," she articulated, painfully. And in that moment, as she put her hand in that of Chuck Mory, across the ocean, her face was very beautiful to see.

ONE HUNDRED PER CENT

THEY had always had two morning papers— he his, she hers. The *Times*. Both. Nothing could illustrate more clearly the plan on which Mr. and Mrs. T. A. Buck conducted their married life. Theirs was the morning calm and harmony which comes to two people who are free to digest breakfast and the First Page simultaneously with no—"Just let me see the inside sheet, will you, dear?" to mar the day's beginning.

In the days when she had been Mrs. Emma McChesney, travelling saleswoman for the T. A. Buck Featherloom Petticoat Company, New York, her perusal of the morning's news had been, perforce, a hasty process, accomplished between trains, or in a small-town hotel 'bus, jolting its way to the depot for the 7.52; or over an American-plan breakfast throughout which seven eighths of her mind was intent on the purchasing possibilities of a prospective nine o'clock skirt buyer. There was no need now of haste, but the habit of years still clung. From eight-thirty to eight thirty-five A. M. Emma McChesney Buck was always in partial eclipse behind the billowing pages of her newspaper.

Only the tip of her topmost coil of bright hair was visible. She read swiftly, darting from war news to health hints, from stock market to sport page, and finding something of interest in each. For her there was nothing cryptic in a headline such as "Rudie Slams One Home"; and Do pfd followed by dotted lines and vulgar fractions were to her as easily translated as the Daily Hint From Paris. Hers was the photographic eye and the alert brain that can film a column or a page at a glance.

Across the table her husband sat turned slightly sidewise in his chair, his paper folded in a tidy oblong. He read down one column, top of the next and down that, seriously and methodically; giving to toast or coffee-cup the single-handed and groping attention of one whose interest is elsewhere. The light from the big bay window fell on the printed page and cameoed his profile. After three years of daily contact with it, Emma still caught herself occasionally gazing with appreciation at that clear-cut profile and the clean, shining line of his hair as it grew away from the temple.

"T. A.," she had announced one morning, to his mystification, "you're the Francis X. Bushman of the breakfast table. I believe you sit that way purposely."

"Francis X——?" He was not a follower of the films.

Emma elucidated. "Discoverer and world's champion exponent of the side face."

"I might punish you, Emma, by making a pun about its all being Greek to me, but I shan't." He returned to Page Two, Column Four.

Usually their conversation was comfortably monosyllabic and disjointed, as is the breakfast talk of two people who understand each other. Amicable silence was the rule, broken only by the rustle of paper, the clink of china, an occasional, "Toast, dear?" And when Buck, in a low, vibrating tone (slightly muffled by buttered corn muffin) said, "Dogs!" Emma knew he was persuing the daily *schrecklichkeit*.

Upon this cozy scene Conservation cast his gaunt shadow. It was in June, the year of America's Great Step, that Emma, examining her household, pronounced it fattily degenerate, with complications, and performed upon it a severe and skilful surgical operation. Among the rest:

"One morning paper ought to be enough for any husband and wife who aren't living on a Boffin basis. There'll be one copy of the *Times* delivered at this house in the future, Mr. Buck. We might match pennies for it, mornings."

It lay there on the hall table that first morning, an innocent oblong, its headlines staring up at them with inky eyes.

"Paper, T. A.," she said, and handed it to him. "You take it, dear."

"Oh, no! No."

She poured the coffee, trying to keep her gaze away from the tantalizing tail-end of the headline at whose first half she could only guess.

"By Jove, Emma! Listen to this! Pershing says if we have one m——"

"Stop right there! We've become pretty well acquainted in the last three years, T. A. But if you haven't learned that if there's one thing I can't endure, it's being fed across the table with scraps of the day's news, I shall have to consider our marriage a failure."

"Oh, very well. I merely thought you'd be——"

"I am. But there's something about having it read to you——"

On the second morning Emma, hurriedly fastening the middle button of her blouse on her way downstairs, collided with her husband, who was shrugging himself into his coat. They continued their way downstairs with considerable dignity and pronounced leisure. The paper lay on the hall table. They reached for it. There was a moment—just the fraction of a minute—when each clutched a corner of it, eying the other grimly. Then both let go suddenly, as though the paper had burned their fingers. They stared at each other,

surprise and horror in their gaze. The paper fell to
the floor with a little slap. Both stooped for it,
apologetically. Their heads bumped. They stag-
gered back, semi-stunned.

Emma found herself laughing, rather wildly.
Buck joined in after a moment—a rueful laugh.
She was the first to recover.

"That settles it. I'm willing to eat trick bread
and whale meat and drink sugarless coffee, but I
draw the line at hating my husband for the price of
a newspaper subscription. White paper may be
scarce but so are husbands. It's cheaper to get
two newspapers than to set up two establishments."

They were only two among many millions who,
at that time, were playing an amusing and fashionable game called Win the War. They did not
realize that the game was to develop into a grim
and magnificently functioning business to whose
demands they would cheerfully sacrifice all that
they most treasured.

Of late, Emma had spent less and less time in
the offices of the Featherloom Company. For
more than ten years that flourishing business, and
the career of her son, Jock McChesney, had been
the twin orbits about which her existence had re-
volved. But Jock McChesney was a man of
family now, with a wife, two babies, and an uncanny advertising sense that threatened to put his

name on the letterhead of the Raynor Advertising
Company of Chicago. As for the Featherloom
factory—it seemed to go of its own momentum.
After her marriage to the firm's head, Emma's
interest in the business was unflagging.

"Now look here, Emma," Buck would say.
"You've given enough to this firm. Play a while.
Cut up. Forget you're the 'And Company' in
T. A. Buck & Co."

"But I'm so used to it. I'd miss it so. You
know what happened that first year of our marriage when I tried to do the duchess. I don't
know how to loll. If you take Featherlooms away
from me I'll degenerate into a Madam Chairman.
You'll see."

She might have, too, if the War had not come
along and saved her.

By midsummer the workrooms were turning out
strange garments, such as gray and khaki flannel
shirts, flannelette one-piece pajamas, and woollen
bloomers, all intended for the needs of women war
workers going abroad.

Emma had dropped into the workroom one day
and had picked up a half-finished gray flannel garment. She eyed it critically, her deft fingers ma-
nipulating the neckband. A little frown gathered
between her eyes.

"Somehow a woman in a flannel shirt always

looks as if she had quinsy. It's the collar. They cut them like a man's small-size. But a woman's neck is as different from a man's as her collarbone is."

She picked up a piece of flannel and smoothed it on the cutting-table. The head designer had looked on in disapproval while her employer's wife had experimented with scraps of cloth, and pins, and chalk, and scissors. But Emma had gone on serenely cutting and snipping and pinning. They made up samples of service shirts with the new neck-hugging collar and submitted them to Miss Nevins, the head of the woman's uniform department at Fyfe & Gordon's. That astute lady had been obliged to listen to scores of canteeners, nurses, secretaries, and motor leaguers who, standing before a long mirror in one of the many fitting-rooms, had gazed, frowned, fumbled at collar and topmost button, and said, "But it looks so—so lumpy around the neck."

Miss Kate Nevins's reply to this plaint was: "Oh, when you get your tie on——"

"Perhaps they'll let me wear a turn-down collar."

"Absolutely against regulations. The rules strictly forbid anything but the high, close-fitting collar."

The fair war worker would sigh, mutter something

about supposing they'd shoot you at sunrise for
wearing a becoming shirt, and order six, grumbling.

Kate Nevins had known Mrs. T. A. Buck in that
lady's Emma McChesney days.   At the end of the
first day's trial of the new Featherloom shirt she
had telephoned the Featherloom factory and had
asked for Emma McChesney.   People who had
known her by that name never seemed able to get
the trick of calling her by any other.

With every fitting-room in the Fyfe & Gordon
establishment   demanding   her   attention,   Miss
Nevins's conversation was necessarily brief.   "Emma McChesney?   .   .   .   Kate Nevins.   .   .   .
Who's responsible for the collar on those Featherloom shirts?   .   .   .   I was sure of it.   .   .   .
No regular designer could cut a collar like that.
Takes a genius.   .   .   .   H'm?   .   .   .   Well, I
mean it.   I'm going to write to Washington and
have 'em vote you a distinguished service medal.
This is the first day since last I-don't-know-when
that hasn't found me in the last stages of nervous
exhaustion   at   six   o'clock.   .   .   .   All   these
women warriors are willing to bleed and die for
their country, but they want to do it in a collar
that fits, and I don't blame 'em.   After I saw the
pictures of that Russian Battalion of Death, I
understood why.   .   .   .   Yes, I know I oughtn't
to say that, but   .   .   ."

By autumn Emma was wearing one of those Featherloom service shirts herself.   It was inevitable that a woman of her executive ability, initiative, and detail sense should be pressed into active service.   November saw Fifth Avenue a-glitter with uniforms, and one third of them seemed to be petticoated.   The Featherloom factory saw little of Emma now.   She bore the title of Commandant with feminine captains, lieutenants, and girl workers under her; and her blue uniform, as she herself put it, was so a-jingle with straps, buckles, belts, bars, and bolts that when she first put it on she felt like a jail.

She left the house at eight in the morning now. Dinner time rarely found her back in Sixty-third Street.   Buck was devoting four evenings a week to the draft board.   At the time of the second Liberty Loan drive in the autumn he had deserted Featherlooms for bonds.   His success was due to the commodity he had for sale, the type of person to whom he sold it, and his own selling methods and personality.   There was something about this slim, leisurely man, with the handsome eyes and the quiet voice, that convinced and impressed you.

"It's your complete lack of eagerness in the transaction, too," Emma remarked after watching him land a twenty-five-thousand-dollar bond pledge, the buyer a business rival of the Featherloom Petticoat Company. "You make it seem a privilege, not a favour. A man with your method could sell sandbags in the Sahara."

Sometimes the two dined downtown together. Sometimes they scarcely saw each other for days on end. One afternoon at 5.30, Emma, on duty bound, espied him walking home up Fifth Avenue, on the opposite side of the street. She felt a little pang as she watched the easy, graceful figure swinging its way up the brilliant, flag-decked avenue. She had given him so little time and thought; she had bestowed upon the house such scant attention in the last few weeks. She turned abruptly and crossed the street, dodging the late afternoon traffic with a sort of expert recklessness. She almost ran after the tall figure that was now a block ahead of her, and walking fast. She caught up with him, matched his stride, and touched his arm lightly.

"I beg your pardon, but aren't you Mr. T. A. Buck?"

"Yes."

"How do you do! I'm Mrs. Buck."

Then they had giggled together, deliciously, and he had put a firm hand on the smartly tailored blue serge sleeve.

"I thought so. That being the case, you're coming home along o' me, young 'ooman."

"Can't do it. I'm on my way to the Ritz to meet a dashing delegation from Serbia. You never saw such gorgeous creatures. All gold and green and red, with swords, and snake-work, and glittering boots. They'd make a musical-comedy soldier look like an undertaker."

There came a queer little look into his eyes. "But this isn't a musical comedy, dear. These men are—— Look here, Emma. I want to talk to you. Let's walk home together and have dinner decently in our own dining room. There are things at the office——"

"S'impossible, Mr. Buck. I'm late now. And you know perfectly well there are two vice-commandants ready to snatch my shoulder-straps."

"Emma! Emma!"

At his tone the smiling animation of her face was dimmed. "What's gone wrong?"

"Nothing. Everything. At least, nothing that I can discuss with you at the corner of Fifth Avenue and Forty-fifth Street. When does this Serbian thing end? I'll call for you."

"There's no telling. Anyway, the Fannings will drive me home, thanks, dear."

He looked down at her. She was unbelievably girlish and distingué in the blue uniform; a straight, slim figure, topped by an impudent cocked hat. The flannel shirt of workaday service was replaced to-day by a severely smart affair of white silk, high-collared, stitched, expensively simple. And yet he frowned as he looked.

"Fisk got his exemption papers to-day." With apparent irrelevance.

"Yes?" She was glancing sharply up and down the thronged street. "Better call me a cab, dear. I'm awfully late. Oh, well, with his wife practically an invalid, and all the expense of the baby's illness, and the funeral—— The Ritz, dear. And tell him to hurry." She stepped into the cab, a little nervous frown between her eyes.

But Buck, standing at the curb, seemed bent on delaying her. "Fisk told me the doctor said all she needs is a couple of months at a sanitarium, where she can be bathed and massaged and fed with milk. And if Fisk could go to a camp now he'd have a commission in no time. He's had training, you know. He spent his vacation last summer at Plattsburg."

"But he's due on his advance spring trip in two or three weeks, isn't he? . . . I really must hurry, T. A."

"Ritz," said Buck, shortly, to the chauffeur. "And hurry." He turned away abruptly, without a backward glance. Emma's head jerked over her shoulder in surprise. But he did not turn. The tall figure disappeared. Emma's taxi crept into the stream. But uppermost in her mind was not the thought of Serbians, uniforms, Fisk, or Ritz, but of her husband's right hand, which, as he turned away from the cab, had been folded tight into a fist.

She meant to ask an explanation of the clenched fingers; but the Serbians, despite their four tragic years, turned out to be as sprightly as their uniforms, and it was past midnight when the Fannings dropped her at her door. Her husband was rather ostentatiously asleep. As she doffed her warlike garments, her feminine canniness warned her that this was no time for explanations. To-morrow morning would be better.

But next morning's breakfast turned out to be all Jock.

A letter from Grace, his wife. Grace McChesney had been Grace Galt, one of the youngest and cleverest women advertising writers in the profession. When Jock was a cub in the Raynor office she had been turning out compelling copy. They had been married four years. Now Jock ruled a mahogany domain of his own in the Raynor suite overlooking the lake in the great Michigan Avenue building. And Grace was saying, "Eat the crust, girlie. It's the crust that makes your hair grow curly."

Emma, uniformed for work, read hasty extracts from Grace's letter. Buck listened in silence.

"You wouldn't know Jock. He's restless, irritable, moody. And the queer part of it is he doesn't know it. He tries to be cheerful, and I could weep to see him. He has tried to cover it up with every kind of war work from Red Crossing to Liberty Loaning, and from writing free full-page national advertising copy to giving up his tobacco money to the smoke fund. And he's miserable. He wants to get into it. And he ought. But you know I haven't been really husky since Buddy came. Not ill, but the doctor says it will be another six months before I'm myself, really. If I had only myself to think of—how simple! But two kiddies need such a lot of things. I could get a job at Raynor's. They need writers. Jock says, bitterly, that all the worth-while men have left. Don't think I'm complaining. I'm just trying to see my way clear, and talking to someone who understands often clears the way."

"Well!" said Emma.

And, "Well?" said T. A.

She sat fingering the letter, her breakfast cooling before her. "Of course, Jock wants to get into it. I wish he could. I'd be so proud of him. He'd be beautiful in khaki. But there's work to do right here. And he ought to be willing to wait six months."

"They can't wait six months over there, Emma. They need him now."

"Oh, come, T. A.! One man——"

"Multiplied by a million. Look at Fisk. Just such another case. Look at——"

The shrill summons of the telephone cut him short. Emma's head came up alertly. She glanced at her wrist-watch and gave a little exclamation of horror.

"That's for me! I'm half an hour late! The first time, too." She was at the telephone a second later, explanatory, apologetic. Then back in the dining-room doorway, her cheeks flushed, tugging at her gloves, poised for flight. "Sorry, dear. But this morning was so important, and that letter about Jock upset me. I'm afraid I'm a rotten soldier."

"I'm afraid you are, Emma."

She stared at that. "Why——! Oh, you're still angry at something. Listen, dear—I'll call for you at the office to-night at five, and we'll walk home together. Wait for me. I may be a few minutes late——"

She was off. The front door slammed sharply. Buck sat very still for a long minute, staring down at the coffee cup whose contents he did not mean to drink. The light from the window cameoed his fine profile. And you saw that his jaw was set.

His mind was a thousand miles away, in Chicago, Illinois, with the boy who wanted to fight and couldn't.

Emma, flashing down Fifth Avenue as fast as wheels and traffic rules would permit, saw nothing of the splendid street. Her mind was a thousand miles away, in Chicago, Illinois.

And a thousand miles away, in Chicago, Illinois, Jock McChesney, three hours later, was slamming down the two big windows of his office. From up the street came the sound of a bugle and of a band playing a brisk march. And his office windows looked out upon Michigan Avenue. If you know Chicago, you know the building that housed the Raynor offices—a great gray shaft, towering even above its giant neighbours, its head in the clouds, its face set toward the blue beauty of Lake Michigan. Until very recently those windows of his office had been a source of joy and inspiration to Jock McChesney. The green of Grant Park just below. The tangle of I. C. tracks beyond that, and the great, gracious lake beyond that, as far as the eye could see. He had seen the changes the year had brought. The lake dotted with sinister gray craft. Dog tents in Grant Park, sprung up overnight like brown mushrooms. Men—mere boys, most of them—awkward in their workaday clothes of office and shop, drilling, wheeling, marching at the noon hour. And parades, and parades, and parades. At first Jock, and, in fact, the entire office staff—heads of departments, writers, secretaries, stenographers, office boys— would suspend business and crowd to the windows to see the pageant pass in the street below. Stirring music, khaki columns, flags, pennants, horses, bugles. And always the Jackie band from the Great Lakes Station, its white leggings twinkling down the street in the lead of its six-foot-six contortionistic drum-major.

By October the window-gazers, watching the parades from the Raynor windows, were mostly petticoated and exclamatory. Jock stayed away from the window now. It seemed to his tortured mind that there was a fresh parade hourly, and that bugles and bands sounded a taunting note.

"Where are *you* ! (sounded the bugle)
　Where are *you?*
　Where are YOU?!!!
　　Where
　　　are
　　　　you?
　Where—are—you-u-u-u——"

He slammed down the windows, summoned a stenographer, and gave out dictation in a loud, rasping voice.

"Yours of the tenth at hand, and contents noted. In reply I wish to say——"

(*Boom!   Boom!   And a boom-boom-boom!*)

"—all copy for the Sans Scent Soap is now ready for your approval and will be mailed to you to-day under separate cover. We in the office think that this copy marks a new record in soap advertising——"

(*Over there!   Over there!   Send the word, send the word over there!*)

"Just read that last line will you, Miss Dugan?"

"Over th—I mean, 'We in the office think that this copy marks a new record in soap advertising——'"

"H'm.   Yes."   A moment's pause.   A dreamy look on the face of the girl stenographer.   Jock interpreted it.   He knew that the stenographer was in the chair at the side of his desk, taking his dictation accurately and swiftly, while the spirit of the girl herself was far and away at Camp Grant at Rockford, Illinois, with an olive-drab unit in an olive-drab world.

"—and, in fact, in advertising copy of any description that has been sent out from the Raynor offices."

The girl's pencil flew over the pad.   But when Jock paused for thought or breath she lifted her head and her eyes grew soft and bright, and her foot, in its absurd high-heeled gray boot, beat a smart left! Left! Left-right-left!

Something of this picture T. A. Buck saw in his untasted coffee cup. Much of it Emma visualized in her speeding motor car. All of it Grace knew by heart as she moved about the new, shining house in the Chicago suburb, thinking, planning; feeling his agony, and trying not to admit the transparency of the look about her hands and her temples. So much for Chicago.

At five o'clock Emma left the war to its own devices and dropped in at the loft building in which Featherlooms were born and grew up. Mike, the elevator man, twisted his gray head about at an unbelievable length to gaze appreciatively at the trim, uniformed figure.

"Haven't seen you around fur many the day. Mis' Buck."

"Been too busy, Mike."

Mike turned back to face the door. "Well, 'tis a great responsibility, runnin' this war, an' all." He stopped at the Featherloom floor and opened the door with his grandest flourish. Emma glanced at him quickly. His face was impassive. She passed into the reception room with a little jingling of buckles and strap hooks.

The work day was almost ended. The display

room was empty of buyers. She could see the back of her husband's head in his office. He was busy at his desk. A stock girl was clearing away the piles of garments that littered tables and chairs. At the window near the door Fisk, the Western territory man, stood talking with O'Brien, city salesman. The two looked around at her approach. O'Brien's face lighted up with admiration. Into Fisk's face there flashed a look so nearly resembling resentment that Emma, curious to know its origin, stopped to chat a moment with the two.

Said O'Brien, the gallant Irishman, "I'm more resigned to war this minute, Mrs. Buck, than I've been since it began."

Emma dimpled, turned to Fisk, stood at attention. Fisk said nothing. His face was unsmiling. "Like my uniform?" Emma asked; and wished, somehow, that she hadn't.

Fisk stared. His eyes had none of the softness of admiration. They were hard, resentful. Suddenly, "Like it! God! I wish I could wear one!" He turned away, abruptly. O'Brien threw him a sharp look. Then he cleared his throat, apologetically.

Emma glanced down at her own trim self—at her stitched seams, her tailored lengths, her shining belt and buckles, her gloved hands—and suddenly and unaccountably her pride in them vanished. Something—something——

She wheeled and made for Buck's office, her colour high. He looked up, rose, offered her a chair. She felt strangely ill at ease there in the office to which she had given years of service. The bookkeeper in the glass-enclosed cubby-hole across the little hall smiled and nodded and called through the open door: "My, you're a stranger, Mrs. Buck."

"Be with you in a minute, Emma," said T. A. And turned to his desk again. She rose and strolled toward the door, restlessly. "Don't hurry." Out in the showroom again she saw Fisk standing before a long table. He was ticketing and folding samples of petticoats, pajamas, blouses, and night-gowns. His cigar was gripped savagely between his teeth and his eyes squinted, half closed through the smoke.

She strolled over to him and fingered the cotton flannel of a garment that lay under her hand. "Spring samples?"

"Yes."

"It ought to be a good trip. They say the West is dripping money, war or no war."

" 'S right."

"How's Gertie?"

"Don't get me started, Mrs. Buck. That girl!

—say, I knew what she was when I married her,
and so did you.   She was head stenographer here
long enough.   But I never really knew that kid
until now, and we've been married two years.
You know what the last year has been for her; the
baby and all.   And then losing him.   And do you
know what she says!   That if there was somebody
who knew the Western territory and could cover
it, she'd get a job and send me to war.   Yessir!
That's Gert.   We've been married two years, and
she says. herself it's the first really happy time
she's ever known.   You know what she had at
home.   Why, even when I was away on my long
spring trip she used to say it wasn't so bad being
alone, because there was always my home-coming
to count on.   How's that for a wife!"

"Gertie's splendid," agreed Emma.   And wondered why it sounded so lame.

"You don't know her.   Why, when it comes to
patriotism, she makes T. R. look like a pacifist.
She says if she could sell my line on the road, she'd
make you give her the job so she could send her man
to war.   Gert says a travelling man's wife ought
to make an ideal soldier's wife, anyway; and that
if I went it would only be like my long Western trip,
multiplied by about ten, maybe.   That's Gertie."

Emma was fingering the cotton-flannel garment
on the table.

Buck crossed the room and stood beside her. "Sorry I kept you waiting. Three of the boys were called to-day. It crippled us pretty badly in the shipping room. Ready?"

"Yes. Good-night, Charley. Give my love to Gertie."

"Thanks, Mrs. Buck." He picked up his cigar, took an apprehensive puff, and went on ticketing and folding. There was a grin behind the cigar now.

Into the late afternoon glitter of Fifth Avenue. Five o'clock Fifth Avenue. Flags of every nation, save one. Uniforms of every blue from French to navy; of almost any shade save field green. Pongee-coloured Englishmen, seeming seven feet high, to a man; aviators slim and elegant, with walking sticks made of the propeller of their shattered planes, with a notch for every Hun plane bagged. Slim girls, exotic as the orchids they wore, gazing limpid-eyed at these warrior *élégants*. Women uniformed to the last degree of tailored exquisiteness. Girls, war accoutred, who brought arms up in sharp salute as they passed Emma. Buck eyed them gravely, hat and arm describing parabolas with increasing frequency as they approached Fiftieth Street, slackening as the colourful pageant grew less brilliant, thinned, and faded into the park mists.

Emma's cheeks were a glorious rose-pink. Head high, shoulders back, she matched her husband's long stride every step of the way. Her eyes were bright and very blue.

"There's a beautiful one, T. A.! The Canadian officer with the limp. They've all been gassed, and shot five times in the thigh and seven in the shoulder, and yet look at 'em! What do you suppose they were when they were new if they can look like that, damaged!"

Buck cut a vicious little semi-circle in the air with his walking stick.

"I know now how the father of the Gracchi felt, and why you never hear him mentioned."

"Nonsense, T. A. You're doing a lot." She did not intend her tone to be smug; but if she had glanced sidewise at her husband, she might have seen the pained red mount from chin to brow. She did not seem to sense his hurt. They went on, past the plaza now. Only a few blocks lay between them and their home; the old brownstone house that had been New York's definition of architectural elegance in the time of T. A. Buck, Sr.

"Tell me, Emma. Does this satisfy you—the work you're doing, I mean? Do you think you're giving the best you've got?"

"Well, of course I'd like to go to France——"

"I didn't ask you what you'd like."

"Yes, sir. Very good, sir. I don't know what you call giving the best one has got. But you know I work from eight in the morning until midnight, often and often. Oh, I don't say that someone else couldn't do my work just as well. And I don't say, either, that it doesn't include a lot of dashing up and down Fifth Avenue, and teaing at the Ritz, and meeting magnificent Missions, and being cooed over by Lady Millionaires. But if you'd like a few statistics as to the number of hundreds of thousands of soldiers we've canteened since last June, I'd be pleased to oblige." She tugged at a capacious pocket and brought forth a smart leather-bound notebook.

"Spare me! I've had all the statistics I can stand for one day at the office. I know you're working hard. I just wondered if you didn't realize——"

They turned into their own street. "Realize what?"

"Nothing. Nothing."

Emma sighed a mock sigh and glanced up at the windows of her own house. "Oh, well, everybody's difficult these days, T. A., including husbands. That second window shade is crooked. Isn't it queer how maids never do. . . . I'll tell you what I can realize, though. I realize that we're going to have dinner at home, reg'lar old-fashioned befo'-de-war. And I can bathe before dinner. There's richness."

But when she appeared at dinner, glowing, radiant, her hair shiningly re-coifed, she again wore the blue uniform, with the service cap atop her head. Buck surveyed her, unsmiling. She seated herself at table with a little clinking of buckles and buttons. She flung her motor gloves on a near-by chair, ran an inquiring finger along belt and collar with a little gesture that was absurdly feminine in its imitation of masculinity. Buck did not sit down. He stood at the opposite side of the table, one hand on his chair, the knuckles showing white where he gripped it.

"It seems to me, Emma, that you might manage to wear something a little less military when you're dining at home. War is war, but I don't see why you should make me feel like your orderly. It's like being married to a policewoman. Surely you can neglect your country for the length of time it takes to dine with your husband."

It was the bitterest speech he had made to her in the years of their married life. She flushed a little. "I thought you knew that I was going out again immediately after dinner. I left at five with the understanding that I'd be on duty again at 8.30."

He said nothing. He stood looking down at his own hand that gripped the chair back so tightly. Emma sat back and surveyed her trim and tailored self with a placidity that had in it, perhaps, a dash of malice. His last speech had cut. Then she reached forward, helped herself to an olive, and nibbled it, head on one side.

"D'you know, T. A., what I think? H'm? I think you're jealous of your wife's uniform."

She had touched the match to the dynamite.

He looked up. At the blaze in his eyes she shrank back a little. His face was white. He was breathing quickly.

"You're right! I am. I am jealous. I'm jealous of every buck private in the army! I'm jealous of the mule drivers! Of the veterinarians. Of the stokers in the transports. Men!" He doubled his hand into a fist. His fine eyes glowed. "Men!"

And suddenly he sat down, heavily, and covered his eyes with his hands.

Emma sat staring at him for a dull, sickening moment. Then she looked down at herself, horror in her eyes. Then up again at him. She got up and came over to him.

"Why, dear—dearest—I didn't know. I

thought you were satisfied. I thought you were happy. You——"

"Honey, the only man who's happy is the man in khaki. The rest of us are gritting our teeth and pretending."

She put a hand on his shoulder. "But what do you want—what can you do that——"

He reached back over his shoulder and found her hand. He straightened. His head came up. "They've offered me a job in Bordeaux. It isn't a fancy job. It has to do with merchandising. But I think you know they're having a devil of a time with all the millions of bales of goods. They need men who know materials. I ought to. I've handled cloth and clothes enough. I know values. It would mean hard work—manual work lots of times. No pay. And happiness. For me." There was a silence. It seemed to fill the room, that silence. It filled the house. It roared and thundered about Emma's ears, that silence. When finally she broke it:

"Blind!" she said. "Blind! Deaf! Dumb! *And* crazy." She laughed, and two tears sped down her cheeks and dropped on the unblemished blue serge uniform. "Oh, T. A.! Where have I been? How you must have despised me. Me, in my uniform. In my uniform that was costing the Government three strapping men. My uniform, that was keeping three man-size soldiers out of khaki. You, Jock, and Fisk. Why didn't you tell me, dear! Why didn't you tell me!"

"I've tried. I couldn't. You've always seen things first. I couldn't ask you to go back to the factory."

"Factory! Factory nothing! I'm going back on the road. I'm taking Fisk's Western territory. I know the Middle West better than Fisk himself. I ought to. I covered it for ten years. I'll pay Gertie Fisk's salary until she's able to come back to us as stenographer. We've never had one so good. Grace can give the office a few hours a week. And we can promote O'Brien to manager while I'm on the road."

Buck was staring at her, dully. "Grace? Now wait a minute. You're travelling too fast for a mere man." His hand was gripping hers, tight, tight.

Their dinner was cooling on the table. They ignored it. She pulled a chair around to his. They sat shoulder to shoulder, elbows on the cloth.

"It took me long enough to wake up, didn't it? I've got to make up for lost time. The whole thing's clear in my mind. Now get this: Jock gets a commission. Grace and the babies pack up and come to New York, and live right here, with me, in this house. Fisk goes to war. Gertie gets well and comes back to work for Featherlooms. Mr. T. A. Buck goes to Bordeaux. Old Emmer takes off her uniform and begins to serve her country—on the road."

At that he got up and began pacing the room. "I can't have you do that, dear. Why, you left all that behind when you married me."

"Yes, but our marriage certificate didn't carry a war guarantee."

"Gad, Emma, you're glorious!"

"Glorious nothing! I'm going to earn the living for three families for a few months, until things get going. And there's nothing glorious about that, old dear. I haven't any illusions about what taking a line on the road means these days. It isn't travelling. It's exploring. You never know where you're going to land, or when, unless you're travelling in a freight train. They're cock o' the walk now. I think I'll check myself through as first-class freight. Or send my pack ahead, with natives on foot, like an African explorer. But it'll be awfully good for me character. And when I'm eating that criminal corn bread they serve on dining cars on a train that's seven hours late into Duluth I'll remember when I had my picture, in uniform, in the Sunday supplements, with my hand on the steering wheel along o' the nobility and gentry."

"Listen, dear, I can't have you——"

"Too late. Got a pencil? Let's send fifty words to Jock and Grace. They'll wire back 'No!' but another fifty'll fetch 'em. After all, it takes more than one night letter to explain a move that is going to change eight lives. Now let's have dinner, dear. It'll be cold, but filling."

Perhaps in the whirlwind ten days that followed a woman of less energy, less determination, less courage and magnificent vitality might have faltered and failed in an undertaking of such magnitude. But Emma was alert and forceful enough to keep just one jump ahead of the swift-moving times. In a less cataclysmic age the changes she wrought within a period of two weeks would have seemed herculean. But in this time of stress and change, when every household in every street in every town in all the country was feeling the tremor of upheaval, the readjustment of this little family and business group was so unremarkable as to pass unnoticed. Even the members of the group itself, seeing themselves scattered to camp, to France, to New York, to the Middle West, shuffled like pawns that the Great Game might the better be won, felt strangely unconcerned and unruffled.

It was little more than two weeks after the night of Emma's awakening that she was talking fast to keep from crying hard, as she stuffed plain, practical blue serge garments (unmilitary) into a bellows suitcase ("Can't count on trunks these days," she had said. "I'm not taking any chances on a clean shirtwaist"). Buck, standing in the doorway, tried hard to keep his gaze from the contemplation of his khaki-clad self reflected in the long mirror. At intervals he said: "Can't I help, dear?" Or, "Talk about the early Pilgrim mothers, and the Revolutionary mothers, and the Civil War mothers! I'd like to know what they had on you, Emma."

And from Emma: "Yeh, ain't I noble!" Then, after a little pause: "This house is going to be so full of wimmin folks it'll look like a Home for Decayed Gentlewomen. Buddy McChesney, aged six months, is going to be the only male protector around the place. We'll make him captain of the home guard."

"Gertie was in to-day. She says I'm a shrimp in my uniform compared to Charley. You know she always was the nerviest little stenographer we ever had about the place, but she knows more about Featherlooms than any woman in the shop except you. She's down to ninety-eight pounds, poor little girl, but every ounce of it's pure pluck, and she says she'll be as good as new in a month or two, and I honestly believe she will."

Emma was counting a neat stack of folded handkerchiefs. "Seventeen—eighteen—— When she comes back we'll have to pay her twice the salary she got when she left. But, then, you have to pay an errand boy what you used to pay a shipping clerk, and a stock girl demands money that an operator used to brag about—nineteen——"

Buck came over to her and put a hand on the bright hair that was rumpled, now, from much diving into bags and suitcases and clothes closets.

"All except you, Emma. You'll be working without a salary—working like a man—like three men——"

"Working for three men, T. A. Three fighting men. I've got two service buttons already," she glanced down at her blouse, "and Charley Fisk said I had the right to wear one for him. I'll look like a mosaic, but I'm going to put 'em all on."

The day before Emma's departure for the West Grace arrived, with bags, bundles, and babies. A wan and tired Grace, but proud, too, and with the spirit of the times in her eyes.

"Jock!" she repeated, in answer to their questions. "My dears, he doesn't know I'm alive. I visited him at camp the day before I left. He thinks he'll be transferred East, as we hoped. Wouldn't that be glorious! Well, I had all sorts of intimate and vital things to discuss with him, and he didn't hear what I was saying. He wasn't even listening. He couldn't wait until I had finished a sentence so that he could cut in with something about his work. I murmured to him in the moonlight that there was something I had long meant to tell him and he answered that dammit he forgot to report that rifle that exploded. And when I said, 'Dearest, isn't this hotel a *little* like the place we spent our honeymoon in—that porch, and all?' he said, 'See this feller coming, Gracie? The big guy with the moustache. Now mash him, Gracie. He's my Captain. I'm going to introduce you. He was a senior at college when I was a fresh.'"

But the peace and the pride in her eyes belied her words.

Emma's trip, already delayed, was begun ten days before her husband's date for sailing. She bore that, too, with smiling equanimity. "When I went to school," she said, "I thought I hated the Second Peloponnesian War worse than any war I'd ever heard of. But I hate this one so that I want everyone to get into it one hundred per cent., so that it'll be over sooner; and because we've won."

They said little on their way to the train. She stood on the rear platform just before the train pulled out. They had tried frantically to get a lower berth, but unsuccessfully. "Don't look so tragic about it," she laughed. "It's like old times. These last three years have been a dream—a delusion."

He looked up at her, as she stood there in her blue suit, and white blouse, and trim blue hat and crisp veil. "Gad, Emma, it's uncanny. I believe you're right. You look exactly as you did when I first saw you, when you came in off the road after father died and I had just taken hold of the business."

For answer she hummed a few plaintive bars. He grinned as he recognized "Silver Threads Among the Gold." The train moved away, gathered speed. He followed it. They were not smiling now. She was leaning over the railing, as though to be as near to him as the fast-moving train would allow. He was walking swiftly along with the train, as though hypnotized. Their eyes held. The brave figure in blue on the train platform. The brave figure in khaki outside. The blue suddenly swam in a haze before his eyes; the khaki a mist before hers. The crisp little veil was a limp little rag when finally she went in to search for Upper Eleven.

The white-coated figure that had passed up and down the aisle unnoticed and unnoticing as she sat hidden behind the kindly folds of her newspaper suddenly became a very human being as Emma regained self-control, decided on dinner as a panacea, and informed the white coat that she desired Upper Eleven made up early.

The White Coat had said, "Yas'm," and glanced up at her. Whereupon she had said:

"Why, William!"

And he, "Well, fo' de lan'! 'F 'tain't Mis' McChesney! Well, mah sakes alive, Mis' McChesney! Ah ain't seen yo' since yo' married. Ah done heah yo' married yo' boss an' got a swell brownstone house, an' ev'thing gran'——"

"I've got everything, William, but a lower berth to Chicago. They swore they couldn't give me anything but an upper."

A speculative look crept into William's rolling eye. Emma recognized it. Her hand reached toward her bag. Then it stopped. She smiled. "No. No, William. Time was. But not these days. Four years ago I'd have slipped you fifty cents right now, and you'd have produced a lower berth from somewhere. But I'm going to fool you. My boss has gone to war, William, and so has my son. And I'm going to take that fifty cents and buy thrift stamps for Miss Emma McChesney, aged three, and Mr. Buddy McChesney, aged six months. And I'll dispose my old bones in Upper Eleven."

She went in to dinner.

At eight-thirty a soft and deferential voice sounded in her ear.

"Ah got yo' made up, Mis' McChesney."

"But this is my——"

He beckoned. He padded down the aisle with that walk which is a peculiar result of flat feet and twenty years of swaying car. Emma followed. He stopped before Lower Six and drew aside the curtain. It was that lower which can always be produced, magically, though ticket sellers, Pullman agents, porters, and train conductors swear that it does not exist. The key to it is silver, but to-night Emma McChesney Buck had unlocked it with finer metal. Gold. Pure gold. For William drew aside the curtain with a gesture such as one of his slave ancestors might have used before a queen of Egypt. He carefully brushed a cinder from the sheet with one gray-black hand. Then he bowed like any courtier.

Emma sank down on the edge of the couch with a little sigh of weariness. Gratefulness was in it, too. She looked up at him—at the wrinkled, kindly, ape-like face, and he looked down at her.

"William," she said, "war is a filthy, evil, vile thing, but it bears wonderful white flowers."

"Yas'm!" agreed William, genially, and smiled all over his rubbery, gray-black countenance. "*Yas 'm !* "

And who shall say he did not understand?

FARMER IN THE DELL

OLD Ben Westerveld was taking it easy. Every muscle taut, every nerve tense, his keen eyes vainly straining to pierce the blackness of the stuffy room—there lay Ben Westerveld in bed, taking it easy. And it was hard. Hard. He wanted to get up. He wanted so intensely to get up that the mere effort of lying there made him ache all over. His toes were curled with the effort. His fingers were clenched with it. His breath came short, and his thighs felt cramped. Nerves. But old Ben Westerveld didn't know that. What should a retired and well-to-do farmer of fifty-eight know of nerves, especially when he has moved to the city and is taking it easy?

If only he knew what time it was. Here in Chicago you couldn't tell whether it was four o'clock ·or seven unless you looked at your watch. To do that it was necessary to turn on the light. And to turn on the light meant that he would turn on, too, a flood of querulous protest from his wife, Bella, who lay asleep beside him.

When for forty-five years of your life you have

risen at four-thirty daily, it is difficult to learn to
loll. To do it successfully you must be a natural-
born loller to begin with, and revert. Bella Westerveld was and had. So there she lay, asleep.
Old Ben wasn't and hadn't. So there he lay,
terribly wide-awake, wondering what made his
heart thump so fast when he was lying so still. If
it had been light, you could have seen the lines of
strained resignation in the sagging muscles of his
patient face.

They had lived in the city for almost a year, but
it was the same every morning. He would open
his eyes, start up with one hand already reaching
for the limp, drab, work-worn garments that used
to drape the chair by his bed. Then he would
remember and sink back while a great wave of
depression swept over him. Nothing to get up for.
Store clothes on the chair by the bed. He was
taking it easy.

Back home on the farm in southern Illinois he
had known the hour the instant his eyes opened.
Here the flat next door was so close that the bedroom was in twilight even at midday. On the
farm he could tell by the feeling—an intangible
thing, but infallible. He could gauge the very
quality of the blackness that comes just before
dawn. The crowing of the cocks, the stamping of
the cattle, the twittering of the birds in the old

elm whose branches were etched eerily against his window in the ghostly light—these things he had never needed. He had known. But here, in the unsylvan section of Chicago which bears the bosky name of Englewood, the very darkness had a strange quality. A hundred unfamiliar noises misled him. There were no cocks, no cattle, no elm. Above all, there was no instinctive feeling. Once, when they first came to the city, he had risen at twelve-thirty, thinking it was morning, and had gone clumping about the flat waking up everyone and loosing from his wife's lips a stream of acid vituperation that seared even his case-hardened sensibilities. The people sleeping in the bedroom of the flat next door must have heard her.

"You big rube! Getting up in the middle of the night and stomping around like cattle. You'd better build a shed in the backyard and sleep there if you're so dumb you can't tell night from day."

Even after thirty-three years of marriage he had never ceased to be appalled at the coarseness of her mind and speech—she who had seemed so mild and fragile and exquisite when he married her. He had crept back to bed, shamefacedly. He could hear the couple in the bedroom of the flat just across the little court grumbling and then laughing a little, grudgingly, and yet with appreciation. That bed-

room, too, had still the power to appall him. **Its**
nearness, its forced intimacy, were daily shocks to
him whose most immediate neighbour, back on the
farm, had been a quarter of a mile away. The
sound of a shoe dropped on the hardwood floor, the
rush of water in the bathroom, the murmur of
nocturnal confidences, the fretful cry of a child in
the night, all startled and distressed him whose
ear had found music in the roar of the thresher and
had been soothed by the rattle of the tractor and
the hoarse hoot of the steamboat whistle at the
landing. His farm's edge had been marked by the
Mississippi rolling grandly by.

Since they had moved into town he had found
only one city sound that he really welcomed: the
rattle and clink that marked the milkman's
matutinal visit. The milkman came at six, and he
was the good fairy who released Ben Westerveld
from durance vile—or had been until the winter
months made his coming later and later, so that he
became worse than useless as a timepiece. But
now it was late March, and mild. The milkman's
coming would soon again mark old Ben's rising
hour. Before he had begun to take it easy six
o'clock had seen the entire mechanism of his busy
little world humming smoothly and sweetly, the
whole set in motion by his own big work-calloused
hands. Those hands puzzled him now. He often

looked at them curiously and in a detached sort of way as if they belonged to someone else. So white they were, and smooth and soft, with long, pliant nails that never broke off from rough work as they used to. Of late there were little splotches of brown on the backs of his hands and around the thumbs.

"Guess it's my liver," he decided, rubbing the spots thoughtfully. "She gets kind of sluggish from me not doing anything. Maybe a little spring tonic wouldn't go bad. Tone me up."

He got a bottle of reddish-brown mixture from the druggist on Halsted Street near Sixty-third. A genial gentleman, the druggist, white-coated and dapper, stepping affably about the fragrant-smelling store. The reddish-brown mixture had toned old Ben up surprisingly—while it lasted. He had two bottles of it. But on discontinuing it he slumped back into his old apathy.

Ben Westerveld, in his store clothes, his clean blue shirt, his incongruous hat, ambling aimlessly about Chicago's teeming, gritty streets, was a tragedy. Those big, capable hands, now dangling so limply from inert wrists, had wrested a living from the soil; those strangely unfaded blue eyes had the keenness of vision which comes from scanning great stretches of earth and sky; the stocky, square-shouldered body suggested power unutilized.

All these spelled tragedy. Worse than tragedy—waste.

For almost half a century this man had combated the elements, head set, eyes wary, shoulders squared. He had fought wind and sun, rain and drought, scourge and flood. He had risen before dawn and slept before sunset. In the process he had taken on something of the colour and the rugged immutability of the fields and hills and trees among which he toiled. Something of their dignity, too, though your town dweller might fail to see it beneath the drab exterior. He had about him none of the high lights and sharp points of the city man. He seemed to blend in with the background of nature so as to be almost indistinguishable from it as were the furred and feathered creatures. This farmer differed from the city man as a hillock differs from an artificial golf bunker, though form and substance are the same.

Ben Westerveld didn't know he was a tragedy. Your farmer is not given to introspection. For that matter any one knows that a farmer in town is a comedy. Vaudeville, burlesque, the Sunday supplement, the comic papers, have marked him a fair target for ridicule. Perhaps even you should know him in his overalled, stubble-bearded days, with the rich black loam of the Mississippi bottomlands clinging to his boots.

At twenty-five, given a tasselled cap, doublet and hose, and a long, slim pipe, Ben Westerveld would have been the prototype of one of those rollicking, lusty young mynheers that laugh out at you from a Frans Hals canvas. A roguish fellow with a merry eye; red-cheeked, vigorous. A serious mouth, though, and great sweetness of expression. As he grew older the seriousness crept up and up and almost entirely obliterated the roguishness. By the time the life of ease claimed him even the ghost of that ruddy wight of boyhood had vanished.

The Westerveld ancestry was as Dutch as the name. It had been hundreds of years since the first Westerveld came to America, and they had married and intermarried until the original Holland strain had almost entirely disappeared. They had drifted to southern Illinois by one of those slow processes of migration and had settled in Calhoun County, then almost a wilderness, but magnificent with its rolling hills, majestic rivers, and gold-and-purple distances. But to the practical Westerveld mind hills and rivers and purple haze existed only in their relation to crops and weather. Ben, though, had a way of turning his face up to the sky sometimes, and it was not to scan the heavens for clouds. You saw him leaning on the plow handle to watch the whirring flight of a partridge across the meadow. He liked farming. Even the drudgery of it never made him grumble. He was a natural farmer as men are natural mechanics or musicians or salesmen. Things grew for him. He seemed instinctively to know facts about the kinship of soil and seed that other men had to learn from books or experience. It grew to be a saying in that section "Ben Westerveld could grow a crop on rock."

At picnics and neighbourhood frolics Ben could throw farther and run faster and pull harder than any of the farmer boys who took part in the rough games. And he could pick up a girl with one hand and hold her at arm's length while she shrieked with pretended fear and real ecstasy. The girls all liked Ben. There was that about his primitive strength which appealed to the untamed in them as his gentleness appealed to their softer side. He liked the girls, too, and could have had his pick of them. He teased them all, took them buggy riding, beaued them about to neighbourhood parties. But by the time he was twenty-five the thing had narrowed down to the Byers girl on the farm adjoining Westerveld's. There was what the neighbours called an understanding, though perhaps he had never actually asked the Byers girl to marry him. You saw him going down the road toward the Byers place four nights out of the seven. He had a quick, light step at variance with his sturdy build, and very different from the heavy, slouching gait of the work-weary farmer. He had a habit of carrying in his hand a little twig or switch cut from a tree. This he would twirl blithely as he walked along. The switch and the twirl represented just so much energy and animal spirits. He never so much as flicked a dandelion head with it.

An inarticulate sort of thing, that courtship.

"Hello, Emma."

"How do, Ben."

"Thought you might like to walk a piece down the road. They got a calf at Aug Tietjens with five legs."

"I heard. I'd just as lief walk a little piece. I'm kind of beat, though. We've got the threshers day after to-morrow. We've been cooking up."

Beneath Ben's bonhomie and roguishness there was much shyness. The two would plod along the road together in a sort of blissful agony of embarrassment. The neighbours were right in their surmise that there was no definite understanding between them. But the thing was settled in the minds of both. Once Ben had said: "Pop says I can have the north eighty on easy payments if—when——"

Emma Byers had flushed up brightly, but had
answered equably: "That's a fine piece. Your
pop is an awful good man."

Beneath the stolid exteriors of these two there
was much that was fine and forceful. Emma
Byers's thoughtful forehead and intelligent eyes
would have revealed that in her. Her mother was
dead. She kept house for her father and brother.
She was known as "that smart Byers girl." Her
butter and eggs and garden stuff brought higher
prices at Commercial, twelve miles away, than
did any in the district. She was not a pretty girl,
according to the local standards, but there was
about her, even at twenty-two, a clear-headedness
and a restful serenity that promised well for Ben
Westerveld's future happiness.

But Ben Westerveld's future was not to lie in
Emma Byers's capable hands. He knew that as
soon as he saw Bella Huckins. Bella Huckins was
the daughter of old Red Front Huckins, who ran
the saloon of that cheerful name in Commercial.
Bella had elected to teach school, not from any
bent toward learning, but because teaching appealed to her as being a rather elegant occupation.
The Huckins family was not elegant. In that day
a year or two of teaching in a country school took
the place of the present-day normal-school di-
ploma. Bella had an eye on St. Louis, forty miles

from the town of Commercial. So she used the
country school as a step toward her ultimate goal,
though she hated the country and dreaded her
apprenticeship.

"I'll get a beau," she said, "that'll take me
driving and around. And Saturdays and Sundays
I can come to town."

The first time Ben Westerveld saw her she was
coming down the road toward him in her tight-
fitting black alpaca dress. The sunset was behind
her. Her hair was very golden. In a day of tiny
waists hers could have been spanned by Ben
Westerveld's two hands. He discovered that
later. Just now he thought he had never seen
anything so fairylike and dainty, though he did not
put it that way. Ben was not glib of thought or
speech.

He knew at once that this was the new school-
teacher. He had heard of her coming, though at
the time the conversation had interested him not
at all. Bella knew who he was, too. She had
learned the name and history of every eligible
young man in the district two days after her
arrival. That was due partly to her own bold
curiosity and partly to the fact that she was boarding with the Widow Becker, the most notorious
gossip in the county. In Bella's mental list of the

neighbourhood swains Ben Westerveld already occupied a two-star position, top of column.

He felt his face redden as they approached each
other.   To hide his embarrassment he swung his
little hickory switch gayly and called to his dog
Dunder that was nosing about by the roadside.
Dunder bounded forward, spied the newcomer, and
leaped toward her playfully and with natural
canine curiosity.

Bella screamed.   She screamed and ran to Ben
and clung to him, clasping her hands about his arm.
Ben lifted the hickory switch in his free hand and
struck Dunder a sharp cut with it.   It was the
first time in his life that he had done such a thing.
If he had had a sane moment from that time until
the day he married Bella Huckins, he would never
have forgotten the dumb hurt in Dunder's stricken
eyes and shrinking, quivering body.

Bella screamed again.   Still clinging to him,
Ben was saying: "He won't hurt you.   He won't
hurt you," meanwhile patting her shoulder reassuringly.   He looked down at her pale face.   She
was so slight, so childlike, so apparently different
from the sturdy country girls.   From—well, from
the girls he knew.   Her helplessness, her utter
femininity, appealed to all that was masculine in
him.   Bella the experienced, clinging to him, felt
herself swept from head to foot by a queer, electric

tingling that was very pleasant but that still had in it something of the sensation of a wholesale bumping of one's crazy bone. If she had been anything but a stupid little flirt, she would have realized that here was a specimen of the virile male with which she could not trifle. She glanced up at him now, smiling faintly. "My, I was scared!" She stepped away from him a little—very little.

"Aw, he wouldn't hurt a flea."

But Bella looked over her shoulders fearfully to where Dunder stood by the roadside, regarding Ben with a look of uncertainty. He still thought that perhaps this was a new game. Not a game that he cared for, but still one to be played if his master fancied it. Ben stooped, picked up a stone, and threw it at Dunder, striking him in the flank. "Go on home!" he commanded, sternly. "Go home!" He started toward the dog with a well-feigned gesture of menace. Dunder, with a low howl, put his tail between his legs and loped off home, a disillusioned dog.

Bella stood looking up at Ben. Ben looked down at her.

"You're the new teacher, ain't you?"

"Yes. I guess you must think I'm a fool, going on like a baby about that dog."

"Most girls would be scared of him if they didn't know he wouldn't hurt nobody. He's pretty big."

He paused a moment, awkwardly. "My name's Ben Westerveld."

"Pleased to meet you," said Bella, twiddling her fingers in assumed shyness.

"Which way was you going? There's a dog down at Tietjens that's enough to scare anybody. He looks like a pony, he's so big."

"I forgot something at the school this afternoon, and I was walking over to get it." Which was a lie. "I hope it won't get dark before I get there. You were going the other way, weren't you?"

"Oh, I wasn't going no place in particular. I'll be pleased to keep you company down to the school and back." He was surprised at his own sudden masterfulness.

They set off together, chatting as freely as if they had known one another for years. Ben had been on his way to the Byers farm, as usual. The Byers farm and Emma Byers passed out of his mind as completely as if they had been whisked away on a magic rug.

Bella Huckins had never meant to marry him. She hated farm life. She was contemptuous of farmer folk. She loathed cooking and drudgery. The Huckinses lived above the saloon in Commercial and Mrs. Huckins was always boiling ham and tongue and cooking pig's feet and shredding cabbage for slaw, all these edibles being destined for the free-lunch counter downstairs. Bella had early made up her mind that there should be no boiling and stewing and frying in her life. Whenever she could find an excuse, she loitered about the saloon. There she found life and talk and colour. Old Red Front Huckins used to chase her away, but she always turned up again, somehow, with a dish for the lunch counter or with an armful of clean towels.

Ben Westerveld never said clearly to himself: "I want to marry Bella." He never dared meet the thought. He intended honestly to marry Emma Byers. But this thing was too strong for him. As for Bella, she laughed at him, but she was scared, too. They both fought the thing, she selfishly, he unselfishly, for the Byers girl, with her clear, calm eyes and her dependable ways, was heavy on his heart. Ben's appeal for Bella was merely that of the magnetic male. She never once thought of his finer qualities. Her appeal for him was that of the frail and alluring woman. But in the end they married. The neighbourhood was rocked with surprise. In fact, the only unsurprised party to the transaction was the dame known as Nature. She has a way of playing these tricks on men and women for the furtherance of her own selfish ends.

Usually in a courtship it is the male who assumes the bright colours of pretence in order to attract a mate. But Ben Westerveld had been too honest to be anything but himself. He was so honest and fundamentally truthful that he refused at first to allow himself to believe that this slovenly shrew was the fragile and exquisite creature he had married. He had the habit of personal cleanliness, had Ben, in a day when tubbing was a ceremony and in an environment that made bodily nicety difficult. He discovered that Bella almost never washed and that her appearance of fragrant immaculateness, when dressed, was due to a natural clearness of skin and eye, and to the way her blonde hair swept away in a clean line from her forehead. For the rest, she was a slattern, with a vocabulary of invective that would have been a credit to any of the habitués of Old Red Front Huckins's bar.

They had three children, a girl and two boys. Ben Westerveld prospered in spite of his wife. As the years went on he added eighty acres here, eighty acres there, until his land swept down to the very banks of the Mississippi. There is no doubt that she hindered him greatly, but he was too expert a farmer to fail. At threshing time the crew looked forward to working for Ben, the farmer, and dreaded the meals prepared by Bella, his wife. She was notoriously the worst cook and housekeeper in the county. And all through the years, in trouble and in happiness, her plaint was the same: "If I'd thought I was going to stick down on a farm all my life, slavin' for a pack of men folks day and night, I'd rather have died. Might as well be dead as rottin' here."

Her school-teacher English had early reverted. Her speech was as slovenly as her dress. She grew stout, too, and unwieldy, and her skin coarsened from lack of care and overeating. And in her children's ears she continually dinned a hatred of farm life and farming. "You can get away from it," she counselled her daughter, Minnie. "Don't you be a rube like your pa," she cautioned John, the older boy. And they profited by her advice. Minnie went to work at Commercial when she was seventeen, an over-developed girl with an inordinate love of cheap finery. At twenty she married an artisan, a surly fellow with anarchistic tendencies. They moved from town to town. He never stuck long at one job. John, the older boy, was as much his mother's son as Minnie was her mother's daughter. Restless, dissatisfied, empty-headed, he was the despair of his father. He drove the farm horses as if they were racers, lashing them up hill and down dale. He was forever lounging off to the village or wheedling his mother for money to take him to Commercial. It was before the day of the ubiquitous automobile. Given one of those present adjuncts to farm life, John would have ended his career much earlier. As it was, they found him lying by the roadside at dawn one morning after the horses had trotted into the yard with the wreck of the buggy bumping the road behind them. He had stolen the horses out of the barn after the help was asleep, had led them stealthily down the road, and then had whirled off to a rendezvous of his own in town. The fall from the buggy might not have hurt him, but he evidently had been dragged almost a mile before his battered body became somehow disentangled from the splintered wood and the reins.

That horror might have served to bring Ben Westerveld and his wife together, but it did not. It only increased her bitterness and her hatred of the locality and the life.

"I hope you're good an' satisfied now," she repeated in endless reproach. "I hope you're good an' satisfied. You was bound you'd make a farmer out of him, an' now you finished the job. You better try your hand at Dike now for a change."

Dike was young Ben, sixteen; and old Ben had no need to try his hand at him. Young Ben was a

born farmer, as was his father. He had come honestly by his nickname. In face, figure, expression,
and manner he was a five-hundred-year throwback
to his Holland ancestors. Apple-cheeked, stocky,
merry of eye, and somewhat phlegmatic. When,
at school, they had come to the story of the Dutch
boy who saved his town from flood by thrusting his
hand into the hole in the dike and holding it there
until help came, the class, after one look at the
accompanying picture in the reader, dubbed
young Ben "Dike" Westerveld. And Dike he
remained.

Between Dike and his father there was a strong
but unspoken feeling. The boy was crop-wise, as
his father had been at his age. On Sundays you
might see the two walking about the farm looking
at the pigs—great black fellows worth almost
their weight in silver; eying the stock; speculating
on the winter wheat showing dark green in April
with rich patches that were almost black. Young
Dike smoked a solemn and judicious pipe, spat expertly, and voiced the opinion that the winter
wheat was a fine prospect. Ben Westerveld,
listening tolerantly to the boy's opinions, felt a
great surge of joy that he did not show. Here, at
last, was compensation for all the misery and
sordidness and bitter disappointment of his married life.

That married life had endured now for more than thirty years. Ben Westerveld still walked with a light, quick step—for his years. The stocky, broad-shouldered figure was a little shrunken. He was as neat and clean at fifty-five as he had been at twenty-five—a habit that requires much personal courage on a farm and that is fraught with difficulties. The community knew and respected him. He was a man of standing. When he drove into town on a bright winter morning and entered the First National Bank in his big sheepskin coat and his shaggy cap and his great boots, even Shumway, the cashier, would look up from his desk to say: "Hello, Westerveld! Hello! Well, how goes it?"

When Shumway greeted a farmer in that way you knew that there were no unpaid notes to his discredit.

All about Ben Westerveld stretched the fruit of his toil; the work of his hands. Orchards, fields, cattle, barns, silos. All these things were dependent on him for their future well-being—on him and on Dike after him. His days were full and running over. Much of the work was drudgery; most of it was back-breaking and laborious. But it was his place. It was his reason for being. And he felt that the reason was good, though he never put that thought into words, mental or spoken. He only knew that he was part of the

great scheme of things and that he was functioning
ably.   If he had expressed himself at all, he might
have said:

"Well, I got my work cut out for me, an' I do it
an' do it right."

There was a tractor now, of course; a phono-
graph with expensive records, so that Caruso and
McCormack and Elman were household words; a
sturdy, middle-class automobile, in which Bella
lolled red-faced in a lacy and beribboned boudoir
cap when they drove into town.   On a Saturday
afternoon you saw more boudoir caps skimming up
and down the main street in Commercial than you
might see in a century of French farces.

As Ben Westerveld had prospered his shrewish
wife had reaped her benefits.   Ben was not the
selfish type of farmer who insists on twentieth-
century farm implements and medieval household
equipment.   He had added a bedroom here, a
cool summer kitchen there, an ice house, a commodious porch, a washing machine, even a crude
bathroom.   But Bella remained unplacated.   Her
face was set toward the city.   And slowly, surely,
the effect of thirty-odd years of nagging was beginning to tell on Ben Westerveld.   He was the finer
metal, but she was the heavier, the coarser.   She
beat him and molded him as iron beats upon gold.

Minnie was living in Chicago now—a good-natured creature, but slack, like her mother. Her surly husband was still talking of his rights and crying down with the rich. They had two children. Minnie wrote of them, and of the delights of city life. Movies every night. Halsted Street just around the corner. The big stores. State Street. The L took you downtown in no time. Something going on all the while. Bella Westerveld, after one of those letters, was more than a chronic shrew; she became a terrible termagant.

When Ben Westerveld decided to concentrate on hogs and wheat he didn't dream that a world would be clamouring for hogs and wheat for four long years. When the time came he had them, and sold them fabulously. But wheat and hogs and markets became negligible things on the day that Dike with seven other farm boys from the district left for the nearest training camp that was to fit them for France and war.

Bella made the real fuss, wailing and mouthing and going into hysterics. Old Ben took it like a stoic. He drove the boy to town that day. When the train pulled out, you might have seen, if you had looked close, how the veins and cords swelled in the lean brown neck above the clean blue shirt. But that was all. As the weeks went on the quick, light step began to lag a little.

He had lost more than a son; his right-hand helper was gone. There were no farm helpers to be had. Old Ben couldn't do it all. A touch of rheumatism that winter half crippled him for eight weeks. Bella's voice seemed never to stop its plaint.

"There ain't no sense in you trying to make out alone. Next thing you'll die on me, and then I'll have the whole shebang on my hands." At that he eyed her dumbly from his chair by the stove. His resistance was wearing down. He knew it. He wasn't dying. He knew that, too. But something in him was. Something that had resisted her all these years. Something that had made him master and superior in spite of everything.

In those days of illness, as he sat by the stove, the memory of Emma Byers came to him often. She had left that district twenty-eight years ago, and had married, and lived in Chicago somewhere, he had heard, and was prosperous. He wasted no time in idle regrets. He had been a fool, and he paid the price of fools. Bella, slamming noisily about the room, never suspected the presence in the untidy place of a third person—a sturdy girl of twenty-two or three, very wholesome to look at, and with honest, intelligent eyes and a serene brow.

"It'll get worse an' worse all the time," Bella's whine went on. "Everybody says the war'll last prob'ly for years an' years. You can't make out alone. Everything's goin' to rack and ruin. You could rent out the farm for a year, on trial. The Burdickers'd take it and glad. They got those three strappin' louts that's all flat-footed or slab-sided or cross-eyed or somethin', and no good for the army. Let them run it on shares. Maybe they'll even buy, if things turn out. Maybe Dike'll never come b——"

But at the look on his face then, and at the low growl of unaccustomed rage that broke from him, even she ceased her clatter.

They moved to Chicago in the early spring. The look that had been on Ben Westerveld's face when he drove Dike to the train that carried him to camp was stamped there again—indelibly this time, it seemed. Calhoun County, in the spring, has much the beauty of California. There is a peculiar golden light about it, and the hills are a purplish haze. Ben Westerveld, walking down his path to the gate, was more poignantly dramatic than any figure in a rural play. He did not turn to look back, though, as they do in a play. He dared not.

They rented a flat in Englewood, Chicago, a

block from Minnie's. Bella was almost amiable
these days. She took to city life as though the
past thirty years had never been. White kid
shoes, delicatessen stores, the movies, the haggling
with peddlers, the crowds, the crashing noise, the
cramped, unnatural mode of living necessitated by
a four-room flat—all these urban adjuncts seemed
as natural to her as though she had been bred in
the midst of them.

She and Minnie used to spend whole days in
useless shopping. Theirs was a respectable neighbourhood of well-paid artisans, bookkeepers, and
small shopkeepers. The women did their own
housework in drab garments and soiled boudoir
caps that hid a multitude of unkempt heads.
They seemed to find a deal of time for amiable,
empty gabbling. Any time from seven to four
you might see a pair of boudoir caps leaning from
opposite bedroom windows, conversing across back
porches, pausing in the task of sweeping front steps,
standing at a street corner, laden with grocery
bundles. Minnie wasted hours in what she called
"running over to ma's for a minute." The two
quarrelled a great deal, being so nearly of a nature.
But the very qualities that combated each other
seemed, by some strange chemical process, to
bring them together as well.

"I'm going downtown to-day to do a little

shopping," Minnie would say. "Do you want to come along, ma?"

"What you got to get?"

"Oh, I thought I'd look at a couple of little dresses for Pearlie."

"When I was your age I made every stitch you wore."

"Yeh, I bet they looked like it, too. This ain't the farm. I got all I can do to tend to the house, without sewing."

"I did it. I did the housework and the sewin' and cookin', an' besides——"

"A swell lot of housekeepin' you did. You don't need to tell me."

The bickering grew to a quarrel. But in the end they took the downtown L together. You saw them, flushed of face, with twitching fingers, indulging in a sort of orgy of dime spending in the five-and-ten-cent store on the wrong side of State Street. They pawed over bolts of cheap lace and bins of stuff in the fetid air of the crowded place. They would buy a sack of salted peanuts from the great mound in the glass case, or a bag of the greasy pink candy piled in vile profusion on the counter, and this they would munch as they went.

They came home late, fagged and irritable, and supplemented their hurried dinner with hastily

bought and so-called food from the near-by delicatessen.

Thus ran the life of ease for Ben Westerveld,
retired farmer. And so we find him lying im-
patiently in bed, rubbing a nervous forefinger over
the edge of the sheet and saying to himself that,
well, here was another day. What day was it?
Le'see now. Yesterday was—yesterday—a little
feeling of panic came over him. He couldn't remember what yesterday had been. He counted
back laboriously and decided that to-day must
be Thursday. Not that it made any difference.

They had lived in the city almost a year now.
But the city had not digested Ben. He was a
leathery morsel that could not be assimilated.
There he stuck in Chicago's crop, contributing
nothing, gaining nothing. A rube in a comic collar
ambling aimlessly about Halsted Street, or State
downtown. You saw him conversing hungrily with
the gritty and taciturn Swede who was janitor for
the block of red-brick flats. Ben used to follow
him around pathetically, engaging him in the
talk of the day. Ben knew no men except the
surly Gus, Minnie's husband. Gus, the firebrand,
thought Ben hardly worthy of his contempt. If
Ben thought, sometimes, of the respect with which
he had always been greeted when he clumped down

the main street of Commercial, Ill.—if he thought
of how the farmers for miles around had come
to him for expert advice and opinion—he said
nothing.

Sometimes the janitor graciously allowed Ben to
attend to the furnace of the building in which he
lived. He took out ashes, shovelled coal. He tinkered and rattled and shook things. You heard
him shovelling and scraping down there, and
smelled the acrid odour of his pipe. It gave him
something to do. He would emerge sooty and
almost happy.

"You been monkeying with that furnace again!"
Bella would scold. "If you want something to do,
why don't you plant a garden in the backyard and
grow something. You was crazy enough about
it on the farm."

His face flushed a slow, dull red at that. He
could not explain to her that he lost no dignity in
his own eyes in fussing about an inadequate little
furnace, but that self-respect would not allow him
to stoop to gardening—he who had reigned over
six hundred acres of bountiful soil.

On winter afternoons you saw him sometimes at
the movies, whiling away one of his many idle
hours in the dim, close-smelling atmosphere of the
place. Tokyo and Petrograd and Gallipoli came
to him. He saw beautiful tiger women twining fair,

false arms about the stalwart but yielding forms of young men with cleft chins. He was only mildly interested. He talked to any one who would talk to him, though he was naturally a shy man. He talked to the barber, to the grocer, the druggist, the street-car conductor, the milkman, the iceman. But the price of wheat did not interest these gentlemen. They did not know that the price of wheat was the most vital topic of conversation in the world.

"Well, now," he would say, "you take this year's wheat crop with about 917,000,000 bushels of wheat harvested, why, that's what's going to win the war! Yes, sirree! No wheat, no winning, that's what I say."

"Ya-as, it is!" the city men would scoff. But the queer part of it is that Farmer Ben was right.

Minnie got into the habit of using him as a sort of nursemaid. It gave her many hours of unearned freedom for gadding and gossiping.

"Pa, will you look after Pearlie for a little while this morning? I got to run downtown to match something and she gets so tired and mean-acting if I take her along. Ma's goin' with me."

He loved the feel of Pearlie's small, velvet-soft hand in his big fist. He called her "little feller," and fed her forbidden dainties. His big brown fingers were miraculously deft at buttoning and unbuttoning her tiny garments, and wiping her soft lips, and performing a hundred tender offices. I think that he was playing a sort of game with himself, and that he pretended this was Dike become a baby again. Once the pair managed to get over to Lincoln Park, where they spent a glorious day looking at the animals, eating pop-corn, and riding on the miniature railway.

They returned, tired, dusty, and happy, to a double tirade.

Bella engaged in a great deal of what she called worrying about Dike. Ben spoke of him seldom, but the boy was always present in his thoughts. They had written him of their move, but he had not seemed to get the impression of its perma-nence. His letters indicated that he thought they were visiting Minnie, or taking a vacation in the city. Dike's letters were few. Ben treasured them, and read and reread them. When the ar-mistice news came, and with it the possibility of Dike's return, Ben tried to fancy him fitting into the life of the city. And his whole being revolted at the thought.

He saw the pimply-faced, sallow youths in their one-button suits and striped shirts standing at the corner of Halsted and Sixty-Third, spitting lan-guidly and handling their limp cigarettes with an amazing labial dexterity. Their conversation was low-voiced, sinister, and terse, and their eyes narrowed as they watched the over-dressed, scarlet-lipped girls go by. A great fear clutched at Ben Westerveld's heart.

The lack of exercise and manual labour began to tell on Ben. He did not grow fat from idleness. Instead his skin seemed to sag and hang on his frame, like a garment grown too large for him. He walked a great deal. Perhaps that had something to do with it. He tramped miles of city pavements. He was a very lonely man. And then, one day, quite by accident, he came upon South Water Street. Came upon it, stared at it as a water-crazed traveller in a desert gazes upon the spring in the oasis, and drank from it, thirstily, gratefully.

South Water Street feeds Chicago. Into that close-packed thoroughfare come daily the fruits and vegetables that will supply a million tables. Ben had heard of it, vaguely, but had never attempted to find it. Now he stumbled upon it and standing there felt at home in Chicago for the first time in more than a year. He saw ruddy men walking about in overalls and carrying whips in their hands—wagon whips, actually. He hadn't seen men like that since he left the farm. The sight of them sent a great pang of homesickness through him. His hand reached out and he ran an accustomed finger over the potatoes in a barrel on the walk. His fingers lingered and gripped them, and passed over them lovingly.

At the contact something within him that had been tight and hungry seemed to relax, satisfied. It was his nerves, feeding on those familiar things for which they had been starving.

He walked up one side and down the other. Crates of lettuce, bins of onions, barrels of apples. Such vegetables!

The radishes were scarlet globes. Each carrot was a spear of pure orange. The green and purple of fancy asparagus held his expert eye. The cauliflower was like a great bouquet, fit for a bride; the cabbages glowed like jade.

And the men! He hadn't dreamed there were men like that in this big, shiny-shod, stiffly laundered, white-collared city. Here were rufous men in overalls—worn, shabby, easy-looking overalls and old blue shirts, and mashed hats worn at a careless angle. Men jovial, good-natured, with clear blue eyes and having about them some of the revivifying freshness and wholesomeness of the products they handled.

Ben Westerveld breathed in the strong, pungent smell of onions and garlic and of the good earth that seemed to cling to the vegetables, washed clean though they were. He breathed deeply, gratefully, and felt strangely at peace.

It was a busy street. A hundred times he had to step quickly to avoid hand truck, or dray, or laden wagon. And yet the busy men found time to greet him friendlily: "H'are you!" they said, genially. "H'are you this morning!"

He was market-wise enough to know that some of these busy people were commission men, and some grocers, and some buyers, stewards, clerks. It was a womanless thoroughfare. At the busiest business corner, though, in front of the largest commission house on the street, he saw a woman. Evidently she was transacting business, too, for he saw the men bringing boxes of berries and vegetables for her inspection. A woman in a plain blue skirt and a small black hat.

He caught a glimpse of white-streaked hair beneath the hat. A funny job for a woman. What weren't they mixing into nowadays! He turned sidewise in the narrow, crowded space in order to pass her little group. And one of the men—a red-cheeked, merry-looking young fellow in white apron—laughed and said: "Well, Emma, you win. When it comes to driving a bargain with you, I quit. It can't be did!"

Even then he didn't know her. He did not dream that this straight, slim, tailored, white-haired woman, bargaining so shrewdly with these men, was the Emma Byers of the old days. But he stopped there a moment, in frank curiosity, and the woman looked up. She looked up, and he knew those intelligent eyes and that serene brow. He had carried the picture of them in his mind for more than thirty years, so it was not so surprising. And time deals kindly with women who have intelligent eyes and serene brows.

He did not hesitate. He might have if he had thought a moment, but he acted automatically. He stood before her. "You're Emma Byers, ain't you?"

She did not know him at first. Small blame to her, so completely had the roguish, vigorous boy vanished in this sallow, sad-eyed old man. Then: "Why, Ben!" she said, quietly. And there was pity in her voice, though she did not mean to have it there. She put out one hand—that capable, reassuring hand—and gripped his and held it a moment. It was queer and significant that it should be his hand that lay within hers.

"Well, what in all get-out are you doing around here, Emma?" He tried to be jovial and easy. She turned to the aproned man with whom she had been dealing and smiled.

"What am I doing here, Joe?" she said.

Joe grinned, waggishly. "Nothin'; only beatin'

every man on the street at his own game, and makin' so much money that——"

But she stopped him there. "I guess I'll do my own explaining." She turned to Ben again. "And what are you doing here in Chicago?"

Ben passed a faltering hand across his chin. "Me? Well, I'm—we're livin' here, I s'pose. Livin' here."

She glanced at him, sharply. "Left the farm, Ben?"

"Yes."

"Wait a minute." She concluded her business with Joe; finished it briskly and to her own satisfaction. With her bright brown eyes and her alert manner and her quick little movements she made you think of a wren—a business-like little wren—a very early wren that is highly versed in the worm-catching way.

At her next utterance he was startled but game. "Have you had your lunch?"

"Why, no; I——"

"I've been down here since seven, and I'm starved. Let's go and have a bite at the little Greek restaurant around the corner. A cup of coffee and a sandwich, anyway."

Seated at the bare little table, she surveyed him with those intelligent, understanding, kindly eyes, and he felt the years slip from him. They were

walking down the country road together, and she
was listening quietly and advising him.

She interrogated him, gently.   But something of
his old masterfulness came back to him.   "No, I
want to know about you first.   I can't get the
rights of it, you being here on South Water, tradin'
and all."

So she told him, briefly.   She was in the commission business.   Successful.   She bought, too,
for such hotels as the Blackstone and the Congress,
and for half a dozen big restaurants.   She gave
him bare facts, but he was shrewd enough and
sufficiently versed in business to know that here
was a woman of wealth and established commercial position.

"But how does it happen you're keepin' it up,
Emma, all this time?   Why, you must be anyway
—it ain't that you look it—but——" He floundered, stopped.

She laughed.   "That's all right, Ben.   I couldn't
fool you on that.   And I'm working because it
keeps me happy.   I want to work till I die.   My
children keep telling me to stop, but I know better
than that.   I'm not going to rust out.   I want to
wear out."   Then, at an unspoken question in his
eyes: "He's dead.   These twenty years.   It
was hard at first when the children were small.
But I knew garden stuff if I didn't know

anything else. It came natural to me. That's all."

So then she got his story from him bit by bit. He spoke of the farm and of Dike, and there was a great pride in his voice. He spoke of Bella, and the son who had been killed, and of Minnie. And the words came falteringly. He was trying to hide something, and he was not made for deception. When he had finished:

"Now, listen, Ben. You go back to your farm."

"I can't. She—— I can't."

She leaned forward, earnestly. "You go back to the farm."

He turned up his palms with a little gesture of defeat. "I can't."

"You can't stay here. It's killing you. It's poisoning you. Did you ever hear of toxins? That means poisons, and you're poisoning yourself. You'll die of it. You've got another twenty years of work in you. What's ailing you? You go back to your wheat and your apples and your hogs. There isn't a bigger job in the world than that."

For a moment his face took on a glow from the warmth of her own inspiring personality. But it died again. When they rose to go his shoulders drooped again, his muscles sagged. At the doorway he paused a moment, awkward in farewell. He blushed a little, stammered.

"Emma—I always wanted to tell you. God knows it was luck for you the way it turned out— but I always wanted to——"

She took his hand again in her firm grip at that, and her kindly, bright brown eyes were on him. "I never held it against you, Ben. I had to live a long time to understand it. But I never held a grudge. It just wasn't to be, I suppose. But listen to me, Ben. You do as I tell you. You go back to your wheat and your apples and your hogs. There isn't a bigger man-size job in the world. It's where you belong."

Unconsciously his shoulders straightened again. Again they sagged. And so they parted, the two.

He must have walked almost all the long way home, through miles and miles of city streets. He must have lost his way, too, for when he looked up at a corner street sign it was an unfamiliar one.

So he floundered about, asked his way, was misdirected. He took the right street car at last and got off at his own corner at seven o'clock, or later. He was in for a scolding, he knew.

But when he came to his own doorway he knew that even his tardiness could not justify the bedlam of sound that came from within. High-pitched voices. Bella's above all the rest, of course, but there was Minnie's, too, and Gus's growl, and Pearlie's treble, and the boy Ed's, and——

At the other voice his hand trembled so that the key rattled in the lock, and he could not turn it. But finally he did turn it, and stumbled in, breathing hard. And that other voice was Dike's.

He must just have arrived. The flurry of explanation was still in progress. Dike's knapsack was still on his back, and his canteen at his hip, his helmet slung over his shoulder. A brown, hard, glowing Dike, strangely tall and handsome and older, too. Older.

All this he saw in less than one electric second. Then he had the boy's two shoulders in his hands, and Dike was saying: "Hello, pop."

Of the roomful, Dike and old Ben were the only quiet ones. The others were taking up the explanation and going over it again and again, and marvelling, and asking questions.

"He come in to—what's that place, Dike?— Hoboken—yesterday only. An' he sent a dispatch to the farm. Can't you read our letters, Dike, that you didn't know we was here now? And then he's only got an hour more here. They got to go to Camp Grant to be, now, demobilized. He come out to Minnie's on a chance. Ain't he big!"

But Dike and his father were looking at each other quietly. Then Dike spoke. His speech was not phlegmatic, as of old. He had a new clipped way of uttering his words:

"Say, pop, you ought to see the way the Frenchies farm! They got about an acre each, and, say, they use every inch of it. If they's a little dirt blows into the crotch of a tree, they plant a crop in there. I never see nothin' like it. Say, we waste enough stuff over here to keep that whole country in food for a hundred years. Yessir. And tools! Outta the ark, believe me. If they ever saw our tractor, they'd think it was the Germans comin' back. But they're smart at that. I picked up a lot of new ideas over there. And you ought to see the old birds—womenfolks and men about eighty years old—runnin' everything on the farm. They had to. I learned somethin' off of them about farmin'."

"Forget the farm," said Minnie.

"Yeh," echoed Gus, "forget the farm stuff. I can get you a job here out at the works for four a day, and six when you learn it right."

Dike looked from one to the other, alarm and unbelief on his face. "What d'you mean, a job? Who wants a job! What you all——"

Bella laughed, jovially. "F'r Heaven's sakes, Dike, wake up! We're livin' here. This is our place. We ain't rubes no more."

Dike turned to his father. A little stunned look

crept into his face. A stricken, pitiful look.
There was something about it that suddenly made
old Ben think of Pearlie when she had been slapped
by her quick-tempered mother.

"But I been countin' on the farm," he said,
miserably. "I just been livin' on the idea of
comin' back to it. Why, I—— The streets here,
they're all narrow and choked up. I been countin'
on the farm. I want to go back and be a farmer.
I want——"

And then Ben Westerveld spoke. A new Ben
Westerveld—no, not a new, but the old Ben
Westerveld. Ben Westerveld, the farmer, the
monarch over six hundred acres of bounteous bot-
tomland.

"That's all right, Dike," he said. "You're going back. So'm I. I've got another twenty years
of work in me. We're going back to the farm."

Bella turned on him, a wildcat. "We ain't! Not
me! We ain't! I'm not agoin' back to the farm."

But Ben Westerveld was master again in his own
house. "You're goin' back, Bella," he said,
quietly. "An' things are goin' to be different.
You're goin' to run the house the way I say, or I'll
know why. If you can't do it, I'll get them in that
can. An' me and Dike, we're goin' back to our
wheat and our apples and our hogs. Yessir!
There ain't a bigger man-size job in the world."

THE DANCING GIRLS

WHEN, on opening a magazine, you see a picture of a young man in uniform with a background of assorted star-shells in full flower; a young man in uniform gazing into the eyes of a young lady (in uniform); a young man in uniform crouching in a trench, dugout, or shell-hole, this happens:

You skip lightly past the story of the young man in uniform; you jump hurriedly over the picture; and you plunge into the next story, noting that it is called "The Crimson Emerald" and that, judging from the pictures, all the characters in it wear evening clothes all the time.

Chug Scaritt took his dose of war with the best of them, but this is of Chug before and after taking. If, inadvertently, there should sound a faintly martial note it shall be stifled at once with a series of those stylish dots . . . indicative of what the early Victorian writers conveniently called a drawn veil.

Nothing could be fairer than that.

Chug Scaritt was (and is) the proprietor and sole owner of the Elite Garage, and he pronounced

it with a long i. Automobile parties, touring
Wisconsin, used to mistake him for a handy man
about the place and would call to him, "Heh, boy!
Come here and take a look at this engine. She
ain't hitting." When Chug finished with her
she was hitting, all right. A medium-sized young
fellow in the early twenties with a serious mouth,
laughing eyes, and a muscular grace pretty well
concealed by the grease-grimed grotesquerie of
overalls. Out of the overalls and in his tight-
fitting, belted green suit and long-visored green
cap and flat russet shoes he looked too young and
insouciant to be the sole owner—much less the
proprietor—of anything so successful and established as the Elite Garage.

In a town like Chippewa, Wisconsin—or in any
other sort of town, for that matter—a prosperous
garage knows more about the scandals of the community than does a barber-shop, a dressmaker-
by-the-day, or a pool-room habitué. It conceals
more skeletons than the catacombs. Chug Scar-
rit, had he cared to open his lips and speak, might
have poured forth such chronicles as to make
Spoon River sound a pæan of sweetness and light.
He knew how much Old Man Hatton's chauffeur
knocked down on gas and repairs; he knew just
how much the Tillotsons had gone into debt for
their twin-six, and why Emil Sauter drove to

Oshkosh so often on business, and who supplied the flowers for Mrs. Gurnee's electric. Chug didn't encourage gossip in his garage. Whenever possible he put his foot down on its ugly head in a vain attempt to crush it. But there was something about the very atmosphere of the place that caused it to thrive and flourish. It was like a combination newspaper office and Pullman car smoker. Chug tried to keep the thing down but there might generally be seen lounging about the doorway or perched on the running board of an idle car a little group of slim, flat-heeled, low-voiced young men in form-fitting, high-waisted suits of that peculiarly virulent shade of green which makes its wearer look as if he had been picked before he was ripe.

They were a lean, slim-flanked crew with a feline sort of grace about them; terse of speech, quick of eye, engine-wise, and, generally, nursing a boil just above the collar of their soft shirt. Not vicious. Not even tough. Rather bored, though they didn't know it. In their boredom resorting to the only sort of solace afforded boys of their class in a town of Chippewa's size: cheap amusements, cheap girls, cheap talk. This last unless the topic chanced to be of games or of things mechanical. Baseball, or a sweet-running engine brought out the best that was in them. At their worst, perhaps, they stood well back in the dim, cool shade of the garage doorway to watch how, when the girls went by in their thin summer dresses, the strong sunlight made a transparency of their skirts. At supper time they would growl to their surprised sisters:

"Put on some petticoats, you. Way you girls run around it's enough to make a person sick."

Chug Scaritt escaped being one of these by a double margin. There was his business responsibility on one side; his very early history on the other. Once you learn the derivation of Chug's nickname you have that history from the age of five to twenty-five, inclusive.

Chug had been christened Floyd (she had got it out of a book) but it was an appendix rather then an appellation. No one ever dreamed of addressing him by that misnomer, unless you except his school teachers. Once or twice the boys had tried to use his name as a weapon, shrieking in a shrill falsetto and making two syllables of it. He put a stop to that soon enough with fists and feet. His virility could have triumphed over a name twice as puerile. For that matter, I once knew a young husky named Fayette who—but that's another story.

The Scaritts lived the other side of the tracks. If you know Chippewa, or its equivalent, you get the significance of that. Nobodys. Not only did they live the other side of the tracks; they lived so close to them that the rush and rumble of the passing trains shook the two-story frame cottage and rattled the crockery on the pantry shelves. The first intelligible sound the boy made was a chesty chug-chug-chug in imitation of a panting engine tugging its freight load up the incline toward the Junction. When Chug ran away—which was on an average of twice daily—he was invariably to be found at the switchman's shanty or roaming about the freight yards. It got so that Stumpy Gans, the one-legged switchman, would hoist a signal to let Mrs. Scaritt know that Chug was safe.

He took his first mechanical toy apart, piece by piece. "Wait till your pa comes home!" his mother had said, with terrible significance. Chug, deep in the toy's wreckage, seemed undismayed, so Mrs. Scaritt gave him a light promissory slap and went on about her housework. That night, before supper, Len Scaritt addressed his son with a sternness quite at variance with his easy-going nature.

"Come here to me! Now, then, what's this about your smashing up good toys? Huh? Whatdya mean! Christmas not two days back and here you go smashing——"

The culprit trotted over to a corner and returned with the red-painted tin thing in his hand. It was as good as new. There may even have been some barely noticeable improvement in its locomotive powers. Chug had merely taken it apart in order to put it together again, and he had been too absorbed to pause long enough to tell his mother so. After that, nothing that bore wheels, internally or externally, was safe from his investigating fingers.

It was his first velocipede that really gave him his name. As he rode up and down, his short legs working like piston-rods gone mad, pedestrians would scatter in terror. His onrush was as relentless as that of an engine on a track, and his hoarse, "Chug-chug! Da-r-r-n-ng! Da-r-r-n-ng!" as he bore down upon a passerby caused that one to sidestep precipitously into the gutter (and none too soon).

Chug earned his first real bicycle carrying a paper route for the Chippewa *Eagle*. It took him two years. By the time he had acquired it he knew so much about bicycles, from ball-bearings to handle-bars, that its possession roused very little thrill in him. It was as when a lover has had to wait over-long for his bride. As Chug whizzed about Chippewa's streets, ringing an unnecessarily insistent bell, you sensed that a motorcycle was already looming large in his mechanism-loving mind. By the time he was seventeen Chug's motorcycle was spitting its way venomously down Elm Street. And the sequence of the seasons was not more inevitable than that an automobile should follow the motorcycle. True, he practically built it himself, out of what appeared to be an old wash-boiler, some wire, and an engine made up of parts that embraced every known car from Ford to Fiat. He painted it an undeniable red, hooded it like a demon racer, and shifted to first. The thing went.

He was a natural mechanic. He couldn't spend a day with a piece of mechanism without having speeded it up, or in some way done something to its belt, gears, wheels, motor. He was almost never separated from a monkey-wrench or pliers, and he was always turning a nut or bolt or screw in his grease-grimed fingers.

Right here it should be understood that Chug never became a Steinmetz or a Wright. He remained just average-plus to the end, with something more than a knack at things mechanical; a good deal of grease beneath his nails; and, generally, a smudge under one eye or a swipe of black across a cheek that gave him a misleadingly sinister and piratical look. There's nothing very magnificent, surely, in being the proprietor of a garage, even if it is the best-paying garage in Chippewa, where six out of ten families own a car, and summer tourists are as locusts turned beneficent.

Some time between Chug's motorcycle and the

home-made automobile Len Scaritt died. The
loss to the household was social more than eco-
nomic.   Len had been one of those good-natured,
voluble, walrus-moustached men who make such
poor providers.   A carpenter by trade, he had always been a spasmodic worker and a steady talker.
His high, hollow voice went on endlessly above
the fusillade of hammers at work and the clatter
of dishes at home.   Politics, unions, world events,
local happenings, neighbourhood gossip, all fed the
endless stream of his loquacity.

"Well, now, looka here.   Take, f'rins'ance, one
these here big concerns——"

After he was gone Mrs. Scaritt used to find herself listening to the silence.   His ceaseless talk
had often rasped her nerves to the point of hysteria,
but now she missed it as we miss a dull ache to
which we have grown accustomed.

Chug was in his second year at the Chippewa
high school.   He had always earned some money,
afternoons and Saturdays.   Now he quit to go to
work in earnest.   His mother took it hard.

"I wanted you to have an education," she said.
"Not just schooling.   An education."   Mittie
Scaritt had always had ambition and a fierce sort
of pride.   She had needed them to combat Len's
shiftlessness and slack good nature.   They had
kept the two-story frame cottage painted and tidy,

had her pride and ambition; they had managed a Sunday suit, always, for Chug; money for the contribution box; pork roast on Sundays; and a sitting room, chill but elegant, with its plump pyramids of pillows, embroidered with impossible daisies and carnations and violets, filling every corner.

Mrs. Scaritt had had to fight for Chug's two years of high school. "He don't need no high school," Len Scaritt had argued, in one of the rare quarrels between the two. "I never had none."

The retort to this was so obvious that his wife refrained from uttering it. Len continued: "He don't go with none of my money. His age I was working 'n' had been for three years and more. You'll be fixing to send him to college, next."

"Well, if I do? Then what?"

"Then you're crazy," said Len, without heat, as one would state a self-evident fact.

That afternoon Mrs. Scaritt went down to the office of the *Eagle* and inserted a neat ad.

LACE CURTAINS DONE UP LIKE NEW. 25 CENTS A PR. MRS. SCARITT, 639 OUTAGAMIE ST.

For years afterward you never passed the Scaritt place without seeing the long skeleton frames of wooden curtain stretchers propped up against the back porch in the sun. Mrs. Scaritt became

famous for her curtains as an artist is known for
his middle distances, his woodland green, or his
flesh tones. In time even the Hattons, who had
always heretofore sent their fine curtains to Milwaukee to be cleaned, trusted their lacy treasures
to Mrs. Scaritt's expert hands.

Chug went to high school on those lace curtains.
He used to call for and deliver them. He rigged
up a shelf-like device on his bicycle handlebars.
On this the freshly laundered curtains reposed in
their neat paper wrappings as unwrinkled as when
they had come from the stretching frame.

At seventeen he went to work in the Elite Garage. He hadn't been there a month before the
owner was saying, "Say, Chug, take a look at this
here bus, will you? She don't run right but I
can't find out what's got into her."

Chug would put his ear to the heart of the car,
and tap its vitals, and count its pulse-beats as a
doctor sounds you with his stethoscope. The
look on his face was that of a violinist who tries
his G-string.

For the rest, he filled gas tanks, changed and
pumped up tires, tested batteries, oiled tappets.
But the thing that fascinated him was the engine.
An oily, blue-eyed boy in spattered overalls, he
was always just emerging from beneath a car, or
crawling under it. When a new car came in, en

route—a proud, glittering affair—he always managed to get a chance at it somehow, though the
owner or chauffeur guarded it ever so jealously.
The only thing on wheels that he really despised
was an electric brougham. Chippewa's well-
paved streets made these vehicles possible. Your
true garage man's feeling for electrics is unprint-
able. The least that they called them was juice-
boxes.

At home Chug was forever rigging up labour-
saving devices for his mother. The Scaritt's
window-shades always rolled; their doorbell
always rang with a satisfactory zing; their suc-
tion-pump never stuck. By the time he was
twenty Chug was manager of the garage and his
mother was saying, "You're around that garage
sixteen hours a day. When you're home you're
everlastingly reading those engineering papers
and things. Your pa at your age had a girl
for every night in the week and two on Sundays."

"Another year or so and I can buy out old
Behnke and own the place. Soon's I do I'm going
to come home in the speediest boat in the barn,
and I'm going to bust up those curtain frames into
kindling wood, over my knee, and pile 'em in the
backyard and make a bonfire out of 'em."

"They've been pretty good friends to us, Chug—
those curtain frames."

"Um." He glanced at her parboiled fingers. "Just the same, it'll be nix with the lace curtains for you."

Glancing back on what has been told of Chug he sounds, somehow, so much like a modern Rollo, with a dash of Alger, that unless something is told of his social side he may be misunderstood.

Chug was a natural born dancer. There are young men who, after the music has struck up, can start out incredibly enough by saying: "What is this, anyway—waltz or fox trot?" This was inconceivable to Chug. He had never had a dancing lesson in his life, but he had a sense of rhythm that was infallible. He could no more have danced out of time than he could have started a car on high, or confused a flivver with a Twelve. He didn't look particularly swanlike as he danced, having large, sensible feet, but they were expert at not being where someone else's feet happened to be, and he could time a beat to the fraction of a second.

When you have practically spent your entire day sprawled under a balky car, with a piece of dirty mat between you and the cement floor, your view limited to crank-case, transmission, universal, fly-wheel, differential, pan, and brake-rods you can do with a bit of colour in the evening. And just here was where Chippewa failed Chug.

He had a grave problem confronting him in his

search for an evening's amusement. Chippewa,
Wisconsin, was proud of its paved streets, its
thirty thousand population, its lighting system,
and the Greek temple that was the new First
National Bank. It boasted of its interurban lines,
its neat houses set well back among old elms, its
paper mills, its plough works, and its prosperity.
If you had told Chippewa that it was criminally
ignoring Chug's crying need it would have put
you down as mad.

Boiled down, Chug Scaritt's crying need was
girls. At twenty-two or three you must have girls
in your life if you're normal. Chug was, but
Chippewa wasn't. It had too many millionaires
at one end and too many labourers at the other
for a town of thirty thousand. Its millionaires
had their golf club, their high-powered cars, their
smart social functions. They were always running down to Chicago to hear Galli-Curci; and
when it came to costume—diamond bracelet, dar-
ing décolletage, large feather fans, and brilliant-
buckled slippers—you couldn't tell their women
from the city dwellers. There is much money in
paper mills and plough works.

The mill hands and their families were well-
paid, thrifty, clannish Swedes, most of them, with
a liberal sprinkling of Belgians and Slavs. They
belonged to all sorts of societies and lodges to

which they paid infinitesimal dues and swore life-long allegiance.

Chug Scaritt and boys of his kind were left high and dry. So, then, when Chug went out with a girl it was likely to be by way of someone's kitchen; or with one of those who worked in the rag room at the paper and pulp mill. They were the very girls who switched up and down in front of the garage evenings and Saturday afternoons. Many of them had been farm girls in Michigan or northern Wisconsin or even Minnesota. In Chippewa they did housework. Big, robust girls they were, miraculously well dressed in good shoes and suits and hats. They had bad teeth, for the most part, with a scum over them; over-fond of coffee; and were rather dull company. But they were good-natured, and hearty, and generous.

The paper-mill girls were quite another type. Theirs was a grayish pallor due to lungs dust-choked from work in the rag room. That same pallor promised ill for future generations in Chippewa. But they had a rather appealing, wistful fragility. Their eyes generally looked too big for their faces. They possessed, though, a certain vivacity and diablerie that the big, slower-witted Swede girls lacked.

When Chug felt the need of a dash of red in the evening he had little choice. In the winter he

often went up to Woodman's Hall.   The dances at
Woodman's Hall were of the kind advertised at
fifty cents a couple.   Extra lady, twenty-five cents.
Ladies without gents, thirty-five cents.   Bergstrom's two-piece orchestra.   Chug usually went
alone, but he escorted home one of the ladies-
without-gents.   It was not that he begrudged the
fifty cents.   Chug was free enough with his money.
He went to these dances on a last-minute impulse,
almost against his will, and out of sheer boredom.
Once there he danced every dance and all the
encores.   The girls fought for him.   Their manner
of dancing was cheek to cheek, in wordless rhythm.
His arm about the ample waist of one of the Swedish girls, or clasping close the frail form of one of
the mill hands, Chug would dance on and on,
indefatigably, until the music played "Home Sweet
Home."   The conversation, if any, varied little.

"The music's swell to-night," from the girl.

"Yeh."

"You're some little dancer, Chug, I'll say.   Honest, I could dance with you forever."   This with a
pressure of the girl's arm, and spoken with a little
accent, whether Swedish, Belgian, or Slavic.

"They all say that."

"Crazy about yourself, ain't you!"

"Not as crazy as I am about you," with tardy
gallantry.

He was very little stirred, really.

"Yeh, you are. I wish you was. It makes no never minds to you who you're dancing with, s'long's you're dancing."

This last came one evening as a variant in the usual formula. It startled Chug a little, so that he held the girl off the better to look at her. She was Wanda something-or-other, and anybody but Chug would have been alive to the fact that she had been stalking him for weeks with a stolid persistence.

"Danced with you three times to-night, haven't I?" he demanded. He was rather surprised to find that this was so.

"Wisht it was thirty."

That was Wanda. Her very eagerness foiled her. She cheapened herself. When Chug said, "Can I see you home?" he knew the answer before he put the question. Too easy to get along with, Wanda. Always there ahead of time, waiting, when you made a date with her. Too ready to forgive you when you failed to show up. Telephoned you when you were busy. Didn't give a fellow a chance to come half way, but went seven eighths of it herself. An ignorant, kindly, dangerous girl, with the physical development of a woman and the mind of a child. There were dozens like her in Chippewa.

If the girls of his own class noticed him at all it was the more to ignore him as a rather grimy mechanic passing briefly before their vision down Outagamie Street on his way to and from dinner. He was shy of them. They had a middle-class primness which forbade their making advances even had they been so inclined. Chug would no more have scraped acquaintance with them than he would have tried to flirt with Angie Hatton, Old Man Hatton's daughter, and the richest girl in Chippewa—so rich that she drove her own car with the chauffeur stuck up behind.

You didn't have to worry about Wanda and her kind. There they were, take them or leave them. They expected you to squeeze their waist when you danced with them, and so you did. You didn't have to think about what you were going to say to them.

Mrs. Scaritt suspected in a vague sort of way that Chug was "running with the hired girls." The thought distressed her. She was too smart a woman to nag him about it. She tried diplomacy.

"Why don't you bring some young folks home to eat, Chug? I like to fuss around for company." She was a wonderful cook, Mrs. Scaritt, and liked to display her skill.

"Who is there to bring?"

"The boys and girls you go around with. Who is it you're always fixing up for, evenings?"

"Nobody."

Mrs. Scaritt tried another tack.

"'I s'pose this house isn't good enough for 'em? Is that it?"

"Good enough!" Chug laughed rather grimly. "I'd like to know what's the matter with it!"

There was, as a matter of fact, nothing the matter with it. It was as spick and span as paint and polish could make it. The curtain-stretching days were long past. There had even been talk of moving out of the house by the tracks, but at the last moment Mrs. Scaritt had rebelled.

"I'll miss the sound of the trains. I'm used to 'em. It's got so I can tell just where my right hand'll be when the seven fifty-two goes by in the morning, and I've got used to putting on the potatoes when I hear the 'leven-forty. Let's stay, Chug."

So they had stayed. Gradually they had added an improvement here, a convenience there, as Chug's prosperity grew, until now the cottage by the tracks was newly painted, bathroomed, electric-lighted, with a cement walk front and back and a porch with a wicker swing and flower baskets. Chug gave his mother more housekeeping money than she needed, though she, in turn, served him meals that would have threatened the waist-line of an older and less active man. There was a banana pie, for instance (it sounds sickish, but wait!) which she baked in a deep pan, and over which she poured a golden-brown custard all flecked with crusty melted sugar. You took a bite and lo! it had vanished like a sweet dewdrop, leaving in your mouth a taste as of nectar, and clover-honey, and velvet cream.

Mrs. Scaritt learned to gauge Chug's plans for the evening by his ablutions. Elaborate enough at any time, on dance nights they amounted to a rite. In the old days Chug's father had always made a brief enough business of the process he called washing up. A hand-basin in the kitchen sink or on the back-porch bench sufficed. The noises he made were out of all proportion to the results obtained. His snufflings, and snortings, and splashings were like those of a grampus at play. When he emerged from them you were surprised to find that he had merely washed his face.

Chug had grease to fight. He had learned how in his first days at the garage. His teacher had been old Rudie, a mechanic who had tinkered around automobiles since their kerosene days, and who knew more about them than their inventor. Soap and water alone were powerless against the grease and carbon and dust that ground themselves into Chug's skin. First, he lathered himself with warm, soapy water. Then, while arms, neck, and face were still wet, he covered them with oil—preferably lubricating oil, medium. Finally he rubbed sawdust over all; great handfuls of it. The grease rolled out then, magically, leaving his skin smooth and white. Old Rudie, while advocating this process, made little use of it. He dispatched the whole grimy business by the simple method of washing in gasoline guaranteed to take the varnish off a car fender. It seemed to leave Rudie's tough hide undevastated.

At twenty-four Chug Scaritt was an upstanding, level-headed, and successful young fellow who worked hard all day and found himself restless and almost irritable toward evening. He could stay home and read, or go back to the garage, though after eight things were very quiet. For amusement there were the pool shack, the cheap dances, the street corner, the Y. M. C. A. This last had proved a boon. The swimming pool, the gym, the reading room, had given Chug many happy, healthful hours. But, after all, there was something——

Chug didn't know it was girls—girls you could talk to, and be with, and take around. But it was. After an hour in the pool, or around the reading table, or talking and smoking, he usually drifted out into the quiet street. He could go home. Or there was Wanda. If he went home he found himself snapping rather irritably at his mother, for no reason at all. Ashamed of doing it. Powerless, somehow, to stop.

He took to driving in the evening: long drives along the country roads, his cap pulled low over his eyes, the wind blowing fresh in his face. He used to cover mile on mile, sitting slumped low on his spine, his eyes on the road; the engine running sweet and true. Sometimes he took Wanda along, or one of the mill girls. But not often. They were disappointed if you didn't drive with one arm around them. He liked being alone. It soothed him.

It was thus that he first met the Weld girl. The Weld girl was the plain daughter of the Widow Weld. The Widow Weld was a musical-comedy sort of widow in French-heeled, patent-leather slippers and girlish gowns. When you met her together with her daughter Elizabeth you were supposed to say, "Not mother and daughter! Surely not! Sisters, of course." Elizabeth was twenty-four and not a success. At the golf-club dances on Saturday night she would sit, unsought, against the wall while her skittish mother tripped it with the doggish bachelors. Sometimes a man would cross the floor toward her and her heart would give a little leap, but he always asked the girl seated two chairs away. Elizabeth danced much better than her mother—much better than most girls, for that matter. But she was small, and dark, and rather shy, and wore thick glasses that disguised the fineness of her black-lashed gray eyes. Now and then her mother, flushed and laughing, would come up and say, "Is my little girl having a good time?" The Welds had no money, but they belonged to Chippewa's fashionable set. There were those who lifted significant eyebrows at mention of the Widow Weld's name, and it was common knowledge that no maid would stay with her for any length of time because of the scanty provender. The widow kowtowed shamelessly to the moneyed ones of Chippewa, flattering the women, flirting with the men. Elizabeth had no illusions about her mother, but she was stubbornly loyal to her. Her manner toward her kittenish parent was rather sternly maternal. But she was the honest sort that congenitally hates sham and pretence. She was often deliberately rude to the very people toward whom her mother was servile. Her strange friendship with Angie Hatton, the lovely and millioned, was the one thing in Elizabeth's life of which her Machiavellian mother approved.

"Betty, you practically stuck out your tongue

at Mr. Oakley!" This after a dance at which Elizabeth had been paired off, as usual, with the puffy and red-eyed old widower of that name.

"I don't care. His hands are fat and he creaks when he breathes."

"Next to Hatton, he's the richest man in Chippewa. And he likes you."

"He'd better not!" She spat it out, and the gray eyes blazed behind the glasses. "I'd rather be plastered up against the wall all my life than dance with him. Fat!"

"Well, my dear, you're no beauty, you know," with cruel frankness.

"I'm not much to look at," replied Elizabeth, "but I'm beautiful inside."

"Rot!" retorted the Widow Weld, inelegantly.

Had you lived in Chippewa all this explanation would have been unnecessary. In that terrifying way small towns have, it was known that of all codfish aristocracy the Widow Weld was the piscatorial pinnacle.

When Chug Scaritt first met the Weld girl she was standing out in the middle of the country road at ten-thirty P.M., her arms outstretched and the blood running down one cheek. He had been purring along the road toward home, drowsy and lulled by the motion and the April air. His thoughts had been drowsy, too, and disconnected.

"If I can rent Bergstrom's place next door when their lease is up I'll knock down the partition and put in auto supplies. There's big money in 'em. . . . Guess if it keeps on warm like this we can plant the garden next week. . . . That was swell cake Ma had for supper. . . . What's that in the road! What's!——"

Jammed down the foot-brake. Jerked back the emergency. A girl standing in the road. A dark mass in the ditch by the road-side. He was out of his car. He recognized her as the Weld girl.

"'S'matter?"

"In the ditch. She's hurt. Quick!"

"Whose car?" Chug was scrambling down the banks.

"Hatton's. Angie Hatton's."

"Gosh!"

Over by the fence, where she had been flung, Angie Hatton was found sitting up, dizzily, and saying, "Betty! Betty!" in what she supposed was a loud cry but which was really a whisper.

"I'm all right, dear. I'm all right. Oh, Angie, are you——"

She was cut and bruised, and her wrist had been broken. The two girls clung to each other, wordlessly. The thing was miraculous, in view of the car that lay perilously tipped on its fender.

"You're a lucky bunch," said Chug. "Who was driving?"

"I was," said Angie Hatton.

"It wasn't her fault," the Weld girl put in, quickly. "We were coming from Winnebago. She's a wonderful driver. We met a farm-wagon coming toward us. One of those big ones. The middle of the road. Perhaps he was asleep. He didn't turn out. We thought he would, of course. At the last minute we had to try for the ditch. It was too steep."

"Anyway, you're nervy kids, both of you. I'll have you both home in twenty minutes. We'll have to leave five thousand dollars' worth of car in the road till morning. It'll be all right."

He did get them home in twenty minutes and the five thousand dollars' worth of car was still lying repentantly in the ditch when morning came. Old Man Hatton himself came into the garage to thank Chug the following day. Chug met him in overalls, smudge-faced as he was. Old Man Hatton put out his hand. Chug grinned and looked at his own grease-grimed paw.

"That's all right," said Old Man Hatton, and grasped it firmly. "Want to thank you."

"That's all right," said Chug. "Didn't do a thing."

"No business driving alone that hour of the

night. Girls nowadays——" He looked around
the garage. "Work here, I suppose?"

"Yessir."

"If there's anything I can do for you? Over
at the mill."

"Guess not," said Chug.

"Treat you right here, do they?"

"Fine."

"Let's see. Who owns this place?"

"I do."

Old Man Hatton's face broke into a sunburst of
laugh-wrinkles. He threw back his head and went
the scale from roar to chuckle. "One on me.
Pretty good. Have to tell Angie that one."

Chug walked to the street with him. "Your
daughter, she's got a lot of nerve, all right. And
that girl with her—Weld. Say, not a whimper
out of her and the blood running down her face.
She all right?"

"Cut her head a little. They're both all right.
Angie wouldn't even stay in bed. Well, as I say,
if there's anything——?"

Chug flushed a little. "Tell you what, Mr.
Hatton. I'm working on a thing that'll take the
whine out of the Daker."

Old Man Hatton owned the Daker Motor plant
among other things. The Daker is the best car
for the money in the world. Not much for looks

but everything in the engine.   And everyone who has ever owned one knows that its only fault is the way its engine moans.   Daker owners hate that moan.   When you're going right it sounds a pass between a peanut roaster and a banshee with bronchitis.   Every engineer in the Daker plant had worked over it.

"Can't be done," said Old Man Hatton.

"Another three months and I'll show you."

"Hope you do, son.   Hope you do."

But in another three months Chug Scaritt was one of a million boys destined to take off a pink-striped shirt, a nobby belted suit, and a long-visored cap to don a rather bob-tailed brown outfit.   It was some eighteen months later before he resumed the chromatic clothes with an ardour out of all proportion to their style and cut.   But in the interval between doffing pink-striped shirt and donning pink-striped shirt.   .   .   .

No need to describe Camp Sibley, two miles outside Chippewa, and the way it grew miraculously, overnight, into a khaki city.   No going into detail concerning the effective combination formed by Chug and a machine gun.   These things were important and interesting.   But perhaps not more interesting than the seemingly unimportant fact that in July following that April Chug was dancing blithely and rhythmically with

Elizabeth Weld, and saying, "Angie Hatton's a smooth little dancer, all right; but she isn't in it with you."

For Chippewa, somehow, had fused. Chippewa had forgotten sets, sections, cliques, factions, and parties, and formed a community. It had, figuratively, wiped out the railroad tracks, together with all artificial social boundaries. Chug Scaritt, in uniform, must be kept happy. He must be furnished with wholesome recreation, fun, amusement, entertainment. There sprang up, seemingly overnight, a great wooden hall in Elm Street, on what had been a vacant lot. And there, by day or by night, were to be had music, and dancing, and hot cakes, and magazines, and hot coffee, and ice cream and girls. Girls! Girls who were straight, and slim, and young, and bright-eyed, and companionable. Girls like Angie Hatton. Girls like Betty Weld. Betty Weld, who no longer sat against the wall at the golf-club dances and prayed in her heart that fat old Oakley wasn't coming to ask her to dance.

Betty Weld was so popular now that the hostess used to have to say to her, in a tactful aside, "My dear, you've danced three times this evening with the Scaritt boy. You know that's against the rules."

Betty knew it. So did Chug. Betty danced so

lightly that Chug could hardly feel her in his arms. He told her that she ran sweet and true like the engine of a high-powered car, and with as little apparent effort. She liked that, and understood.

It was wonderful how she understood. Chug had never known that girls could understand like that. She talked to you, straight. Looked at you, straight. Was interested in the things that interested you. No waist-squeezing here. No cheap banter. You even forgot she wore glasses.

"I'm going to try to get over."

"Say, you don't want to do that."

"I certainly do. Why not?"

"You're—why, you're too young. You're a girl. You're——"

"I'm as old as you, or almost. They're sending heaps of girls over to work in the canteens, and entertain the boys. If they'll take me. I'll have to lie six months on my age."

Rudie was in charge of the garage now. "That part of it's all right," Chug confided to the Weld girl. "Only thing that worries me is Ma. She hasn't peeped, hardly, but I can see she's pretty glum, all right."

"I don't know your mother," said the Weld girl.

"Thasso," absent-mindedly, from Chug.

"I'd—like to."

Chug woke up. "Why, say, that'd be fine! Listen, why don't you come for Sunday dinner. I've got a hunch we'll shove off next week, and this'll be my last meal away from camp. They haven't said so, but I don't know—maybe you wouldn't want to, though. Maybe you—we live the other side of the tracks——"

"I'd love to," said the Weld girl. "If you think your mother would like to have me."

"Would she! And cook! Say!"

The Widow Weld made a frightful fuss. Said that patriotism was all right, but that there were limits. Betty put on her organdie and went.

It began with cream soup and ended with short-cake. Even Chug realized that his mother had outdone herself. After his second helping of shortcake he leaned back and said, "Death, where is thy sting?" But his mother refused to laugh at that. She couldn't resist telling Miss Weld that it was plain food but that she hoped she'd enjoyed it.

Elizabeth Weld leaned forward. "Mrs. Scaritt, it's the best dinner I've ever eaten."

Mrs. Scaritt flushed a little, but protested, politely: "Oh, now! You folks up in the East End——"

"Not the Welds. Mother and I are as poor as can be. Everybody knows that. We have lots of doylies and silver on the table, but very little to eat. We never could afford a meal like this. We're sort of crackers-and-tea codfish, really."

"Oh, now, Miss Weld!" Chug's mother was aghast at such frankness. But Chug looked at the girl. She looked at him. They smiled understandingly at each other.

An hour or so later, after Elizabeth had admired the vegetable garden, the hanging flower-baskets, the new parlour curtains ("I used to do 'em up for folks in town," said Mrs. Scaritt, "so's Chug could go to high school." And "I know it. That's what I call splendid," from the girl), she went home, escorted by Chug.

Chug's hunch proved a good one. In a week he was gone. Thirteen months passed before he saw Elizabeth Weld again. When he did, Chippewa had swung back to normal. The railroad tracks were once more boundary lines.

Chug Scaritt went to France to fight. Three months later Elizabeth Weld went to France to dance. They worked hard at their jobs, these two. Perhaps Elizabeth's task was the more trying. She danced indefatigably, tirelessly, magnificently. Miles, and miles, and miles of dancing. She danced on rough plank floors with cracks an inch wide between the boards. She danced in hospitals, châteaux, canteens, huts; at Bordeaux,

Verdun, Tours, Paris. Five girls, often, to five
hundred boys. Every two weeks she danced out a
pair of shoes. Her feet, when she went to bed at
night, were throbbing, burning, aching, swollen.
No hot water. You let them throb, and burn, and
ache, and swell until you fell asleep. She danced
with big blond bucks, and with little swarthy
doughboys from New York's East Side. She
danced with privates, lieutenants, captains; and
once with a general. But never a dance with Chug.

Once or twice she remembered those far-away
Chippewa golf-club dances. She was the girl who
used to sit there against the wall! She used to look
away with pretended indifference when a man
crossed the floor toward her—her heart leaping a
little. He would always go to the girl next to her.
She would sit there with a set smile on her face,
and the taste of ashes in her mouth. And those
shoddy tulle evening dresses her mother had
made her wear! Girlish, she had called them. A
girl in thick-lensed glasses should not wear tulle
evening frocks with a girlish note. Elizabeth had
always felt comic in them. Yet there she had sat,
shrinking lest the odious Oakley, of the fat white
fingers and the wheezy breath, should ask her
to dance.

She reflected, humorously, that if the miles of
dancing she had done in the past year were placed

end to end, as they do it in the almanac's fascinating facts, they must surely reach to Mars and return.

Whenever the hut door opened to admit a tall, graceful, lean brown figure her heart would give a little leap and a skip. As the door did this on an average of a thousand times daily her cardiac processes might be said to have been alarmingly accelerated.

Sometimes—though they did not know it—she and Chug were within a half hour's ride of each other. In all those months they never once met.

Elizabeth Weld came back to Chippewa in June. The First National Bank Building seemed to have shrunk; and she thought her mother looked old in that youthful hat. But she was glad to be home and said so.

"It has been awful here," said the Widow Weld. "Nothing to do but sew at the Red Cross shop; and no sugar or white bread."

"It must have been," agreed Elizabeth.

"They're giving a dance for you—and dinner— a week from Saturday, at the golf club. In your honour."

"Dance!" Elizabeth closed her eyes, faintly. Then, "Who is?"

"Well, Mr. Oakley's really giving it—that is, it was his idea. But the club wanted to tender some fitting——"

"I won't go."

"Oh, yes, you will."

Elizabeth did not argue the point. She had two questions to ask.

"Have the boys come back?"

"What boys?"

"The—the boys."

"Some of them. You know about dear Harry Hatton, of course. Croix de——"

"What have they done with the Khaki Club, where they used to give the dances?"

"Closed. Long ago. There was some talk of keeping it open for a community centre, or something, but it fell through. Now, Betty, you'll have to have a dress for Saturday night. I wonder if that old chiffon, with a new——"

Chug Scaritt came home in September. The First National Bank Building seemed, somehow, to have shrunk. And his mother hadn't had all that gray hair when he left. He put eager questions about the garage. Rudie had made out, all right, hadn't he? Good old scout.

"The boys down at the garage are giving some kind of a party for you. Old Rudie was telling me about it. I've got a grand supper for you to-night, Chug."

"Where's this party? I don't want any party."

"Woodman's Hall, I think they said. There was some girl called up yesterday. Wanda, her name sounded like. I couldn't——"

"Don't they give dances any more at the Soldiers' Club down on Elm?"

"Oh, that's closed, long. There was some talk of using it for what they called a community club. The *Eagle* was boosting for a big new place. What they called a Community Memorial Centre. But I don't know. It kind of fell through, I guess."

"I won't go," said Chug, suddenly.

"Go where, Chug?"

But instead of answering, Chug put his second question.

"Have you seen—is that—I wonder if that Weld girl's back."

"My, yes. Papers were full of it. Old Oakley gave her a big dance, and all, at the Country Club. They say——"

A week later, his arm about Wanda's big, yielding waist, he was dancing at Woodman's Hall. There was about her a cheap, heavy scent. She had on a georgette blouse and high-heeled shoes. She clung to Chug and smiled up at him. Wanda had bad teeth—yellow, with a sort of scum over them.

"I sure was lonesome for you, Chug. You're some dancer, I'll say. Honest, I could dance with you all night." A little pressure of her arm.

Somewhere in the recesses of his brain a memory cell broke. Dimly he heard himself saying, "Oh, they all tell me that."

"Crazy about yourself, ain't you!"

"Not as crazy as I am about you," with tardy gallantry.

Then, suddenly, Chug stopped dancing. He stopped, and stepped back from Wanda's arms. Bergstrom's two-piece orchestra was in the throes of its jazziest fox-trot number. Chug stood there a moment, in the centre of the floor, staring at Wanda's face that was staring back at him in vacuous surprise. He turned, without a word, and crossed the crowded floor, bumping couples blindly as he went. And so down the rickety wooden stairs, into the street, and out into the decent darkness of Chippewa's night.

THE END

The University of Illinois Press
is a founding member of the
Association of American University Presses.

University of Illinois Press
1325 South Oak Street
Champaign, IL 61820-6903
www.press.uillinois.edu